OUR DAILY BREAD

OUR DAILY BREAD

A Novel

J ACKIE A LEXANDER

T URNER

200 4th Avenue North • Suite 950
Nashville, Tennessee 37219

445 Park Avenue • 9th Floor
New York, NY 10022

www.turnerpublishing.com

Our Daily Bread

This book is a work of fiction. Names, characters, places, and events are products of the author's
imagination or are used fictitiously. Any resemblance to actual incidents, locales, or persons, living
or dead, is entirely coincidental.

Cover design by laura beers design
Cover photograph: istockphoto.com, lbd
Author photograph: Alexander Berg / www.alexberg.com

Library of Congress Cataloging-in-Publication Data

Alexander, Jackie.
 Our daily bread : a novel / Jackie Alexander. -- 1st ed.
    p. cm.
 ISBN 978-0-9830405-0-7
1. Racially mixed people--Fiction. 2. Fathers and sons--Louisiana--Fiction. 3. Grandparent and
child--Louisiana--Fiction. 4. Domestic abuse--Fiction. 5. Voyages and travels--Fiction. I. Title.
 PS3601.L35378O97 2012
 813'.6--dc23
                              2012014187
Printed in the United States of America
12 13 14 15 16 17 18—0 9 8 7 6 5 4 3 2 1

To the Jackson and Stephens families,
along with the unforgettable characters of my childhood in Louisiana,
all of whom have provided me with a lifetime of stories to share.

ACKNOWLEDGEMENTS

When I heard that literary agent Diane Gedymin was interested in meeting me after seeing *Joy,* a film for which I'd written the screenplay, her name sounded familiar. It soon dawned on me that I had read her name only days before in the first line of the acknowledgments for *The Measure of a Man*, an autobiography by Sidney Poitier; he was, without a doubt, the main reason I became an actor, which in turn led me to become a writer. If Diane had worked with Sir Sidney, I wanted to work with her! I immediately phoned to set up an office meeting, but after the call ended, I realized that I still had no idea what she wanted.

Since meeting her I've grown to learn that the only thing Diane wanted, then and now, is to help me in any way she can. That I had no experience writing a book seemed to be of little importance to her; she believed I had it in me to write a novel, and in turn, convinced me to believe it also. Over the years, she has answered every call, responded to every e-mail, and taken the time to critique my work honestly; most memorably commenting on the first sixty-four pages submitted to her that, "This is not working at all; you need to throw all of this away, and start over." What is truly amazing about her though, is her continued faith in me, shown in what she said next: "When you come up with something new, I'll give it a read, and we'll go from there." Writing *Our Daily Bread* has been the most artistically gratifying experience of my life; it would never have happened without Diane. I am eternally thankful for her guidance in writing this novel, but that feeling pales in comparison to my gratitude for her friendship.

Writing can be a terrifying experience without the encouragement and support of a trusted friend; thankfully I was blessed to have Marcelle Gover in my corner. Marcelle has read every draft of *Our Daily Bread* countless times, editing typos and grammar along the way; no small feat for a novel that started at over four hundred pages, and for a time was being completely revised every few months. But Marcelle always treated this tedious task as if I were doing her a favor; going so far as to thank me for allowing her to do work most others would have shunned. Thank you, Marcelle, for always being there.

I am also grateful to the following people for their advice and support while working on this project: Willie and Shirley Jackson, Sharon Burns, Lee Borom, Christi Frantom, Alexis Hurley and Inkwell Management, Adrienne Ingrum, Jennifer Kane, Alexis Kaplan, Adrienne Lotson, Marjorie Moon and The Billie Holiday Theatre, Ronald and Pam Scipio, and Victoria Stapf. And to everyone who took the time to read some incarnation of this novel over the past eight years, thank you!

PART I

EIGHTH GRADE

An Uninvited Guest

I've always wanted to be a hero. As a child, each night I'd imagine dangerous scenarios, then doze off dreaming of clever ways to save the day. It was in this carefully constructed world of dreams I was most happy. Earl delighted in waking me back to reality.

Earl was the kingpin among my grandfather's chickens. An unusually large rooster with auburn and black feathers that gave him a regal look, he ascended to this level of prominence mainly due to a characteristic he shared with underworld kingpins, the propensity for unthinkable violence. If rooster or hen dared question his leadership, punishment was swift and sometimes deadly. Earl also taught any misguided child who wandered into our yard that a rooster should not be chased. Each morning at sunrise, he took his position on the porch outside my window and sounded the alarm signaling the start of a new day. Every day I looked out onto the porch in annoyance at Earl, only to be stared down into submission. Something about a chicken's eyes, Earl's in particular, gave me the creeps; he had an icy stare that made me uneasy. My father had that same icy stare.

Thirteen is a rough age for a child, and if you're a child of scandal, it's nearly unbearable. Such was my life on Sunday, September 8, 1974, the day before I started eighth grade. My paternal grandfather was raising me; my grandmother passed away when I was three, and although both my parents were alive, neither was in a position to care for me. My mother was living as an invalid in a nursing home after suffering a vicious beating, reportedly at the hands of my father. I say "reportedly" because this was a story my grandfather never believed, despite my father's conviction.

"My boy ain't had nothing to do with what happened to Sarah, I can tell you that as sure as I'm standing here," he insisted.

My father received a life sentence in Angola State Penitentiary. His fate was an ironic one since life in Angola was the nightmarish threat he reserved for me upon any infraction of his numerous house rules.

"What's wrong with you, Boy?" he'd roar. "You wanna end up in Angola? They'll lock your ass up for life and make a punk out of a skinny little runt like you!"

These threats had scared me, but at the time I was too young to understand their full implications. At thirteen, now grasping the true meaning behind his words, I wondered what life in Angola would make of my father.

My mother's parents disowned her when she married my father, because she was white, and he was black. It disturbed me that parents would disown their child solely based on who she loved. More disturbing was the justification of this action I overheard adults express.

"You can't blame them, embarrassing the family like that," they snickered.

My mother's present condition miraculously healed all wounds with her parents, although it didn't change the way they felt about me. I occasionally ran into them when I visited Mama in the nursing home, but it was clear to me I shouldn't expect any birthday cards.

"She ain't doing too well today, so don't stay too long," Mrs. Boutte coldly informed my grandfather and me on one of our monthly visits.

Mr. and Mrs. Boutte was how I addressed my mother's parents. I could never bring myself to call them Grandma or Grandpa, which they didn't seem to mind. Mrs. Boutte was a short gaunt woman with dark brown hair and freckled leathery skin, who wore a frown as a constant expression. I remember Mama commenting on how attractive her mother was as a young girl, but the harshness of Mrs. Boutte's current appearance robbed her of any beauty. Mr. Boutte was a tall lanky man, with unusually dark skin for a white person. His attire always consisted of snakeskin cowboy boots, an oversized silver belt buckle, and a green *John Deere* cap. Throughout my childhood he appeared to be rendered speechless by the sight of me; I never heard the man speak a word. Normally on our encounters he just averted his eyes, grimacing as if suddenly struck with intense pain.

Mama had three brothers, but as did Mr. and Mrs. Boutte, they chose not to acknowledge the blood we shared. With no one else to turn to, my grandfather's home was a sanctuary.

We lived in a small two-bedroom wooden house in LaPlace, Louisiana. The house was painted white, with red trim, and located at the rear of a dead-end dirt road. Behind the house there was nothing but woodland, every inch of it serving as my playground. Da-dee, that's what I called my grandfather, was retired after working for the Southern Union Railroad Company for fifty years. He stood six feet five inches, weighed two hundred and forty pounds, and even at seventy-four years old, he was solid as a rock. Da-dee had the largest hands I'd ever seen. I remember him having to use a pencil to dial our old rotary-style telephone because his fingers couldn't fit in the holes. His complexion was described as *blue black*, a result of years working under an unforgiving Louisiana sun. His dark skin, combined with his clean-shaven head and face made him glisten after working up a sweat. He epitomized what the legendary John Henry must have looked like.

There weren't many demands placed on me, outside of expectations that I do well in school, and take care of chores around the house. Da-dee and I got along quite well, our only bone of contention being the house temperature.

"Da-dee, can we please put on the air conditioners?" I pleaded every night during summer months.

"We don't need them," he always answered. "If you just open your window, you'll get a nice breeze in your room."

"But there is no breeze, it's a hundred degrees outside," I whined.

"Well just turn up the fan. But them air conditioners have it too cold in here at night."

In summer months it was over ninety degrees at night, which is miserable sleeping weather without taking into consideration the brutal humidity. There were two air conditioning units in the house, one in Da-dee's bedroom, and the other in the living room, which was located directly across from my bedroom. Da-dee conceded to running the air conditioners during the day, but insisted they weren't needed at night.

"You sleep with that cold air blowing on you, you sure to catch a head cold," he warned.

My solution to the problem on nights when I could not bear the heat was to simply wait until he was asleep, a state that was announced by his snoring, and then turn on the air conditioner in the living room.

"Kevin, you turn this thing on last night?" Da-dee would ask the next morning.

"Yeah, but just because the breeze died down," I would answer, flirting as close to sarcasm as I dared.

We didn't get a chance to spend much time together Monday through Friday due to my schooling and homework, combined with Da-dee's various work projects. He had a little red woodshed behind the house where he built and repaired furniture for people in the area. The building had no air conditioning and one window. I wondered how he could work in that unbearable heat, but old habits die hard, I guessed. Saturdays were also busy for Da-dee, who worked most of the day and used Saturday night to prepare his sermon for the next day. Da-dee was a Baptist minister. Sundays, however, were great. After church we spent the entire day together. We would take in lunch at a local restaurant and talk about the *good old days* as Da-dee called them.

"All Mama and Poppa had to give my brothers and sisters and me was love, but that was more than enough," Da-dee said. I envied him.

Besides Da-dee, my best friend was Duke, the dog he brought home for me when I came to live with him.

"Every boy should have a dog," Da-dee said.

Duke was a mutt of unknown origins. With his smooth coat of tan and black hair, he would have resembled a German Shepherd were it not for his abnormally large head. A big dog, he not only weighed more than I did, but was taller than me when standing on his hind legs. Duke was my constant companion when I was at home. Whether it was a safari into the dense woods behind our house, or a plain old game of catch, he was never tired of me. Duke's size also made him good protection, although he too lived in fear of Earl.

Overall, life at the house was good. It was life away from it that was a daily trial.

The world held few welcomes for me. I didn't seem to fit in anywhere, in part because other people didn't know how to place me.

I had inherited my mother's white complexion, but bore my father's black features. It was apparent that I wasn't white, but I didn't look black, either. In our town if you weren't clearly identifiable as one or the other, you were a curiosity.

"Hey, what are you?" kids asked when meeting me for the first time.

"My mama is white, and my daddy is black," I politely explained.

"So what does that make you?" they demanded to know, as if a choice must be made before the relationship could move forward.

"I don't know, I guess black."

Da-dee always told me I was black. "If you got black blood in you, regardless of what else you might have in you, people in this country go'n think of you as black," he said. I accepted this answer, although the question remained a source of irritation.

Another problem was my size. I was puny for a thirteen-year-old, and anyone looking to enhance his status as a tough guy on the playground needed only look in my direction. Factor in my love of books, which I openly displayed by choosing to read during recess as opposed to playing baseball or whatever sport was in season, and I was a bona fide target in any schoolyard.

"It's recess, Kevin, you little weirdo, why are you reading?" kids taunted as I sat with my nose buried in a book.

"I just wanna finish this chapter," I replied, thinking this logical answer would suffice.

"Finish it after recess!" they responded, kicking the book from my hands.

I remember feeling that the world treated me as if I were an uninvited guest.

As I lay in bed Sunday night drenched in sweat, listening for Da-dee's snoring so I could turn on the air conditioner, my singular hope for the new school year was that I could maintain the surreptitious existence I had created for myself. Everyone knew the stories about my parents' scandalous union, my mother being attacked, and my father's subsequent imprisonment, but even in our small town, after three years, these stories had grown tiresome. Little did I know the next morning my checkered past would once again become the talk of the town.

JOHNNY MO'

The phone woke me before Earl that first Monday morning of the new school year. Da-dee was even shocked by the time of the call.

"Who on God's green earth calling here this early?" he pondered aloud.

We received few phone calls at any time of the day. A call before the sun rose was legitimately a curious one.

"Hello, Matthews residence," Da-dee answered, as I scrambled to turn off the air conditioner.

The clock read four a.m. I was instantly struck with fear. Mama, something has happened to Mama, I thought.

"Praise God! I'll be down there this morning!" Da-dee cried, hanging up the phone. I could hear his hurried footsteps rushing back to his room to get dressed. Caught up in his excitement he began to sing, *"Jesus, can make a way, somehow, Oh yes he can!"* After a few minutes his head popped into my room. "Kevin, I got to run down to the hospital, you sure you got everything you need for school today?"

"Yeah, what happened?"

"You got lunch money?"

"I got everything I need, Da-dee, but what happened?"

"It's Johnny, he out of his coma!" he said, his head vanishing from my doorway.

"What?" I asked, springing from the bed to catch him before he left. "When? How?"

"I'll fill you in on everything this evening when you get home from school," he yelled, walking out the front door.

I knew I wouldn't be able to sleep another wink. This was great news. After a week of worrying, Johnny was on the road to recovery.

His name was Jonathan Morgan, but everyone called him Johnny Mo'. He hired himself out as assistant, delivery person, or messenger to anyone with a few dollars to pay him or a free meal to feed him. Johnny was a big man, owning the build of a middle linebacker years after his playing career had ended, muscular but having put on some extra pounds around the waist. He was dark skinned, almost as dark as Da-dee, and was never seen without some sort of hat on his head.

"Johnny don't wanna get too black, no sir," he said.

He wore a mustache and beard that were constantly in need of grooming, and was perpetually sweating, even on cold days. I was never certain how old Johnny was, although I believe he was somewhere in his fifties. He became a local legend for his ability to walk long distances.

"Johnny can walk over all of God's creation and not get tired," Da-dee said.

Johnny walked all day, every day. Da-dee said he once walked from LaPlace to Baton Rouge, a distance of at least fifty miles, after discovering that James Brown was performing there.

"Mr. Please, Please, Please! Gotta see him! Yes sir, gotta be there!" he told anyone who asked about the concert.

Adults described Johnny as being *touched*. This condition was the result of a blow to the head with a Louisville Slugger. I heard that when Johnny was younger, he had fallen in love with a married woman. The woman, after being questioned by her husband about the affair, claimed Johnny raped her. The husband, angered by what he heard, forced his wife to invite Johnny to the house. When Johnny walked through the door, the husband took a homerun swing to the back of his head. Johnny survived, but was never the same. He would be shuttled in and out of the state hospital for the mentally ill in Jackson, Louisiana for almost twenty years. Johnny was petrified of the place. You couldn't even mention the name Jackson in his presence.

"No Jackson for Johnny! No sir! That's a bad place, Jackson a bad place! Don't wanna go there! No sir!"

Despite his condition, Johnny was a trusted and reliable worker. He had an uncanny ability to relay error-free anything he heard or witnessed. I once looked on in disbelief as Da-dee verbally instructed

Johnny on a detailed list of materials he needed for a specific project, and then sent him to the hardware store to pick them up.

"Ain't you go'n write it down for the people at the store?" I asked, confused by my grandfather's faith in a man who often didn't know what day of the week it was. "There's no way he go'n remember all that."

Johnny returned with every item Da-dee asked for. "All God's children have special gifts, no matter how the world judges them," Da-dee said. Johnny was indeed special.

Although a man of his size roaming up and down the road talking to himself might make some people nervous, Johnny was as gentle as a lamb. People around LaPlace genuinely liked him, and it had saddened everyone when he was sideswiped by a car and left for dead in a ditch. Johnny was destitute with no insurance, so he was taken to Charity Hospital in New Orleans, the one place that would care for him. There, he clung to life with little prospects for survival. I was kept abreast of his condition because Da-dee took on the responsibility of making sure Johnny received the proper care. In his own way, Da-dee was Johnny's hero.

Later that morning, I was brimming with excitement as I waited for the school bus, little if any of it having to do with school. When the bus pulled up to my stop, Ms. Bertha, our next-door neighbor, called to me from her kitchen window, "Kevin, don't get on the bus!"

She didn't need to tell me twice. I waved the bus on and ran toward her house, Duke running along behind me.

"What happen, Ms. Bertha? I ain't going to school today?"

"No, Baby. Your grandfather called and he wants you to stay at the house. He on his way home right now."

"What happened? Is Johnny okay?"

"Johnny? What you talking about, Baby?"

"Da-dee went to see him at the hospital this morning. They say he go'n be alright."

"Preacher (that's what everyone called Da-dee) ain't said nothing about that, he was in a bit of a rush on the phone, but praise God if that's the case," Ms. Bertha said, waving her right hand towards the heavens. "Anyway, he just wanted me to catch you before you got on the bus. Said for you to wait at the house for him, he on his way."

"Okay."

"You had breakfast?"

"Yes ma'am."

"Okay, Baby. You tell Preacher to let me know how Johnny doing soon as he get back, you hear?"

Ms. Bertha was a life-long friend of Johnny's. She was a small woman, with a voice like a megaphone.

"When you little like us, Baby, you got to make sure folks listen," she explained to me.

I liked Ms. Bertha. Her husband had passed away, and her two sons and their families lived in another town, so she loved having me around her house for company. I cut her grass and did other yard work, and she always rewarded me with a freshly baked treat. Ms. Bertha also thought I was the most handsome boy in the neighborhood, albeit having questionable reasons for doing so.

"This boy sure do have good hair, just like white folks," she would say, laughing and running her hand through my hair. "And this pretty skin, Baby, you go'n have to fight the girls off when you grow up."

Ms. Bertha was color struck. Her reddish complexion, full lips, prominent cheekbones, and thick jet-black hair were features that revealed her own mixed ancestry, African American and Native American, a fact she took pride in announcing.

"My mother was half Cherokee Indian," she boasted.

Ms. Bertha didn't know how to drive a car, so she was always at home. Each day, she fixed herself near the window in her favorite rocking chair, where she could look out to catch any newsworthy activity. Here, endless phone conversations detailed the goings on in our small town: a conspiracy at the church involving misappropriated funds, accusations that good farmland she rightfully owned was outright stolen by a white family from the next town, rumors about who was cheating on whom, and above all else there were conversations on how good the Lord was.

"I know the Lord done gave me everything I got," she confessed. "That's why I get on my knees and thank him every day."

As I walked back to the house, Duke wanted to play a game of fetch, but I was too distracted. Da-dee didn't believe in me missing school days for any reason, and I couldn't understand why he told me to stay home on the first day. I went into the house, turned on the air conditioner, and sat fidgeting in the living room trying to figure out what could have happened. It was three hours before Da-dee returned home, but what he told me, I would have never guessed had it taken him three years.

"Just Like I Told Ya'll"

I heard a car pull into the driveway and raced to the window. It was Da-dee's pick-up truck as expected, but what I didn't expect was the police car that pulled in behind. Da-dee got out of his truck and waited as, to my amazement, Jim Brady, the town's Chief of Police, stepped out of the car.

Jim Brady was a big man, almost as big as Da-dee, with snow-white hair and pale skin that was always sunburned. He wore a tan Stetson cowboy hat in tandem with his police uniform, and mirrored sunglasses that shielded his piercing blue eyes. In his late fifties, Chief Brady had held the position of police chief for twenty years, and from what I heard, he didn't intend on giving it up any time soon.

"The only way Brady go'n leave that office is in a box," the men in our town joked.

Chief Brady was also what older black men described as a "hard but fair white man." He treated everyone equally, regardless of race, an uncommon trait among police officers in our town. Only one thing mattered with him, the law.

I watched as Chief Brady and Da-dee spoke for a moment, then both turned and headed for the house. I quickly ducked, so I wouldn't be seen spying from the window. Seconds later I heard the front door open.

"Kevin, Kevin, come in here," Da-dee called out from the living room. Although I knew I'd done nothing wrong, I was unable to move. I considered slipping out of my bedroom window to avoid whatever questions awaited me in the other room. "Kevin, you in here?" Da-dee shouted.

"Yes sir, be right there."

My fear apparently preceded my arrival; because before I got in the room Chief Brady yelled out, "No need to be scared, Son."

"What's wrong?" I asked, hugging the doorway and peering into the room.

"Kevin, you know Chief Brady, don't you?" Da-dee asked.

"Yes sir. Hello, Chief Brady."

"How you doing, Son?" he asked, taking off his glasses and smiling while shaking my hand. He was attempting to put me at ease, but it didn't work.

"I'm okay."

"Now I know this won't be easy, Kevin, but we need to talk to you about what happened to your mama," Da-dee said, ushering me over to the sofa and taking a seat next to me.

"What happened to Mama? What do you mean?"

"Chief Brady just needs to go over a few things about what you saw that morning, and if you remember anything from the night before."

"Like what?" I asked, my right leg shaking uncontrollably.

"Like was anyone else at the house that night," Chief Brady said. "Maybe somebody stop by to visit your mama, and you heard them talking."

"I don't think so."

"What about the next morning," Chief Brady said. "Did your daddy say anything to you about what happened?"

"I already told you everything I knew back when it happened. Besides, it's been a long time, and I try not to think about it. I don't remember much anymore," I lied. Three years had passed, but I remembered every detail of that morning. I couldn't imagine why they were asking me about it now. I had answered every conceivable question during my father's trial.

"I know it's been a long time," Da-dee said. "But we need you to try real hard and see if you remember anything else. Something you might a thought was strange but didn't mention before."

I could feel the tears coming. I was terrified. I'm not sure if it was the prospect of reliving that morning, or the fear that they knew I was lying.

"I don't remember, it was a long time ago," I said, my voice cracking. "Why are you asking me about this?"

"Kevin, Johnny say he saw a man hurt your mama the night before you found her," Da-dee said. "He say the man wasn't your daddy."

"But it was him!" I yelled, standing from the sofa. "I found him on top of her. Her face was all swollen and she wasn't moving! I know he did it to her!"

"Okay, okay, take it easy," Da-dee said, standing and hugging me, patting my back to calm me down. "Come on, and sit back down." We both sat back down on the sofa, Da-dee's arm around me for support. "Now, I know you found him in the room with her, but you didn't see him hurt her, did you?" It was true, I hadn't seen my father hurt Mama that morning, but it was an act I had witnessed in the past.

"The thing is, Son, Morgan described what he saw that night pretty darn good," Chief Brady said. "He say it wasn't your daddy who he saw arguing with your mama that night, and your daddy wasn't the man who hurt her."

"Who's Morgan?" I asked.

"That's Johnny," Da-dee said.

"What does Johnny know about this?" I asked.

"Well, when I got to the hospital this morning, he was conscious. He started crying when he saw me, saying how sorry he was for not saving Junior," Da-dee said. Junior was how most people referred to my father. "He said he dreamt that he was burning in hell for not saving Junior, and had to make things right. He said the Lord had lifted him from the flames in the dream and warned that his telling what he saw was the only thing that would save him from eternal damnation."

"What are you talking about?" I asked. "If Johnny knew something, why didn't he say anything?"

"He was scared," Chief Brady said.

"Scared of what?"

"It ain't what he was scared of, it's who he was scared of," Chief Brady said.

"Huh?"

"Go ahead and tell him, he needs to know," Chief Brady said to Da-dee.

"Kevin, Johnny say the man he saw hurt your mama was Jesse Boutte," Da-dee said. I couldn't believe what I was hearing. Mama and Mr. Boutte hadn't spoken to each other in years, why would he hurt her now? It doesn't make sense, I thought. "Johnny say he saw them arguing that night," Da-dee continued. "Said he was walking by the house and heard yelling from inside. When he went to the window to see what was happening, say he saw Jesse throw your mama to the floor."

"Why didn't he just tell somebody?" I asked.

"Say Jesse saw him looking in the window, and come out and chased him off. Told him if he said anything, no one would believe him, and he would make sure they locked him up in Jackson forever," Chief Brady said. "Morgan ran off scared, but come back later that night to see if your mama was okay. Said when he looked in the window again, Jesse was gone, and your mama was in bed. Said her face was all bloody, and she wasn't moving. Now I wouldn't even pay much attention to what he saying, but Morgan described that room exactly the way we found it. No way he knows that unless he saw it."

My head was spinning at this point. Da-dee and Chief Brady continued questioning me, but I insisted I remembered nothing. Eventually, Da-dee said I should go to my room and get some rest, and we would talk about it later. He then walked Chief Brady out to his car. I made my way back to the window to eavesdrop on their conversation.

"Preacher, you should probably talk to Diaz, he defended your boy, right?" Chief Brady asked.

"That's right, Mr. Diaz defended him," Da-dee said.

"You need to talk to him about maybe trying to get a new trial. I'm go'n talk to Jesse, but you go'n need more than Morgan's word to get anywhere. Folks just ain't go'n believe the story he telling."

"I don't know why not, like you said, ain't no way Johnny know them details without seeing it with his own eyes. Just like I told ya'll, my boy ain't had nothing to do with what happened to Sarah."

"That's My Blood Running Through Your Veins"

Earl was right on cue the next morning, but I was already awake. I hadn't slept a wink. It wasn't Johnny's story that kept me awake, nor was it the heat. All night I was hounded by the memory of Mama being attacked. Normally these memories brought me to tears, but today I felt nothing but anger. I walked over to the window and Earl was pacing back and forth arrogantly staring, daring me to return his gaze. This was a daily competition that I never won, but today there was a fury in my stare that momentarily paralyzed Earl. After a few seconds, he began to peck at the ground, diverting his eyes and walking away. This retreat was not enough for me. I opened the window, grabbed a baseball, and threw a missile directly at Earl's head. I missed, but my point was made. Earl clucked in anger, reluctantly leaving the porch defeated for the first time.

I returned to bed, lying there stewing until Da-dee called me for breakfast at eight. He had told me the night before that I didn't have to go to school. It hadn't been twenty-four hours since Johnny first told his story, but the town was already abuzz. Da-dee, knowing I would be a target on that first day, decided to give me a reprieve.

"I'm going to see your daddy today," he said, as I took a seat at the table. Da-dee visited my father regularly. He never asked me to go, and I never wanted to. "Got to give him the news, Chief says with this kind of evidence they might be able to get a new trial."

"That would be a mistake."

"Kevin, your daddy ain't a perfect man, I know that. He didn't do right by you or your mama, but they got him locked up for something he didn't do. You got to see that ain't right," Da-dee said, handing me a plate of grits and eggs. I didn't say anything. "Well, I'll be gone for most of the day. You sure you go'n be okay here by yourself?"

"I'll be just fine," I said, not looking up from my plate.

"That's what I figured. Bertha said you could stop by there for lunch if you want. If not, got plenty of ham, bologna, and cold cuts in the ice box for you to make a sandwich or something."

I knew Da-dee wanted me to go with him to visit my father, but I had no intention of granting him that wish.

Normally having a day off from school and not being sick was cause for celebration, but not this day. I tried to read, but couldn't escape my thoughts. It felt like my head was going to explode. Da-dee often said that fresh air can clear your head, so I decided to go fishing. Not knowing how long I would be gone, I decided to pack a lunch for the trip. I searched the icebox and found some ham, bologna, salami, cheese, olives, and peppers, which I combined to create a king-sized muffuletta sandwich. I had a bag of potato chips from my lunch the day before, so all I needed now was dessert, and nothing other than a Hubig's lemon pie would do. Hubig's lemon pies were made at a local bakery, and individually wrapped. They were Da-dee's and my favorite, so the pantry was always stocked. I added a pie to my lunch bag, and then filled up two canteens of water, knowing it was hot outside. I then loaded up my backpack for the trip.

I stepped out the front door at noon and was instantly slapped in the face by the heat. It was the kind of weather that makes your clothes stick to you after taking a few steps, and causes each breath to be a challenge. I reasoned it would be cooler once I made it to the creek. Before leaving, I thought it wise to stop by Da-dee's woodshed to borrow a stick in case I ran into anything that required me to have a weapon. Da-dee owned ten walking sticks of different lengths and weights carved from oak trees. He didn't need them to assist him in walking, so I'm not quite sure why there were so many. After grabbing a proper-sized stick, I sought out companionship. Duke happily joined me.

I headed out for a creek deep in the woods behind our house where I kept a small boat and a fishing pole. After walking less than ten minutes Duke began barking and growling. I scanned the area around us, and spotted a blue runner snake standing in the weeds. Blue runner snakes are exactly what they sound like; blue snakes that are very fast. Most people wouldn't believe it, and I really never understood how they do it, but they can stand straight up. Don't ask me on what because I don't know. Now blue runners aren't poisonous, and there is really nothing to fear from them, but that was normally of little consequence in my mind. On any other day I would have fled in the opposite direction without delay; but today I didn't move. As with Earl, I stared at the snake with no fear, my anger forging a newfound boldness within me. Duke, of course, took off in hot pursuit of the snake. After exhausting himself with no success, he returned, and we continued on our way.

Needing a break from the heat, I stopped under a huge pecan tree for some shelter from the sun and a quick drink of water. These trees were scattered throughout the woods, and you could pick the pecans and sell them. The going rate was thirty cents a pound. I decided to turn part of the morning into a money-making venture. Pecan season didn't start for a few weeks, but I was certain I could turn a profit. A resourceful woodsman, I used my weapon, the stick, as a tool for retrieving the pecans. I found low hanging branches, and alternated swinging the stick knocking down a cluster, and tossing the stick into the tree taking down several. The second of my methods resulted in a knot on the back of my head after misjudging where the stick was going to land. I soon grew tired, and decided to move on. I checked my bag to see how many pecans I had picked, and realized my earnings would be a disappointment.

The woods were full of life; rabbits, armadillos, and squirrels all sent Duke on mad dashes in every direction. He never caught anything. When we finally made it to the creek, I decided to have lunch. I pulled out my muffuletta sandwich and potato chips, with Duke staring longingly at my food. I gave in to his begging, and shared my sandwich with him, although his cries were of no use when it came to my Hubig's lemon pie.

After eating, I cleared away the branches and leaves that covered my boat, and flipped it over onto the bank. I then pulled out my fishing pole, which I stored beneath the boat in a Hefty garbage bag. Needing bait, I dug up some worms, most of which were bigger than the minnows I'd be attempting to catch. I was now ready to set sail. Duke would have to stay behind, which I think he preferred. My boat was not in the greatest condition. It wasn't very big, and considering the numerous holes that were patched up in the most haphazard ways, how it stayed afloat eluded me. Then again, it wasn't much of a creek. The creek bed was covered with fallen limbs and rocks, and many times I had to get out of the boat and loosen some obstruction in order to continue on my trek. Luckily today, rains from the previous week had deepened the creek enough for smooth sailing. I got in the boat and used Da-dee's walking stick to launch it from the bank. I baited my line and tossed it in the water, then sat back in the boat awaiting a bite, of what I have no idea. I had fished in this creek many times, but never caught anything.

Floating down the creek, my mind strayed back to Johnny's story. For the first time, I entertained the idea that I was wrong about my father. He had been abusive to Mama and me, but was it possible he was wrongly convicted? Then I remembered the way he looked at me when I found him in bed that morning, Mama's unconscious body lying beside him. He never said a word. He just stared at me. As quickly as my father's innocence entered my mind, the memory of his stare erased it.

As I sat in the boat lost in thought, my fishing pole dipped in the water. I was so surprised I wasn't sure what to do. My first instinct was to let the pole go, I mean what on earth could be pulling on it? Dismissing my fears, I began to pull on the line with all my might. After a brief struggle, the pole snapped back out of the water knocking me down. When I checked the end of my line, there was nothing there, including my worm. I looked in the water and spotted a large snapping turtle swimming from under the boat. These turtles were known to rip the fingers off of anyone within snapping range. The turtle swam up to the edge of the creek and made its way onto land, where Duke cornered it. I jumped out of the boat and pulled it onto shore. Duke was sniffing the turtle, which had vanished into its shell. Angered by this invasion of privacy, the turtle took a swipe at Duke's nose, SNAP! Shocked and frightened, Duke quickly backed away, and began barking at the turtle, which cleverly retreated back into the safety of its shell. After a few seconds of intimidation tactics from a safe distance, Duke ventured back in close, nudging the turtle and flipping it onto its back. I walked over and began to prod the turtle with Da-dee's stick. I tried putting the stick into the holes of the shell, spinning the shell around, and I even flipped it over a couple of times. Then right as my attention was wavering, the turtle took a bite at me, SNAP! I dodged the attack, but tripped and fell in the process. Fearful I might still be in snapping range; I scrambled away on my knees. But after catching my breath, the anger seasoning within me since the moment I awoke took control of my body. I jumped to my feet, grabbed Da-dee's stick, and began sadistically pounding on the shell of the turtle. BAM! BAM! BAM! Duke, disturbed by my actions, continually circled the turtle and me not making a sound. Then, as abruptly as I started, I stopped. Duke studied me cautiously, fearing he might be my next target. I stood there, out of breath, staring down at the turtle. It was lying on its back motionless, its shell cracked. When I bent down to get a closer look, I saw an image that will remain with me for the rest of my life. Eggs, I could see eggs. The turtle was pregnant. Horrified by what I saw, I dropped the stick, and ran away as fast as I could.

After running for what seemed an eternity, I reached the house and collapsed. I sat on the ground in the middle of the backyard trying to catch my breath, with the sun blinding me, and tears streaming down the sides of my face. Then I heard my father's voice so clearly; it was as if he were whispering to me through the trees.

"That's my blood running through your veins; you and me, we one and the same."

This was my father's response to my declarations of hate toward him whenever he yelled at or hit Mama. Now haunted by his voice, I hated him more than ever.

"The Choice Is Yours"

"Hiding is no solution to a problem," Da-dee said when I joined him at the breakfast table Friday morning. "You have to face life's storms head on." After allowing me to stay home four days, this was his way of telling me it was time to start the eighth grade. I think he felt it best for me to start on a Friday, so I would have the weekend to recover from the abuse I was destined to receive. "I already spoke with the school about you being absent, so all you need to do is go ahead to class," Da-dee said. "And another thing, I don't want you to pay attention to no nonsense you hear today."

Johnny's story greatly upset the white community, who branded it as a shameful slander on one of the most respected men in town. They believed Da-dee concocted the story in hopes of freeing his son.

"You call yourself a religious leader, you go'n burn in hell for this!" an anonymous woman screamed into the phone, mistaking me for Da-dee.

The black community believed the accusations, but took a strange sort of pleasure in the possibility that my mother's attacker was her own father.

"Much as Boutte hate niggers, don't surprise me one bit!" I overheard Mr. Benny say, laughing. Mr. Benny was the town know-it-all. "His daughter living with one, having babies with one, I'm surprised that crazy biscuit burner ain't beat her ass sooner."

Da-dee knew children echoed the sentiments of their parents. I already wasn't the most popular kid, and events of the past few days weren't going to help. As we sat quietly finishing breakfast, an overwhelming sense of dread engulfed me. The first day of school had been a constant worry of mine before any of this happened. My plan was to go as unnoticed as possible, for as long as possible. I was in desperate need of a new plan.

Da-dee drove me to school, since sparing me the bus ride was the least he could do. As I walked through the halls, crowded because no one wanted to be outside due to the heat, I was pleasantly surprised to find no one paid much attention to me; being ignored on this day felt like a blessing. I found a nice deserted corner and tried to keep a low profile. It wasn't until the bell rang that I realized I didn't know where any of my classes were. Since I missed the first four days of school, I didn't have my class schedule. I made my way to the administration office and found no one there but Mrs. Raymond, one of the school secretaries.

"Good morning, Mrs. Raymond, my name is Kevin Matthews. I was out the first couple of days and I need to pick up my class schedule."

"I know who you are, Kevin," she said, smiling. "I'll be with you in one minute." It was as if nothing happened. She didn't ask any questions or give me any funny looks. I took a seat, and seconds later she returned with my schedule. "Kevin, you made it into the X section," she said cheerfully, handing me a schedule card. X sections were the school system's attempt at recognizing gifted students, and separating them so their underachieving classmates would not impede their learning. "Congratulations!"

"Thanks," I mumbled.

"The two Mrs. Jones teach the class; you know where their room is, right?"

"Yes ma'am, I do. Thank you."

"You're welcome."

I couldn't believe it, not one question. Maybe no one will ask me about it, I thought.

I left the office and headed for class. I knew this was the real test, kids don't hold back. I walked into the room, freezing at the doorway as all eyes zeroed in on me.

"Good morning, Kevin," Mrs. Jones said.

"Good morning, Kevin," the second Mrs. Jones repeated from the back of the room.

"Good morning," I replied.

"We've been expecting you," the first Mrs. Jones added. "Why don't you see Mrs. J and she'll get you up to speed."

I nodded in agreement and made my way to the back of the class where the second Mrs. Jones was seated at her desk.

"Have a seat, Kevin," Mrs. Jones said. "The way this class works is Mrs. Jones teaches the first three courses in the morning, and after lunch I, the students refer to me as Mrs. J to avoid confusion, teach the last three, then you see Mr. Ryan for physical education. Here are your textbooks."

"Thanks," I said, taking the books.

"Now you can use your locker if you like, or you can leave books you don't need for homework at your desk. No other students use this classroom. Any questions?"

"No ma'am."

"Okay then, have a seat. Everyone's in alphabetical order, so you'll be behind Tammy," she said, pointing out an empty desk.

I walked to my seat, looking around at the faces in the classroom. I knew everyone, most of the kids having been in my class the year before. Although X sections didn't start until eighth grade, certain students were mysteriously placed in the same classes as far back as second grade.

"Psssst. Psssst. Hey, Kevin," whispered Kirk Taylor, a classmate since kindergarten.

"What?" I asked.

"You been sick?"

"Quiet, Kirk," Mrs. Jones said. "Let Kevin get settled in."

Was it possible no one knew about Johnny's story? This was one of the most uneventful mornings of my school career.

When the lunch bell rang, I was relieved that not one person had commented on the resurgence of my troubled home life. Not wanting to push my luck, I headed straight for the library. Although it was against the rules to eat in the library, I never got caught, and figured I could eat there undisturbed. I found the perfect spot, a desk near the back hidden by bookshelves.

The peace and quiet of the library allowed me my first stress-free moment of the day. Unfortunately, as soon as I was freed from the worries of school, the events of the past few days invaded my mind. I still didn't know what to make of Johnny's story. Mama knew all the answers, but they were safer in her head than if they were locked in

Fort Knox. Without warning I could feel my eyes tearing up. Over the past four days the mere thought of Mama had injected me with a sadness I could not bear. I desperately wanted to see her. As I sat there crying, I heard some kids approaching down the aisles.

"I saw him come in here," one of them said. *Are they looking for me?* Right then, Dylan Patin's head popped around the corner. "Here's the little jungle bunny," Dylan whispered to someone, who I wasn't sure. Then I saw him, James Boutte, my first cousin, although he never referred to me as such.

"Cover his mouth!" James said.

Before I could yell for help, Josh Boutte, James's twin brother who I hadn't seen behind me, grabbed me around the neck, and Dylan covered my mouth.

"Shove him in here," James whispered, not wanting to alarm any of the librarians.

They dragged me into a maintenance closet. My perfect spot in the library turned out to be perfect for an ambush.

"Look, he crying already. Let the little bastard go," James said, shutting the door. "And if you yell, I swear we'll break every bone in your body." Dylan and Josh pushed me to the floor. "I'm warning you if that crazy old coon you live with don't stop spreading lies about my grandpa, we go'n kick your ass."

"Da-dee ain't made up nothing, he ain't even the one who saw what happened," I said, standing and boldly wiping the tears from my eyes.

"No, he convinced some nut to do his lying for him," James said. "Old nigger ain't brave enough to do it himself."

After hearing words like nigger, jungle bunny, and coon countless times in my life, I was immune to reaction. I remained calm, subtly scanning the room and noticing a two-foot lead pipe lying on the floor. As James continued on with his tirade of insults aimed at my entire family, including my mother, his aunt, I nudged my way closer to where the pipe lay.

"The problem started with that slut-whore mama of yours," James ranted.

Those were the last words he got out before I grabbed the pipe and leveled him with a blow to the jaw.

"OH SHIT!" yelled Josh, as blood gushed from James's face. "GET HIM!"

"Don't do it," I warned them, wielding the pipe. "Either I walk out of here right now, or at least one of you will know how James feels. The choice is yours."

After glancing down at James writhing in agony, a pool of blood collecting around his face, Dylan and Josh backed away. I cautiously made my way to the door.

"We go'n get you for this, Kevin," Josh said.

"Or maybe I'll get you first," I said, smiling and backing out of the door.

I left the library and headed straight for the principal's office. I was known to be a model student, while James, Josh, and Dylan were notorious troublemakers. I told the principal what happened, explaining that I was left with no choice in my actions. After looking into my story, he agreed, and I received no punishment.

Word of the incident spread fast, and by the time I boarded the bus home that afternoon, I was a hero. I wasn't the first black kid James had bullied, and there were nothing but black kids on my bus. They surrounded me, pleading for details.

"How many of his teeth did you knock out?" one asked.

"Was he crying?" asked another.

I ignored them, not saying anything. After all, most of the kids asking the questions picked on me as often as James did. Annoyed by my silence, Melvin Lawes, an ignoramus who often exiled me from neighborhood games due to my pale complexion, plopped down next to me.

"Answer the questions, man!" Melvin demanded. "Answer the questions or else!"

"Or else what?" I replied.

Melvin was the toughest kid on the bus; hell, Melvin was one of the toughest kids in school. I knew everyone was thinking my earlier triumphs had gone to my head, everyone except Melvin. After a brief staring contest, he stood in the aisle, a stunned expression masking his face.

"What's going on?" shouted Mr. Franklin, our bus driver. "Melvin, sit down."

Melvin did just that in a seat near the back of the bus. I knew every kid on the bus was wondering why Melvin didn't clobber me. What they didn't see, and what Melvin did, was the pair of scissors I pulled from my bag. Melvin also saw in my eyes that I was not afraid to use them.

I wore a huge smile the rest of the bus-ride home, silently vowing never to be picked on again. No longer would I need to dream of being a hero, I thought. From this day forward, I, the conscious Kevin Matthews, would solve any problem that arose right then and there.

"We Got Company"

I stepped off the bus Friday evening feeling quite pleased with myself. It felt like an oven when I walked into the house, so I turned on the air conditioner.

"Who here?" shrieked a voice, startling me. "Who here?"

The voice was coming from the attic. I remembered that Johnny was being released from the hospital, and Da-dee planned on bringing him home to stay with us. He thought it was safer than Johnny's previous residence, wherever that was.

"That you, Johnny?" I asked. "It's me, Kevin."

"Kevin at school."

"No, Johnny, this is Kevin."

"First day, Kevin at school."

I knew this exchange presented no foreseeable end, so I decided to go up and say hello. When I climbed the narrow stairs to the attic, I couldn't believe my eyes. What was once a dusty, cobweb-filled storage room was now a nicer room than mine, not to mention bigger. I knew Da-dee had been spending a lot of time in the attic over the past four days, but it was so hot up there, I hadn't bothered to go up and see what he was doing. Da-dee had painted the room, re-done the floors, and even cut a window into the wall. Johnny was seated on a twin bed next to the window, dressed in an old pair of Da-dee's pajamas. He looked perfectly healthy.

"Hey, Johnny, how you feeling? You look good!"

"Hey, Kevin. Preacher man taking care of Johnny," he said, standing, and surveying the room with his arms stretched open.

"I know, Johnny. How are you?"

"Preacher man taking care of Johnny. Yes sir. No Jackson for Johnny," he said, with a loud laugh. "Preacher man taking care of Johnny."

"I know, Johnny. You wanna come downstairs? I turned on the air conditioners, so it'll be a lot cooler down there in a little while."

"I got a window."

"I know, but the air conditioning will make it more comfortable."

"I got a window, nice breeze," Johnny said, pointing to the open window.

"What breeze?" I asked under my breath.

"Kevin been reading at school, yes sir, first day."

"Yeah, today was my first day," I said, turning to leave the attic.

"First day, yes sir, first day! Eighth grade!"

I knew this was Johnny's way of asking me to stay, so I decided to share the day's events with him. He was always a great audience, much better than Duke.

"Johnny, I'll tell you all about my first day of school, but you have to come downstairs, it's too hot up here for me."

Johnny agreed, following me downstairs into the living room. I began by telling him about the bus incident involving Melvin Lawes. Melvin often harassed Johnny also, so I knew he would enjoy that story.

"Melvin a scaredy cat! Ha-ha!" Johnny squealed in delight. "Scared of Kevin! Yes sir, Melvin a scaredy cat!"

After repeating the story more than five times at Johnny's request, I insisted we move on. I told him I was in the X section, a class for smart kids.

"Kevin smart; yes sir, Preacher man say 'that boy got a good head on his shoulders,'" Johnny said.

I then made the mistake of telling him that both my teachers were named Mrs. Jones, thinking he might find it funny. After what felt like hours, Johnny accepted my teachers having the same name, although he thought it was confusing, even for smart kids.

I saved the best story for last. I was going to tell Johnny how I cracked James Boutte's jaw. I began by explaining how I found what I thought to be a quiet safe spot in the back of the library to eat my lunch.

"Kevin been reading at school, yes sir! Preacher man say that boy smart!" Johnny said, grinning.

"So right as I'm about to eat my lunch, I hear these voices in the aisles," I said. "I heard one of them say 'Here's the little jungle bunny.'"

"Biscuit burners call Kevin a bad name."

"Right then is when I saw him, James Boutte," I continued.

The words barely escaped my lips before Johnny went ballistic.

"No Boutte! No sir! No sir! Johnny ain't going to Jackson! No Boutte!" Johnny screamed, racing back up the stairs into the attic.

"Calm down, Johnny!" I said, chasing behind him. "I ain't talking about Mr. Boutte, I'm talking about his grandson, James."

"Johnny ain't going to Jackson! No sir! No Jackson!" Johnny said, erratically pacing in circles around the attic.

"No, Johnny you not going to Jackson. Preacher man take care of Johnny."

"Preacher man take care of Johnny. Preacher man and Kevin take care of Johnny, right?"

"Yeah, Preacher man and Kevin take care of Johnny."

After a few more minutes, during which he paced around the room scratching his head and talking to himself, Johnny began to calm down. He sat back on the bed and stared out the window.

"It's okay, Johnny, everything go'n be okay." Johnny didn't reply. He just sat there staring out the window. I noticed his eyes beginning to tear up. "Johnny, we ain't go'n let you go to Jackson. You go'n stay here with us."

"Johnny saw Boutte hurt your mama," he said, turning to look up at me. "Johnny go'n burn in hell if he don't help Junior, going to Jackson he do."

"You ain't going to Jackson, Johnny, I promise."

"Johnny in trouble, Kevin," he said, trembling.

"It's go'n be okay, Johnny, everything go'n be okay. Lay down and get some rest."

Johnny laid down in bed, curling up in a ball on his side. I stood and watched as this huge man lay in bed crying like a frightened child. Johnny was stuck between hell and Jackson, two places in which he saw no difference. I was wrong to think that Johnny didn't know what was in store for us in the coming weeks. Johnny may not have commanded all of his senses, but he knew Mr. Boutte was a powerful man in our town. He couldn't put Johnny back in Jackson right away, but sooner or later, if Johnny continued to tell this story, Mr. Boutte or someone else in town would make sure he ended up there. If ever there was someone in need of saving, Johnny was that someone. My triumphs from earlier in the day meant nothing to me. I found myself once again to be an impotent hero, unable to protect the innocent.

I climbed down the stairs, besieged by thoughts of what Johnny saw that night. I rubbed my eyes and found I was crying. Seconds later, I heard Da-dee's truck pull into the driveway. I quickly escaped out the back door, not wanting him to see me in this condition, and headed for the woods, Duke chasing after me.

"Kevin, where you going?" Da-dee yelled. "We got company!"

MAMA

"Washed in the blood of the lamb!" Da-dee preached. "Jesus Christ shed his blood on the cross at Calvary, and once we accept him, everlasting life is ours!"

Da-dee spent most of the night explaining to Johnny that once he was saved, he became a child of God and could not go to hell. Baptism was the solution to Johnny's dilemma.

"Boutte can't hurt Johnny after tomorrow, no sir! And Johnny ain't go'n burn in hell when he die either, go'n ride in a golden chariot, yes sir! Go'n sit at the table with the king!" Johnny said, laughing at the breakfast table Saturday morning.

Johnny was going to be baptized the following day. Baptisms were normally done on the first Sunday of the month (the following day was the third Sunday), but Johnny's excitement allowed for no delay. Da-dee agreed to make an exception.

"Kevin, I was thinking, maybe we can visit your mama today," Da-dee said.

"Okay," I said, grinning from ear to ear.

Mama had been in my thoughts constantly over the past few days, and I was so excited I couldn't finish my breakfast. It had been a rough week, and more than anything else in the world, I wanted to see Mama.

Sarah Ann Matthews had long silky curly black hair that used to tickle my nose when she kissed me goodnight. I had heard black people use the phrase "blue eyed devils," but Mama's crystal blue eyes were those of a saint. She was tall for a woman, five feet eleven inches, with an olive complexion that made her skin appear newly tanned. Coupled with my father, who inherited Da-dee's dark complexion and stood six feet two inches, I found them to be a striking duo, although the rest of the world seemed blind to the beauty I found in their union.

My parents had met when they were in high school. My father was a star basketball player, and Mama was a cheerleader. Schools in LaPlace were segregated at the time, but the black high school didn't have a gymnasium, so their games were played at the white high school. Mama first spotted my father while at cheerleader practice. A relationship such as theirs was strictly taboo, but Mama knew what she liked when she saw it.

"Running up and down that court, the man reminded me of a fudgesicle on a hot day, mouth watering," she joked with Ms. Linda.

Even though most of Mama's friends deserted her, Ms. Linda remained faithful, and was her only confidant. They were both cheerleaders, and Ms. Linda was one of the few people who knew of my parents' high school romance.

"Your mama's a special woman, Kevin. People described her as being colorblind, but Sarah was aware of every color God created. She delighted in the beauty of the human rainbow," Ms. Linda said, after Mama was attacked. "She has a special light burning in her. She passed that light on to you. You might feel like she's been taken away from you, but as long as that light burns within you, she will always be with you."

Ms. Linda died of breast cancer the following year.

As I got older, I was puzzled how Mama remained with my father in such a destructive relationship. She was a smart woman by all accounts, so it must have been more than mere physical attraction. *What did she love about him? Why had she stayed with him? Was love really that blind?* These were questions to which I had no answers. Being so young before Mama was hurt, the only question I ever thought to ask was, "Why does Daddy hit you?"

"His ego won't allow him to find peace or accept love," Mama answered, confusing me even more.

I occasionally asked Da-dee about my parents, but he was never comfortable talking about their relationship. "They loved each other" was all I could get out of him. With Ms. Linda passing away before I was old enough to ask the questions that now plagued me, there was no one left to supply the answers.

Mama was not a complete mystery to me. I remembered everything she told me about her life. She was the oldest of four children, and the only girl. Unlike her brothers, who were constantly in trouble, Mama caused her parents no worries. She excelled as a student, and graduated high school at the top of her class. After high school, Mama attended Columbia University in New York, earning a Bachelor's degree in English. It was an experience she relished.

"I'd heard people say that everyone should live in New York at some point in their life. Those people knew what they were talking about," she said.

During her sophomore year in college, Mama spent a semester in Paris with the Gautreaux family as part of a student foreign exchange program.

"Twenty-five Rue Muller, that was my address," Mama told me. She said the house was only a few blocks from the Basilique Sacré Coeur, a Catholic Church in Montmartre; a section of Paris. Mama loved the church. "Just sitting in the pews of Sacré Coeur brought about a sense of peace and tranquility within me like no other place I've ever been," she wistfully said to Ms. Linda.

Mama said that Sacré Coeur sat on a majestic rise above Paris, and on many evenings she would climb to the top of the dome in the church, and take in the city lights below. It was from this vantage point she fell in love with Paris.

Mama became close friends with the Gautreauxes' daughter, Nicholle, and spent three subsequent summers with them, becoming fluent in French over the course of her visits. It was a skill Mama attempted to pass on to me, but I hadn't spoken the language since she was attacked.

Mama said she and Nicholle were the toast of Paris. They spent their days in museums, and evenings in cafés discussing politics, life, and love while being courted by countless suitors. I enjoyed picturing my beautiful mother, and what I imagined to be her equally stunning friend Nicholle, being pampered by the richest men in France. This was the life Mama deserved.

Nicholle and Mama kept in contact through letters and occasional phone calls. I always spoke to Nicholle when she phoned, proudly reciting any newly learned French, to her delight. I wondered if Nicholle was aware of what happened to Mama.

Mama credited her exposure to different cultures and ethnicities while living in New York and France for allowing her to reject the racist ideas of her family.

"To accept something you know to be morally unjust is the first step to corrupting your soul, and racism by anyone is nothing if not morally unjust," she said.

After hearing rumors about my parents in high school, Mr. and Mrs. Boutte had been thrilled at their daughter's choice of attending Columbia, thinking it would separate her from my father. But after graduation, Mama returned to Louisiana, and to my father. She took a job as an English teacher at a high school in New Orleans, and soon after married my father.

"If you wanna ruin your life, I can't stop you, but I won't be a part of it," Mrs. Boutte told Mama.

"Long as you married to a nigger, you no daughter of mine," Mr. Boutte said.

Mama never told me these things, but my father repeated her parents' words many times. I knew their disownment of her was painful.

"What's wrong, Mama, don't you like my card?" I asked, after finding her in the bathroom crying one Mother's Day.

"Yes, Baby, it's beautiful."

"Then what's wrong?"

"I just wish I could give my mama a card," she said, sniffling through her tears.

Whenever I felt sorry for myself, I remembered that for Mama things were a lot worse. To have a mother who didn't want you was undoubtedly a harsher fate than the one I suffered.

Mama found solace in her faith. She was raised Catholic and attended church every Sunday with me at her side. Like everything else in our town, religions were split along racial lines; whites were Catholics, and blacks were Baptists. This being the case, our attendance was not greatly appreciated during Sunday services at St. Paul Catholic Church.

· "I don't like this church, they don't want us here," I said to Mama, after detecting the hostility aimed in our direction.

"This is God's house, and we are God's children. And God is one parent who is always welcoming of his children, regardless of race."

"But can't we try another church, maybe another religion?"

"It's not the religion that's the problem, it's ignorance. Don't ever allow ignorance to come between you and your beliefs."

Mama didn't fare much better with neighborhood residents, of which she was the only white person.

"Much money as her people got, she can't find herself a decent white man?" black women questioned.

The men all appeared to be under the impression that Mama was some sort of sexual deviant who craved black men.

"White women freaky I tell you, and once they get a taste of that black meat, well like they say, 'once you go black,'" I overheard a group of black men discussing outside the corner store as I sat in the car awaiting Mama's return. "That's Junior boy she got in that car."

"I done told you triflin' Negroes you ain't go'n be drinking outside my store!" yelled Mr. Frank, chasing the men away.

Mr. Frank was not only the store owner, but also our next-door neighbor. He was a little man, but fierce, allowing no "tomfoolery," as he called it, anywhere on his property.

"Don't pay them fools no mind, they drunk off that liquor," he told me.

Mr. Frank was very fond of Mama. There was a large garden behind his house where he grew vegetables and flowers to sell at the store. His wife had been the primary caretaker, and after she died, Mama took over the responsibilities of caring for the flowers.

"I can't grow a weed, but your mama, she got the touch. That's a gift from God, to nurture things, help them grow. My Betty was blessed with it, your mama, she got it too," he told me.

Mr. Frank now lived alone. He had one daughter, Mary, but she was attending college at Southwestern University in Lafayette. Even though he was in his late forties, I felt I could talk to him about anything. I spent more time with Mr. Frank than I did with my own father. He was a great cook, his specialty being seafood gumbo, and he often invited Mama and me over for dinner.

"Nothing completes a good meal like good company," he said.

Mr. Frank went out of his way to make Mama feel like part of the community; everyone else continually emphasized she wasn't.

"You don't belong here, that's my problem," a black woman answered, after Mama, never being one to back down, challenged her attitude.

Mama's life was far from perfect, but she never complained.

"Who's the luckiest woman in the world?" she asked each night, tucking me into bed.

"You are," I replied.

"And why is that?"

"Because you got me!"

Mama's life revolved around me. She quit her job to become a full-time mom after having me, and put all her energy into raising and educating me. With Mama's tutelage, I was reading at three years old.

"Books are your passport to endless adventures," she said.

We read everything from Dr. Seuss to Shakespeare. Whenever my father said the material was too advanced for a child my age, Mama smiled and said, "Sometimes a kid can understand things better than adults." This response derived from one of our bedtime readings of the greatest adventure story ever told, the Bible.

"Why did God let his only son die?" I asked one night. "Didn't he love Jesus?"

"For God so loved the world, that he gave his only begotten son, that whosoever believeth in him should not perish, but have everlasting life," Mama read.

"So God loved us so much, he sacrificed his own son to save us?"

"Yes, Baby, God loved us so much, he sacrificed his own son to save us."

"Would you sacrifice me to save the world?"

"No, Kevin. I'm not that strong, Baby," she said, with a sigh.

"That's why God had to save the world, right? Because nobody is that strong."

"I guess no one is. I never thought about it that way. Well, smart guy, you taught me something new tonight; what do you think about that?" she asked, tickling my sides.

"I guess sometimes a kid can understand things better than adults," I said, laughing, and squirming under the covers.

"I guess they can," she agreed, squeezing me in her arms, and kissing me goodnight.

Mama doted on me, and I her. I was the picture perfect description of a mama's boy. I went everywhere with her. Whether it was a trip to the hairdresser or shopping, I was there.

"Boy, why don't you go outside and play, instead of hanging under your mama so much," my father suggested.

"He's not hanging under me, we just enjoy each other's company," Mama said, with a wink in my direction.

Mama made me feel loved like no one else could, and I couldn't imagine anyone ever would again.

❄   ❄   ❄

Da-dee and I left on our trip to visit Mama after breakfast. It was a two-hour drive from our home in LaPlace. Da-dee never played the radio, and normally we enjoyed the ride in silence, the wind rushing through the windows our only music.

"I spoke with Mr. Diaz yesterday about what they go'n do with Johnny's story," Da-dee said, thirty minutes into our trip. "He wants to talk to you about what happened."

"I told you and everybody else everything I saw back when it happened."

"Yeah, but he just need to go over it, maybe you remembered something new over the years."

"Like what?"

"I don't know; that's why he wants to talk with you, planning on filing a motion for a new trial."

"I don't remember anything else."

"Well, he just wants to talk to you."

"When?"

"Like to do it as soon as possible, wants to talk to you and your daddy before he interview Johnny. I told him I'd bring you by after school on Monday."

"You believe Johnny, don't you?"

"I don't think Johnny lying, if that's what you asking me. I think he saw what he say he saw, we just got to figure out what that was."

"A lot of folks say you told him to tell that story in order to get my daddy out of jail."

"Folks say a lot of stuff, don't make it true."

"But you don't think he did it, do you?"

"Kevin, your daddy done a lot of wrong in his life, we both know that all too well. He had a lot of anger trapped up inside of him, didn't know what to do with it. But he loved your mama, loved that woman more than you'll ever know. Now I know you probably don't believe that, I can understand why, but I know as sure as I'm sitting here, he loved her. He was ashamed of the way he treated the two of you, told me that himself. I accepted the jury's verdict, but I never was able to bring myself to believe that Junior could hurt Sarah like that, never will until I hear it from his lips. He my boy and I love him."

We drove the rest of the way in silence.

Mama now lived at Cabrini Nursing Home, which was located along a stretch of deserted highway on the outskirts of Slidell, Louisiana. Mr. and Mrs. Boutte chose Cabrini Home because it was considered to be the best nursing home in the state. I found it to be the most depressing place in the world.

The complex consisted of five huge gray stone buildings, all in dire need of a paint job, surrounded by swampland. Bars shielded many of the buildings' windows, causing it to look more like a jail than a nursing home. When you walked through the front doors you were hit with the smell of Lysol, and the people who worked there all seemed angered by their chosen profession. I really hated the place.

Mama was housed on the second floor of Building Three. My sole consolation in her current residence was that she was unaware of her surroundings. She had suffered what the doctors referred to as "Traumatic Brain Injury" when she was attacked. Her resulting condition was called global aphasia. I was told this meant portions of her brain responsible for language and communications had undergone extensive damage, making it difficult for her to speak or understand anyone. In the years following, she developed Alzheimer's disease, a common side effect from this type of injury. These days, Mama rarely attempted to speak, and it was anyone's guess if she understood anything we said, or even knew who we were.

Da-dee and I arrived a little before noon, and went to register in Building One. You were required to sign in and issued a visitor's pass.

"Any visitors for Sarah Boutte?" Da-dee subtly asked the guard manning the registration desk.

"Can't keep track, but I don't think so," he said, preoccupied with his morning paper. "Check the list, if somebody been here you'll see the name."

I watched as Da-dee signed in and scanned the other names on the list. He always checked, but today, more than any other, I knew he didn't want to run into Mr. and Mrs. Boutte. After signing in, the guard handed him our visitor's badges.

"Okay, let's go," Da-dee said, smiling and handing me my badge. His smile signaled their names were not on the list.

We made our way over to Building Three and up to the second floor. When we walked into Mama's room, we found her in a familiar position, seated in a chair next to a barred window, staring out onto the side of Building Four. She was dressed in a white hospital gown, and her hair was pulled back in a ponytail. Mama was still a beautiful woman. From her appearance alone, you wouldn't have known anything was wrong with her.

"How you doing today, Sarah?" Da-dee asked. Mama looked in our direction, and then turned back to her view of Building Four. "Been a crazy week back at the house, so me and Kevin decided to sneak away and pay you a visit. Yeah, got a lot going on, even got a baptism tomorrow at the church. Go'n baptize Johnny."

Mama always liked Johnny. "There's goodness in Johnny," she used to say.

"Well, I'm go'n leave you and Kevin alone," Da-dee said. "Got to go make my rounds. Sarah, I'll sit and talk with you when I get back." Da-dee knew other residents of Cabrini Home, who he always took time to visit. "I'll be back in an hour or so, okay?" he said to me. "Give you and your mama some time alone."

"Okay," I said.

For some reason, I couldn't bring myself to sit down after Da-dee left. I just stood in the middle of the room, staring at Mama, while she stared out at Building Four.

"You belong in here?" I heard a voice ask from the hallway seconds later.

I turned to find a short fat woman dressed in a nurse's outfit.

"I'm visiting my mama," I said, showing her my visitor's badge.

"That your mama?" she asked, glancing at Mama, then back at me.

"Yes ma'am, that's my mama."

"Okay then," she said cautiously.

I watched as she turned and walked away. When I turned back to face Mama, she was looking directly at me, smiling. That smile was all I ever needed. I took a seat next to her, and started talking about old times. She occasionally looked at me smiling, but for the most part she continued to stare out at Building Four. It didn't matter though; I now knew why I wanted to visit her. I was simply a boy who needed to talk to his mother.

THE CARTWRIGHTS

The house was full of excitement when Earl sounded his alarm Sunday morning. I walked into the kitchen and found Johnny seated at the table dressed in a brand new double-breasted black suit, white shirt, and bright gold tie, an early baptism gift from Ms. Bertha.

"Johnny look like the preacher man! Yes sir!" Johnny said, standing to model his new duds. Da-dee had shaved Johnny's head and face. "Going down in the river Jordan today!"

"You look sharp, Johnny," I said.

"Going down in the river Jordan today, yes sir! Kevin go'n come see?"

"Yeah, I'm coming."

"Y'all ready for some breakfast?" Da-dee asked.

"Can't eat 'fore you go in the water," Johnny said.

"I think you'll be okay," Da-dee said.

DoRight Baptist Church services began at nine o'clock on Sunday mornings. Da-dee built the church in 1950 with his own hands, and had been its only Pastor. It was a charming little sanctuary, painted white with blue trim. The church held about two hundred people, and there wasn't an empty seat on this morning, with the crowded pews proving a magnet for the heat. Da-dee had given in to pressure from church members and installed central air conditioning, but even with it blowing full blast, there were fans waving on each row.

I was one of the junior ushers. We, along with the senior ushers, were in charge of seating people, picking up collections, delivering messages to church officials, and making sure there was no talking during the service. There were four junior ushers, and six senior ushers. We stood in strategically placed locations along the walls, where every church member could easily gain our attention. Today I made sure to get a spot near the front of the church where I would have a good view.

Johnny was seated on the front pew, along with the church deacons. He was grinning from ear to ear. His handsome appearance surprised many of the congregation.

"Don't tell me God ain't good. Look what he done for Johnny," I heard countless people repeat.

Service began with a welcome address from Ms. Bertha, who was the head Deaconess of the church.

"Giving honor to God, Pastor Matthews, Church officers and members. Today is a very special day for all of us. We are blessed to welcome home one of God's children"

"Amen!" cried the congregation.

"Many people look at Brother Johnny and say that life has been unfair to him. But as you look around at all the people who have come out this morning to share the happiness of this day with him, you ask yourselves 'how can a man who is so loved by his friends, not be thought of as having a blessed life."

"Yes Lord!" said the congregation.

Ms. Bertha walked over to where Johnny was seated. "Brother Johnny, it brings my heart great joy to see this day. We've known each other since we was children and I want you to know, I love you, Brother." Johnny stood and hugged Ms. Bertha, gripping her in a bear hug that swallowed her from view.

After Ms. Bertha's address, there was a music selection. This was the thing I loved most about our church, the music. It was amazing. The choir, dressed in their blue robes with gold sashes, stood as the organist began playing.

"*At the cross. Where I first saw the light. And the burdens of my heart rolled away.*" The church joined in, and I could feel goose bumps up and down my arms.

After the choir selection, there were more testimonials about God's love, and of course, more singing. When it came time for Tithes and Offerings, the collection plates overflowed. This was all a prelude to Da-dee's sermon.

Da-dee was dressed in a long black robe with a red sash around his neck. He sat alone behind the pulpit in a huge wooden chair, with smaller chairs to the left and right for any visiting preachers who might drop by. The seats were elevated above the pulpit, allowing Da-dee to look out onto the congregation with an unobstructed view. His appearance from this position was nothing less than commanding. After a final hymn, Da-dee stood, slowly stepped down to the podium, and examined the congregation.

"Baptism is to be immersed or dipped in water as an open testimony of being identified with Jesus Christ's own death, burial, and resurrection. It announces to the world that you have received Jesus Christ as your Lord and Savior, and you will spend eternal life after death with Him," he said calmly. This was Da-dee's approach when delivering a sermon. He started off slow, defining for the congregation what the day's lesson centered around. He sounded somewhat like a teacher delivering a classroom lecture. "In Matthew twenty-eight and nineteen, Jesus said to his disciples 'Go ye therefore, and teach all nations, baptizing them in the name of the Father, and of the Son, and of the Holy Ghost.' Now there are those in our community who will say that my taking Brother Johnny into my home and teaching him of the glory of our Lord was an act generated by selfish desires. By now we all know of the situation involving Brother Johnny's knowledge of events that might free my son. But I am here to tell you that I am a disciple of Jesus and my sole desire is to bring another of God's children home."

"Amen! Yes Sir!" yelled the congregation.

Da-dee turned his focus to Johnny. "Brother Johnny, the bible tells us in Matthew three, verse sixteen, that after Jesus was baptized 'the heavens were opened unto him, and he saw the Spirit of God descending like a dove, and lighting upon him.'"

I looked at Johnny, wondering if he comprehended any of the things Da-dee was saying. All doubt was erased when I noticed a tear sliding down his cheek. Johnny had not yet been baptized, but the "lighting" Da-dee referred to had already taken place.

Da-dee continued on with his sermon, his excitement building with each scripture read. He would say a few words and then grunt and clap his hands for emphasis, after which he repeated the last few words of his first statement, and then grunted again. He was in constant movement in the pulpit during this whole time.

"In Mark sixteen, sixteen, huh! Jesus promises the world, huh! He said 'He that believeth and is baptized,' I say 'He that believeth and is baptized, shall be saved!' But the Lord also warns us, huh! He warns us that, 'he that believeth not', huh, I say 'he that believeth not, shall be dammed!'" Da-dee preached, dancing in circles around the pulpit, with beads of sweat cascading down his face, while cries of "Yes sir!" and "Speak Pastor!" rang out from the congregation. "Therefore to be baptized and believe in Jesus is to choose to live with him eternally in heaven, and to not be baptized and not believe is to choose to live with Satan eternally in hell!" Then he squealed out a line as if singing it and speaking it at the same time. "Eternally with Jesus at rest in peace, or eternally with Satan in fire and turmoil!"

Right at that moment Ms. Bertha, along with several other church members, began to *get happy*. *Get happy* was described as being filled with the *Holy Ghost*, and was experienced only by adults. Ms. Bertha began screaming and jumping, and speaking in some unknown language. "Mon-na-tock Mushi, fu-sho-long du, fu-sho-long-du!" she babbled.

This the adults referred to as *speaking in Tongues*. It was the usher's job to physically restrain those who *got happy* so they wouldn't hurt themselves. Of course this was a job for the senior ushers. Ms. Bertha and the others would have crushed my fellow junior ushers and me. No, our job was to get water and wave fans in an attempt to calm them down. As I rushed to Ms. Bertha's side, cup of water and fan in hand, I noticed Johnny sitting alone on the pew; all the deacons had stood to assist in calming down church members. Oblivious to the chaos around him, he sat there crying with a huge smile on his face, his eyes focused on Da-dee. Then, without warning as always, Da-dee spoke the last few lines of his sermon calmly; the same as he had began.

"To be baptized is a choice that each person born into this world must make. It is the most important choice you will make during your life on this earth," he said, pulling out a handkerchief and wiping the sweat from his face. "Brother Johnny has made his choice."

"Praise God! Praise God!" cried the congregation.

"Please rise as the choir leads us out in song," Da-dee instructed the church.

"Let us go down to Jordan. Let us go down to Jordan my Lord. Let us go down to Jordan, and be baptized."

Ms. Bertha, after calming down, led Johnny into the church office to prepare for the baptism. The church members filed out the doors and headed to the rear of the church where the baptismal pool was located. I slipped out through a side door so I could get a spot in front. The congregation continued to sing as we waited for Johnny and Da-dee, who emerged from the church's back door a few minutes later. Da-dee still wore his black robe with the red sash, but Johnny now wore an all white outfit: shirt, pants, and socks, with a white bandana tied around his head. Da-dee climbed into the pool first, and blessed the waters. He then signaled for Johnny, taking his hand and leading him to the middle of the pool.

"Jonathan Paul Morgan, do you believe that Jesus died for your sins in order that you may have everlasting life?"

"I do, yes sir. I do!" Johnny answered.

"Then according to your confession of faith, I now baptize you in the name of the Father, the Son, and the Holy Spirit, Amen." Da-dee then dunked Johnny's head under the water.

"Glory be to God!" Ms. Bertha yelled out.

"I'm gonna lay down my burdens, down by the riverside. Way down! Down by the riverside. Way down! Down by the riverside. I'm gonna lay down my burdens, down by the riverside, I ain't go'n study war no more," the congregation sang, as Da-dee embraced Johnny, their tears blending with the water from the pool.

Ms. Bertha hosted a dinner for Johnny in her backyard after the baptism. All the church members were invited. It was a delightful afternoon, the heat taking the day off and allowing a cool breeze to blow. Ms. Bertha often cooked meals for Johnny and knew all of his favorites. There was fried catfish, barbecued ribs, collard greens, red beans and rice, macaroni and cheese, potato salad, candied yams, and a host of assorted cakes and pies. Johnny sampled every dish available.

"You go'n make yourself sick, Johnny," Ms. Bertha said.

"Not today," Johnny said, sopping up the gravy from his red beans with a huge slice of cornbread. "Johnny feel mighty good, yes sir!"

People sat on blankets in the backyard eating, as Da-dee took on all comers in a game of horseshoes. Around five o'clock, an evening rainstorm caught everyone by surprise. We hurriedly moved the food inside, everyone getting soaked in the process, but nothing could dampen people's spirit on this day. Folks stood under Ms. Bertha's garage talking until the rain lightened. Everyone laughed and spoke of what a blessed day we had enjoyed, before being chased home by mosquitoes arriving for their evening feast. After helping Ms. Bertha clean up, Johnny, Da-dee, and I made it home a little before seven o'clock.

"Bonanza should be coming on, Kevin," Da-dee said.

"Oh yeah!" I said, turning on the television. "Come on, Johnny, you know this show, right?"

The theme song for Bonanza blared from the television and Johnny quickly answered my question as he excitedly hummed along to the music. Da-dee took a seat in his recliner, and Johnny and I stretched out on the floor. The opening of the show featured the three main characters, Ben, Hoss, and Little Joe all riding up on their horses.

"That just like us!" Johnny shouted, pointing at the television. "Preacher man-Ben, Johnny-Hoss, and Kevin-Little Joe! Yes Sir! We just like the Cartwrights!"

After watching Bonanza and a great episode of Gunsmoke, one that caused Johnny to make comparisons between Da-dee and Matt Dillon, not to mention Ms. Bertha and Ms. Kitty, the three of us sat and rehashed the day's events. I didn't get in bed until ten o'clock.

"Kevin, you sleep yet?" Da-dee asked, popping his head into my room.

"No, not yet."

"I wanted to remind you tomorrow after school, we need to go down and see Mr. Diaz. I'll pick you up after class and we'll drive over to his office."

"I know."

"I'll be waiting for you out front of the school when your last class is over. You just come on out and find me."

"Okay."

There was no need to remind me. Although my visit with Mama, and Johnny's baptism served to temporarily take my mind off the meeting with Mr. Diaz, the dread of reliving the worst day of my life haunted me. I kneeled to say my prayers, a nightly ritual that began years before with Mama kneeling next to me:

Our Father, Who Art In Heaven,
Hallowed Be Thy Name.
Thy Kingdom Come.
Thy Will Be Done,
On Earth As It Is In Heaven.
Give Us This Day, Our Daily Bread.
And Forgive Us Our Trespasses,
As We Forgive Those Who Trespass Against us.
And Lead Us Not Into Temptation,
But Deliver Us From Evil.
For Thine Is The Kingdom,
And The Power,
And The Glory,
Forever, And Ever, Amen.

And God, please help me get through tomorrow.

As I pulled back my bed covers, I noticed a streak of lightening crackling across the night sky. Shortly thereafter, I heard the porch being pummeled by a thunderous rainstorm, Mother Nature setting the tone for the next day. I crawled into bed knowing there would be little sleep for me.

I Said Nothing

As far back as I can remember, life with my father had been chaotic. I would come home from school to find the house quiet one day, and the next day there would be arguing and screaming. I began a practice of listening at the door when I came home. If it was quiet, I went in; otherwise I occupied myself away from the house, normally visiting Mr. Frank at his store until things settled down.

My parents' relationship was not always tumultuous; there were moments when they honestly seemed to love each other. I remember nights being awakened by soft jazz ballads playing in the living room. I would peek out of my bedroom door to find them dancing, or cuddled together on the sofa sipping wine. Some mornings I found them in the same spot as I had last seen them the night before, Mama's head buried in my father's chest, his in her curly black locks. They looked so peaceful at these times I just stood watching them.

"What's wrong, Baby?" Mama asked one morning, after awaking to find me staring at her and my father.

"You and Daddy look nice laying on the sofa like that."

My words brought tears to her eyes. She knew, as I did, this was sadly not the norm. The problem was my father's temper. He was angered by the smallest transgression, especially one I committed. There were times when my mere presence aggravated him.

"Why don't you go outside and play, boy, I'm trying to get some rest. I'm tired of looking at you," he complained to me one Saturday morning as I watched cartoons.

Mama didn't like him, or anyone else for that matter, raising their voice to me, so an argument was bound to follow.

"Lester, don't talk to him like that, he's just watching TV, he's not bothering you," she said.

"TV blaring this early in the morning, I ain't entitled to peace and quiet in my own house, that what you telling me, woman?" he hollered in her direction.

It was downhill from there, as they began screaming at each other. These arguments became so commonplace that most times I ignored them. My parents could be yelling like someone was being killed, while I sat on the sofa watching television or reading a book. My only reaction would be to turn up the television to drown out the noise, or go into my room shutting the door to do so. Following these arguments, my father always felt guilty, begging Mama's forgiveness.

"I'm sorry, Sarah, you just make me so mad sometimes," he said. "You know I love you, the last thing in the world I wanna do is hurt you."

Mama remained mad for a few days, but eventually she forgave him, and I would hear jazz music once again seeping into my room late at night.

My father said he didn't want to harm Mama, but I was convinced he didn't have a problem doing so with me.

"Boy, you go'n make me hurt you sooner or later," he'd warn whenever he thought I crossed the line, a line whose boundaries were a complete mystery to me. These threats were accompanied by a menacing stare, one that would burn right through me. Sometimes I wished he would just go ahead and hit me, at least that way it would be over and done with, but there was no end to his stare.

In the end, however, my father's threats were empty, since he never once struck me. *Why was I spared the rod, even in his most ill-tempered moments?* The reason was simple; Sarah Ann Matthews would not allow it.

"Lester, you hit my baby one time and I promise I'll leave you, as sure as there's a God in heaven, I'll leave you for good," she warned one evening, after my father grabbed me by the neck to strike me for taking Mama's side in an argument.

My father responded by wearing the same stunned look Melvin Lawes wore on the bus when I threatened him with my scissors. He knew Mama was fully prepared to follow through on her promise. She had already left him once, the year before I was born. I learned of this news one night when I overheard my parents arguing, my father saying he couldn't handle it if Mama left him again. I later asked Mama about it, but she said they were discussing something that happened a long time ago, and was no longer important. I knew Mama leaving was a fear that hounded my father.

Although most of my parents' fights never went beyond shouting matches, occasionally they became violent and very frightening. The worst example I can recall before Mama was attacked happened just nine days prior.

Thursday, June 17, 1971, my tenth birthday, started out as a great day. Mama cooked my favorite breakfast, blueberry pancakes and bacon, and after I finished eating, she wheeled in my birthday present, a silver and red Schwinn Sting Ray bicycle, with ape-hanger handlebars and a banana seat. Mama didn't see me for the rest of the day. When I finally made it home, Mama had cooked my favorite dish for dinner, Crawfish Etouffee. She then surprised me with tickets for us to see a touring production of *Purlie*, being performed at the Saenger Theatre in New Orleans at eight o'clock that evening. This was to be my introduction into the world of live theatre. "Nothing can compare to live theatre," Mama said.

My father was working that day; he was a supervisor at a chemical plant. He wouldn't make it home until after five, so the plan was Mama and I would have dinner alone, with my father eating something on the job. We would wait until he got home to blow out the candles on my birthday cake, a Devil's food chocolate cake with chocolate icing, also one of my favorites; and then he would get dressed. We would leave no later than seven o'clock, since the trip to the theatre took about thirty minutes.

After stuffing myself with crawfish, I took a bath, got dressed, and sat in the living room watching television. I was wearing my favorite purple pullover with black pants and dress shoes.

"You have to dress fancy for the theatre, it's not like going to the movies," Mama told me.

Mama was wearing a sleeveless black summer dress, gold hoop earrings, and an opal pendant that hung from a gold chain around her neck. The pendant had been a gift from Nicholle when Mama lived in France.

As the clock neared six forty-five, I noticed Mama becoming increasingly agitated. She had broken the front axle on her car after swerving to miss a dog and hitting a large pothole. The car was still in the shop, and without my father we had no transportation to the theatre.

"Maybe he got stuck in traffic," I said.

Mama said nothing. At seven, with no word from my father, she phoned Mr. Frank.

"Mr. Frank, hi, this is Sarah. It's Kevin's birthday and we've got tickets to a show tonight in New Orleans. You know my car's in the shop and Lester hasn't made it home. I would just hate for Kevin to miss the show and I was wondering—really, well thank you so much!"

"Is Mr. Frank go'n take us?" I asked.

"Look, we've got an extra ticket, and we'd love to have you join us," she continued. "Great! We're already dressed, we'll be right over." Mama hung up the phone and lit the candles on my cake. "Mr. Frank is going to take us to the play, but before we leave, come make a wish and blow out the candles on your cake."

I turned off the television and ran to the table. "I wish,"

"Don't say your wish out loud, or it won't come true."

I silently made my wish and blew as hard as I could, blowing out all ten candles in one attempt. Mama then cut several pieces of cake, wrapping them up for the drive. I couldn't have been happier. I was looking forward to the show, but dreaded going anywhere with my father. You never knew when he would explode. My wish was that Mr. Frank would become my new father. He knew how to treat us.

Mama seemed agitated as we settled into Mr. Frank's burgundy Lincoln Continental for the trip to the theatre, but he had her laughing before we backed out of the driveway.

"Temptin' Temptations!" he yelled out mid verse, while passionately singing along to *Ain't Too Proud To Beg*, which blared from the car stereo. Mr. Frank loved the Temptations; their music was in constant rotation on his eight-track player. By the time we hit the highway that took us into New Orleans, Mr. Frank had moved on to love songs. "I know you know this one," he said to Mama, smiling, as the opening notes to *Just My Imagination* rose from the speakers. "Come on, Sarah, sing with me," he pleaded. She was helpless to his charms, and soon joined in; both of them singing in keys of their own creation.

I sat in the backseat eating a piece of my birthday cake, silently saying a prayer thanking God for allowing Mr. Frank to be our theatre companion.

We arrived in New Orleans at seven-thirty. By the time Mr. Frank parked in a garage on Rampart Street, we had twenty minutes to make it to the theatre before the curtain went up. As we walked, me in the middle, Mr. Frank and Mama each holding one of my hands, the excitement of the evening began to take hold. Mama told me that the lead character was a Preacher, just like Da-dee, and some of the play took place in a church. I had visited Da-dee's church and my mind raced with questions as to what the show held in store for me: *Was he a better preacher than Da-dee? How big would the church be? Would the choir be as good as the one at Da-dee's church?* I wasn't even in the theatre, but I was convinced Mama was right; nothing can compare to live theatre.

We turned onto Canal Street, and the flashing lights spelling out **SAENGER** that sat above the theatre marquee sent chills down my back.

"Mr. Frank, could you please get a picture of Kevin and me under the marquee?" Mama asked, pulling out her camera.

"Yeah, good idea!" Mr. Frank said, taking the camera.

Mama and I hurried under the marquee and Mr. Frank, after repositioning the camera in every conceivable fashion, snapped the picture.

"Now let me get one of you and Kevin," Mama said.

"We can get one of all three of you if you like," an older black couple offered.

"Oh, thank you so much," Mama said, handing them the camera.

I stood in front, Mr. Frank hugging Mama behind me.

"Okay, say cheese," the woman said, with her husband acting as the photographer.

"CHEESE!"

"Thank you again," Mama said, as the man handed her the camera. "Are you going to the show?"

"Yes ma'am, we certainly are," the man said.

"Us too, it's my son's birthday," Mama said.

"Well Happy Birthday!" they both said.

"You are in for a treat young man," the woman said. "There's nothing like live theatre."

"Oh my, that is such a beautiful cameo you're wearing," Mama said to the woman. "My Nana wore one just like that."

"Thank you, this was actually given to me by my grandmother," the woman said, smiling and touching the cameo. "Kind of a family heirloom."

"Well, it's beautiful. Thanks again for the picture," Mama said.

"Oh, you're welcome darling, I just hope it comes out. It looks like it'll be such a nice family shot," the woman said. "Enjoy the show."

Mr. Frank was at least ten years older than Mama, and about five inches shorter, so I couldn't imagine that the couple thought they were married, but that concept was quite appealing to me.

When we entered the lobby of the theatre, I was surprised to find that the majority of the theatregoers were black. I had never seen so many black people dressed up like that, except the few times I visited Da-dee's church. Mama was right; you had to dress fancy for the theatre.

We took our seats, and there it was on stage, *Big Bethel Church*, the setting for the musical. As the lights went down, I could hardly sit still from anticipation.

The show ended around ten-thirty p.m., and it was better than I ever imagined. *Purlie*, the lead character, was indeed a master showman in the pulpit, every bit Da-dee's equal at delivering a sermon. The dancing was unlike anything I had ever seen, and the singing, to my surprise, was better than any I experienced in local churches. My favorite song was *Walk Him up the Stairs*, a song about saving sinners from hell, which *Purlie* sang with a full choir backing him up. The whole evening was fantastic. The show was also Mr. Frank's first live theatre experience.

"That's a lot more exciting than TV. Tell you the truth, I don't know how they remember all them lines doing all that singing and dancing," he said.

As excited as I was at the end of the show, I was still asleep less than ten minutes into the trip home, the spacious backseat of Mr. Frank's Lincoln proving to be just as inviting as my own bed. When we made it home shortly before midnight, my father was nowhere to be found.

"That's a damn shame I tell you!" Mr. Frank said at the door, thinking I was asleep in Mama's arms. "It's the child's birthday. You need to leave that man, Sarah. He ain't no good."

"I know, Mr. Frank, I know," Mama said.

Mama thanked Mr. Frank and said goodnight. She carried me into my bedroom and helped me put on my pajamas. After saying my prayers with me, she tucked me into bed, kissed me goodnight, and stood to leave my room. I could tell something was wrong.

"You going to bed, Mama?"

"Not right now, Baby, go to sleep."

Knowing Mama was upset, I couldn't fall back to sleep. I got out of bed and went to my door, cracking it open and looking out. I watched as Mama turned off all of the lights in the house and took a seat at the kitchen table. After watching quietly from my bedroom for a few minutes, Mama not moving from her seat, I walked out to see what she was doing.

"Mama, why you sitting in the dark?"

"I'm fine, Baby, you go to sleep, Mama is fine."

"But why you——,"

"Go to bed, Kevin!"

Frightened by her response, I quickly went back to my room. A few moments later, Mama came in and sat next to me on the bed.

"I'm sorry, Baby, Mama didn't mean to yell at you. I'm just a little upset."

"You mad at Daddy?"

"I am, but I shouldn't have yelled at you."

"Why are you sitting in the dark?"

"I just want to talk to your daddy."

"When is he coming home?"

"I don't know, but I'm going to be up when he gets here. Did you
enjoy the show?"

"Yeah, it was great. I liked *Gitlow*, he was funny."

"He sure was, wasn't he?" she said, running her hands through my
hair. "Who's the luckiest woman in the world?"

"You are."

"And why is that?"

"Because you got me," I said, grinning.

"That's right, because I got you," she said, kissing me on the forehead. "Good night, Baby."

With those words, everything was okay. I watched as she closed the
door to my bedroom, and I fell off to sleep.

"What you go'n do?" my father yelled, jolting me awake hours later.
"You ever try to leave me woman, and I'll kill you, you hear me, I'll
kill you!"

I ran into the living room and found Mama kneeling on the floor,
my father standing above her, a handful of her hair in his hand, a gun
pointed to her temple.

"No! Don't hurt my mama!"

"Go back to bed, Baby, it's okay" Mama cried, blood trickling from
her nose.

My unexpected appearance unnerved my father. He turned to face
me, releasing Mama.

"I don't need this shit, I tell you I don't need it!" he yelled, and then
stormed out of the house.

Mama stood, running to the door and locking it. I could hear the roar
of the engine on my father's royal blue Mustang as he pulled out of the
driveway, tires screeching. Mama told me to get dressed and we went
next door to Mr. Frank's house. We spent the night in his guest room.

❋　❋　❋

On the morning Mama was attacked I remember getting out of bed
and finding the door to my parents' bedroom closed. I thought it odd
that Mama was not awake. It was a Saturday, so it wouldn't have been

unusual for my father to be sleeping one off from the night before, but Mama normally would have been up by the time I awoke at eight. After entertaining myself with cartoons for an hour, I became hungry. I considered eating cereal, but all week I had been itching for Mama's blueberry pancakes and bacon. Although she had made an exception on my birthday, she normally made this meal only on Saturday mornings. "This way you'll appreciate it more," she said. I decided to wake her up. I had waited all week, and I wanted my pancakes.

I opened the door to my parent's bedroom, and the events of the previous night screamed out at me. A chair was tossed on its side in the middle of the room, a frame containing my parents wedding picture was shattered on the floor, an empty suitcase lay open on the bed, and clothing was strewn all over the room. My father was lying on his side in bed next to Mama, with his left arm and leg draped across her. From where I stood in the doorway, he was completely shielding Mama from view. I walked to the side of the bed where she was lying and the first thing I noticed was her eye. It was swollen shut and discolored. I moved closer to the bed and saw that her lip was puffy and split. There was also a gash across her temple. It then occurred to me that her entire face was swollen, and it appeared she wasn't breathing. Fear instantly raced through me. I turned to run from the room and tripped over one of Mama's many beauty products, which cluttered my path. The sound of my falling woke my father. He looked around the room for the noise, but was then frozen by Mama's appearance. It was as if he were seeing her in this condition for the first time. He then turned his attention to me, our eyes locking in a brief staring contest. I scrambled to my feet.

"What did you do to Mama?" My father didn't answer. "What did you do to Mama?" I cried once more, running from the room. I left the house and ran into Mr. Frank's front yard. "Mr. Frank, Mr. Frank!" I yelled running under the garage.

"What's the matter, Kevin?" Mr. Frank asked, sprinting from his front door to meet me.

"It's Mama, Daddy hurt Mama! I don't think she's breathing."

Mr. Frank pulled me into the house and called the police. The next thing I remember was seeing my father taken from the house in handcuffs. Mr. Frank kept me inside until the ambulance took Mama away, but he wanted me to see my father.

"Look at him!" he demanded. "Don't ever forget what that bastard did to your Mama, you hear me!"

I looked on as police officers, Chief Brady among them, lead my father out of the house. My father glanced in my direction as the officers placed him in the backseat of the patrol car, but he looked right through me. I was certain Mama was dead. I wanted to yell out to him that I knew he killed her. I wanted to tell him how much I hated him because he took her from me. Instead, I just watched as the police car drove away with him in the backseat. I said nothing.

A Way Out

After telling my story to Mr. Diaz, I suffered another sleepless night. I was already at the window by the time Earl made his way onto the porch Tuesday morning. Upon seeing me, he stopped dead in his tracks. Surprisingly, I felt no satisfaction from his fear. I simply closed the curtains and returned to bed, lying there until Da-dee called me for breakfast.

"Me and Mr. Diaz going out to take your daddy's statement, so I'll be gone most of the day," Da-dee said. "Bertha go'n cook something for you and Johnny, so you just stop by there for supper when you get home from school."

"Where Johnny at now?"

"He left out of here about an hour ago, been out there in the field picking pecans. Bertha told him she was go'n fix him a pie if he pick the pecans. I told both of them ain't no pecans on them trees yet, still too early in the year."

"When Mr. Diaz go'n talk to Johnny?"

"First thing tomorrow morning, after that he go'n prepare the paperwork for the appeal; say we got a good chance at a new trial."

Normally Da-dee's bright outlook regarding my father's fate annoyed me, but today I felt no emotional response whatsoever. I sat at the breakfast table drained, the events of the previous day having sucked all the energy from my body. I was tired of the whole situation, and just wanted things to go back to the way they were before Johnny told his story. I longed for an escape.

The blank expression I wore that morning at school announced to the world my state of mind.

"You alright, Kevin?" Kirk asked. "You look like a zombie."

"I'm just tired, that's all."

"Okay, class, we're going to start this morning by discussing Fitzgerald's *The Great Gatsby*," Mrs. Jones said.

The book was assigned the first day of class as part of our one book per week reading schedule. Although I was out the first day, and therefore missed the assignment, I had read the book of my own volition the year before. I found it to be a colossal bore, focusing on people whose problems in life were more self-induced than based in reality.

"Kevin, can I speak with you?" Mrs. J called from the back of the room, rescuing me from a discussion I dreaded.

I turned to find a man I had never seen before seated at her desk. He looked like any number of the male teachers at our school, pale and slim with silver framed glasses, but was dressed more like a businessman, wearing a gray pinstripe suit, light blue shirt, dark blue tie, and freshly polished black Florsheim shoes.

"Kevin, Jim Willis," he said, standing and shaking my hand. "I've heard some very impressive things about you. It's nice to finally meet you."

The first thing I noticed about him, aside from his expensive attire, was his speech. He spoke really proper, and didn't sound like the other white people in our town.

"Mr. Willis is an old college friend of mine," Mrs. J said.

"Hello. Nice to meet you also, Mr. Willis," I said.

"Mrs. Jones, or should I say Mrs. J?" he asked, laughing.

"It does help to avoid confusion," Mrs. J said.

"Well, Kevin, Mrs. J contacted me regarding your choice of high schools next year," he continued.

"My choice of high schools? We only have one high school in town, I didn't know I had a choice."

"That's true, Kevin, there's only one high school in town, but Mr. Willis is here to speak with you about St. Ann's Catholic Academy Boarding School for Boys in New Orleans," Mrs. J said to me.

"Catholic Boarding School?" I asked, my first thought being I wasn't Catholic. I had attended Catholic churches with Mama when I was younger, but Da-dee baptized me at DoRight, a Baptist church.

"You see, Kevin, Mrs. J contacted me because in reviewing your school records for inclusion in her class, she felt you were an exceptional student," Mr. Willis said.

"Thanks," I replied, feeling gratitude for such praise was required. "But, I'm not Catholic."

"That's not a problem; you're not required to be Catholic in order to attend the school. You see, St. Ann's offers five four-year scholarships to deserving minority students who, due to economic conditions, would otherwise not be able to attend the school," he said. "After reviewing your records and talking with some of your previous instructors, I thought you might be an ideal candidate."

"I don't understand."

"It's really quite simple. I submit your name to the school's board as a candidate for one of the scholarships. You will be asked to write an essay on reasons why you feel attending St. Ann's would be beneficial to your academic career. We'll set up an appointment for you and your family. You live with your grandfather, correct?"

"Yes sir."

"We'll set up an appointment for you and your grandfather to come in for an interview and a visit so both of you have a chance to see the campus, and in a few months, we'll notify you if you've been awarded the scholarship."

"Then I would go to school in New Orleans next year?"

"That's right. You would live on campus Monday through Friday, coming home on weekends."

"It's an excellent opportunity, Kevin," Mrs. J said. "St. Ann's will provide more of a challenge for you. The one thing I've heard from your teachers is you're a little bored by the material presented to you here."

"I would go to school at St. Ann's for all four years of high school?" I asked.

"That's the idea," Mr. Willis said. "The only requirement is that you maintain a B average."

"What if I don't maintain a B average?"

"Well, the first month you're placed on probation, and you have the next semester to bring your grades up," Mr. Willis said. "If you don't, you're in jeopardy of losing your scholarship the next year."

"I don't think that will be a cause for concern," Mrs. J said, smiling.

"I know you're probably a little nervous about the idea of living away from home, having to make new friends and all, but like Mrs. J said, this is a great opportunity for you," Mr. Willis said. "Our students get recruited by the top universities in the country."

Mr. Willis was giving his best sales pitch, unaware that his persuasion was the last thing I needed. *Make new friends? Who were the old friends?* True, I would miss Da-dee, Johnny, Ms. Bertha, Mr. Frank, and Duke, but that's about all I could imagine I would miss of LaPlace. St. Ann's may have been a great opportunity as Mr. Willis alleged, but in my mind the only thing that mattered was that St. Ann's was not in LaPlace.

I spoke with Mr. Willis a while longer, and then he gave me some brochures about the school for Da-dee to read. He said he would call Da-dee and schedule an appointment for us to come to the school for a visit the following week.

"Take care, Kevin," he said, shaking my hand as he prepared to leave. "Linda, I'll speak with you soon."

"Good seeing you, Jim," Mrs. J said, as Mr. Willis left the classroom.

"You went to college with Mr. Willis?" I asked Mrs. J.

"Sure did."

"Where did you go?"

"We went to Tulane University."

"He's from New Orleans?"

"No, Jim's from New York."

That explains the way he talks, I thought. "He came here to go to school?"

"Sure did."

"He didn't wanna go back to New York after he finished school?" I asked, not understanding why anyone wouldn't want to live in New York.

"He went back to New York for graduate school, but missed New Orleans so much, he moved back down after he finished."

"Where did he go to graduate school?"

"Columbia University. Ivy League school, maybe you'll go there someday, going to St. Ann's definitely makes that a possibility."

I felt my body come alive. Columbia University was where Mama went to school. It was located in a city that I dreamt of living. After a week of dreading each coming day, I was now presented with something to look forward to, something to focus on. St. Ann's represented a way out.

I got off the bus that afternoon in high spirits. Needing to share my news with someone I thought would appreciate it, and knowing Da-dee wasn't home, I decided to pay Mr. Frank a visit. I stopped in the house to drop off my book bag and ask Johnny if he wanted to go with me to Mr. Frank's store, but when I called out to him in the attic, he didn't answer. I hope he's not still out in the field picking pecans, I thought. Johnny tended to over-do everything. I left the house and hopped on my bike, then headed over to Mr. Frank's store.

"Kevin, where you going, Baby?" Mrs. Bertha yelled from her window.

"I'm going down to see Mr. Frank, he asked me to stop by."

"You not hungry? I got some meatloaf and white beans cooked in here."

"No ma'am. I ain't hungry right now; I'll eat when I get back. Tell Da-dee where I went if he get home before I come back?"

"I'll tell him."

"Oh, Ms. Bertha, you seen Johnny?"

"Last I saw him he was headed down the road to Bo's place to sell what was left of the pecans he picked."

"He picked enough to sell?"

"Lord, yes! Picked enough for me to make him two pies and still had a sack full left over. He was out there all day long. I don't know how he found that many, Preacher say it ain't even pecan season yet. You be careful on the road with that bike, you hear me?"

"Yes ma'am," I yelled, my bike kicking up dirt as I sped out of the driveway.

"I don't allow no foul language on these premises!" Mr. Frank yelled, as I pulled into the store parking lot.

I saw Melvin Lawes and his cronies jumping onto their bikes as Mr. Frank chased them from the store.

"Forget you old man," Melvin said, peeling out of the driveway.

"You'll remember me if I catch you, I guarantee you that!" Mr. Frank shouted.

"What did Melvin do?" I asked Mr. Frank, parking my bike in front of the store.

"Cursing like a grown man who done lost his job, that's what he did, and right in front of grown folks. Boy ain't got no home training, I tell you."

"He was cursing right in front of you?"

"I guess it ain't his fault, his daddy ain't worth a good God damn! Who go'n teach him any better," Mr. Frank reasoned. "So what brings you by?"

"Got some good news."

"Well, come on in the store, it's too hot to talk out here," he said, wiping sweat from his forehead. "You go get yourself an ICEE, got a new flavor, watermelon."

Mr. Frank always asked that I test out new flavored ICEEs. When we went into the store, Mrs. Washington, my fifth grade teacher, was waiting at the counter with a gallon of milk and a carton of eggs.

"That child has no respect for his elders," Mrs. Washington said.

"Ain't that the truth, I tell you, I don't know what's wrong with these kids today," Mr. Frank said.

"Hi, Mrs. Washington," I said, heading toward the ICEE machine.

"Hi, Kevin. I hear you had a visitor today," she said, smiling.

"Yes ma'am."

"I hope everything works out, you really deserve it, Baby."

"I guess she talking about your good news, right?" Mr. Frank asked.

"Oh, you don't know, Kevin's been offered a scholarship to St. Ann's Catholic Academy in New Orleans," Mrs. Washington blurted out, cheating me of delivering the good news to Mr. Frank. "You know those Catholic schools are much better than the public ones."

"You don't say," Mr. Frank said, beaming.

"The man——," I began to say.

"What man?" Mr. Frank asked.

"Jim Willis, he helps run the school up there," Mrs. Washington said, allowing me no room to speak. "He's a friend of Linda Jones, she's Kevin's teacher. You see Linda spoke to him about Kevin, and he came down here today personally to talk to Kevin about the school. Linda says Kevin has to go through the application process, but she's sure they're going to take him." Will I get to tell any of this story, I thought.

"You don't say? St. Ann's, huh?" Mr. Frank asked, his smile broadening with each detail.

"Top boarding school in the state," Mrs. Washington added, grabbing her grocery bag and heading toward the store's exit. "Well I got to go, but don't be so modest, Kevin, tell Frank what happened."

"I think you pretty much covered everything," I said, finishing off my ICEE and tossing it into the trashcan.

"So, Kevin, what did the man tell you?" Mr. Frank asked.

"He said——,"

"Said the top colleges in the country recruit their students, I tell you, this is a real opportunity for Kevin," Mrs. Washington interrupted once more, before leaving.

"St. Ann's, well I'll be," Mr. Frank said. "Top school in the state and they want little old Kevin Matthews from right here in LaPlace."

"Mr. Willis didn't say anything was definite, I still have to apply and everything," I said.

"Boy, your mama sure would been proud. I don't know why I'm saying would, it's your mama spirit that's watching out for you, guiding you. She knew all about this happening even before St. Ann's did. Yeah, don't think she don't know about what done happened."

"They say I got to live at school during the week, then come home on the weekends."

"That's good, you don't need to be with these fool children we got around here. No, you need to be around folks headed in the same direction you are."

"What does that mean?"

"You too big for this place, it can't do nothing but trap you. People got small minds in this town, Kevin. They can't see past what they been told to expect from life."

"I don't understand."

"What I mean is, you got dreams. You always talking about going to France and living in New York like your mama did. How many other people around here you hear talk about going any further than New Orleans?"

"Mr. Willis went to Columbia University just like Mama. Mrs. J say I might be able to go there to if I go to St. Ann's." I was excited to relay the one bit of news not divulged by Mrs. Washington.

"You can go anywhere you want, Kevin."

"You know I ain't even really been offered the scholarship yet."

"I wouldn't worry about that, like I said, your mama watching over you. You told Preacher yet?"

"No, he ain't home, they taking my daddy's statement today down at the prison."

"They are, huh?" Mr. Frank said, his disposition quickly changing.

"Yeah, Da-dee think they can get him a new trial," I said, feeling Mr. Frank out for a response.

"Oh really."

"You know with Johnny testimony and all."

"Uh-huh," Mr. Frank said, revealing nothing.

"You think my daddy did it?" I asked, realizing that no opinion was forthcoming unless I pressed Mr. Frank.

"Well, Kevin, you know I ain't never been one to beat around the bush with you, so I'm go'n shoot you straight. Like I told you the day it happened, I know your daddy did it."

"But what about Johnny, he said he saw Mr. Boutte——,"

"I don't know what Johnny saw. And Lord knows Boutte ain't no good, but Junior the one who hurt your mama. It hurt me to stand here and tell you that, but it's best you face the truth."

"I guess you right."

"Your daddy ain't no good, Kevin, he got evil in him. Now, I don't understand it, never have. Preacher and your grandma, well, I ain't never met two more decent, giving, loving, Christian people in my life, but Junior, something went wrong with him. The way he treated your mama and you, he just ain't got no good in him, that's all I can say."

Mr. Frank was the only adult who spoke so openly in my presence about the disdain he held for my father.

I continued discussing with Mr. Frank all the great opportunities St. Ann's could present to me until I became hungry and decided to go home and get something to eat.

"Hey, how was that watermelon ICEE?" Mr. Frank asked, before I left the store.

"It was pretty good. The strawberry kind is still the best though."

"Yeah, I thought the same thing. You keep me posted on how your visit goes, okay? You on your way, boy, you on your way!"

With the sun having gone down and a cool evening breeze blowing up against my direction, the ride home was infinitely more enjoyable. As I turned onto our road I noticed the sign on the corner:

DEAD END

I have to get into St. Ann's, I thought.

When I made it to the house, Da-dee hadn't made it home. I rode over to Ms. Bertha's for supper.

"Child, I was wondering where you was," she said, spotting me from her window, telephone in hand. "Late as it is, you must be starving."

"Yes ma'am, I am," I said, parking my bike under her porch.

"Let me call you back, Martha, Kevin here. Preacher ain't home so I cooked for him. I'll call you back later, but you call me if you hear anything about that other issue we was discussing," Ms. Bertha said, hanging up the phone as I walked into the house. "So, St. Ann's boarding school, huh?" Martha was Mrs. Washington's first name; she had beaten me to the punch once again. "Martha say that's the best school in the state," Ms. Bertha said, as I took a seat at the kitchen table.

"That's what they tell me," I said, annoyed.

"Preacher know?"

"No ma'am. I just found out today."

"Lord, he go'n be so proud. I'm proud of you too, Baby," she said, kissing me on the forehead.

"Well I ain't been accepted yet, I still have to go through the application process."

"Martha say you definitely go'n get in with your grades. Say ain't no telling what kind of opportunities going to that school could lead to."

"I know."

"It's a blessing, I tell you, cause ain't nothing for you to do staying around here. I can tell you that. Just like I told my boys, 'get out of LaPlace any way you can, cause white folks in this town ain't go'n let you accomplish but so much,'" she said, dishing up my supper.

"Johnny come back by here?"

"He stopped by to get something to eat and pick up his pies. Bo done got him all upset. Johnny say he cheated him on how much he paid him for the pecans he picked. He asked me where you was, then said he was going home to watch television. What time Preacher due back?"

"I don't know. He had to go to Angola today, they taking my daddy's statement."

"Yes, Praise God, Preacher say they might get a new trial for him," Ms. Bertha said, placing a plate of white beans and meatloaf in front of me that could have easily fed three people. This was the only thing I hated about eating at Ms. Bertha's house. She was a great cook, but she served you too much food. She said it was okay if you didn't eat it all, but I felt obligated to finish whatever she put on my plate. I always left her house with my stomach too stuffed. "So, if I got it right, you go'n be staying at the school during the week, and come home on the weekends?" she asked.

"Yes ma'am."

"I don't know if I like that, but I guess Preacher can't be driving all that way every day to take you back and forth."

"Yeah, I guess not. I don't mind though, that is if I get in."

"What you mean if? Martha say you go'n get in, ain't no question about that."

Mrs. Washington was really turning up the pressure on my getting into St. Ann's. I was beginning to feel I would let everyone down if I didn't.

Just then, the phone rang, startling me. Ms. Bertha's phone featured the loudest ringer I had ever heard. She claimed such excessive volume was needed to assure her of not missing a call if she were outside. This explanation never made sense to me since she was never outside, and forever within arms' reach of the phone.

"Hello," Ms. Bertha answered, snatching up the phone after one ring. "Who this, Benny? Yeah, he went down there today. Kevin eating at the table right now." It was Mr. Benny calling to find out how things were going in Da-dee's attempt to get my father a new trial. "They got to give him a new trial, Johnny done told them what he saw," Ms. Bertha shouted into the phone. "Yeah, that's true, cause Lord knows white folks can make things look the way they want them to, you ain't lying about that." Ms. Bertha believed in my father's innocence. Having heard Johnny's story, she was now convinced my father was framed. "Look Benny, I'll call you after I speak with Preacher. Yeah, I'll call you back tonight. Bye."

"You think they go'n give my daddy a new trial?" I asked.

"I don't know, Baby, they should with everything Johnny done told them, but who knows?"

"So you don't think my daddy did it?"

"Well Johnny saw Boutte do it, told me himself."

"You talked to Johnny about what he saw?"

"He sat right where you sitting just yesterday and told me how he saw Boutte hurt your mama. Poor soul thought he was go'n burn in hell for not doing anything until Preacher baptized him on Sunday."

For the past week I had debated in my mind what Johnny saw that night, but had yet to ask him. I knew telling the story made him upset and I thought it best not to talk to him about it. Ms. Bertha pointed out something that I had failed to realize. Johnny no longer feared punishment from God or Mr. Boutte, so he shouldn't have a problem talking about what he saw that night. I was halfway through the mountainous plate of food Ms. Bertha served me, when I felt an urgent need to talk to Johnny about his story.

"Ms. Bertha, can you wrap this up for me to take home?" I asked, not wanting her to think I was going to waste the food.

"You full?"

"No, it's just I promised Johnny I was go'n watch TV with him, so I'll just finish eating at home," I lied.

"Baby, Johnny go'n be fine, finish eating your food, we talking."

RING! The phone rang.

"Hello," Ms. Bertha answered, once again allowing but one ring. "What? Child, I knew something was going on with them people, you just don't keep to yourself like that, not talking to nobody."

Knowing Ms. Bertha was now distracted by whatever juicy gossip she was being told, I saw my opportunity to get out of there.

"I'm going so you can talk on the phone, Ms. Bertha. I'll just bring the plate back tomorrow."

"Okay, Baby, I'm sorry, but I do need to take this call."

"That's alright."

"I saw him at the grocery store, look right in my face and ain't said a word," she continued, caught up in her phone conversation.

Not capable of taking another bite of the food, I stopped in the back yard to let Duke finish off my supper. I felt my nerves getting the better of me as I considered the best way of approaching Johnny regarding his story. I'll just ask him flat out what he saw, I thought. After a week of speculation, I was going to get to the bottom of Johnny's story.

I walked into the house and found the television blaring, an empty pie pan on the floor.

"Johnny, come down here for a minute," I yelled. I turned off the television and walked to the stairs leading up to the attic. "Johnny, come down here, I need to talk to you." Johnny didn't answer. I made my way up the stairs into the attic. The room was dark, but I could see Johnny lying in bed. "Johnny, you sleeping?"

There was no answer.

"'I am the resurrection, and the life: he that believeth in me; though he were dead, yet shall he live: And whosoever liveth and believeth in me shall never die,'" Da-dee serenely read from the pulpit, choosing to dispense with his normal theatrics on this day.

The doctors, after declaring eight days earlier that Johnny's recovery from being hit by a car could not be explained, were at a loss once again in explaining what caused Johnny to pass away less that seventy-two hours after securing his place in heaven. Da-dee held no reservations about what had happened.

"'Reverend Matthews, we can't explain what caused Mr. Morgan to wake from his coma, he's lucky to be alive.' That's what the doctors told me last Monday when I arrived at the hospital," Da-dee said to the congregation. "You see, Church, the doctors were looking at Johnny's recovery through the eyes of the world. I'm here to tell you that what was going on was being dictated from a higher plane."

"Yes, Lord," said the congregation.

"When Brother Johnny spoke to me on that morning, the first thing he told me was 'I dreamt I was burning in hell, and the Lord lifted me from the flames.' The explanation the doctors searched for was a simple one. The Lord, after deciding to call home one of his children, wanted Brother Johnny to get right with his God before he died. I'm here to tell you, Church, Brother Johnny did just that. He was baptized, he gave his life to Jesus, and now he will live eternally with Jesus in heaven."

"Praise God!" the congregation shouted.

"Friends, let me tell you a story. Last Friday, when Brother Johnny told me he wanted to be baptized, your wise Pastor told him that we didn't do baptisms on the third Sunday of the month. Well, Brother Johnny would have none of our earthly rules. He told me 'Preacher man, I got to go down in the river Jordan on Sunday, I can't wait no longer.' You think the Lord wasn't in control of what was happening? Can I get an Amen?"

"Amen!"

"The Lord knew his child was coming home Tuesday night, and Johnny knew he had to get right with his God. Revelation fourteen, verse thirteen tells us 'Blessed are the dead which die in the Lord from henceforth: Yea, saith the Spirit, that they may rest from their labours; and their works do follow them.' Brother Johnny is at rest from his labors, Glory be to God!"

"Amen!"

"Jesus said 'In my Father's house are many mansions.' Church, I'm here to let you know that Brother Johnny is at home with Jesus," Da-dee concluded.

Most people think of funerals as sad occasions, but the prevailing emotion in the church that morning was one of great joy.

"I cry because I'm happy, I cry because I'm free!" the choir sang, echoing the apparent sentiments of everyone, because although there were many who cried, all appeared happy.

As she had done the past Sunday, Ms. Bertha invited the entire congregation over to her house for dinner after the funeral. It was one of the most glorious September days ever experienced in LaPlace, a breezy, sunny sixty degrees, with the clouds resembling soft white pillows on a light blue bed in the heavens. People laughed and talked, reveling in their memories of Johnny.

"They say the Lord will walk with you, but I don't know if he can keep up with Johnny, no sir!" Mr. Frank said, laughing.

"The Lord said he will prepare a table before you, but he better prepare two tables the way Johnny eat," Ms. Bertha said.

I noticed Da-dee sitting alone under a large oak tree in the backyard. I couldn't help but wonder if he was upset because with Johnny passing before a new trial was secured, it was doubtful my father would ever be freed. I decided to go over and keep him company.

"You want me to get you anything to eat?" I asked. "Ms. Bertha said the food's going fast."

"No, not right now."

"Why you sitting over here all by yourself? You upset about something?"

"No, quite the opposite," he said, wearing a peaceful smile.

"Then what?"

"Well, I'm go'n miss my friend, Lord knows that's the truth, but I'm just sitting here in awe of how good God has been to me."

"You mean still being alive?"

"I am grateful for that," he said, chuckling at my question. "But, Kevin, the Lord blessed me by allowing me to be the instrument by which one of his children was saved. Through God's grace I was able to bring my friend home to Jesus before he passed."

"Never thought about it that way."

"This is truly a blessed day."

"Ain't you upset about my daddy? Probably won't get a new trial without Johnny to tell what he saw."

"Your daddy fate in the Lord's hands," he said, standing and placing his arm around my shoulders. "Now come on, I better go over here and get something to eat. Johnny might not be here, but Frank sure is, and to be honest I don't know who eat the most, him or Johnny," Da-dee said, laughing as we walked over to join the others.

Later that evening I had a chance to discuss with Da-dee the possibility of my going to St. Ann's the next year. He said he was proud of me and knew I would be selected for the scholarship. "Your mama go'n be so excited to hear this news," he said. Da-dee always spoke of Mama as if she were still aware of what was going on, as if she were still a part of my life.

That night I said my prayers, adding a special request for God to take care of Johnny, and crawled into bed a little melancholy. Although I shared the earnest belief that Johnny was in a better place, just like Da-dee, I knew I would miss him. A very small circle of people defined my life in LaPlace. First Ms. Linda, and now Johnny had passed away. There would be no new trial for my father, not that I held any desire to welcome him back into my world, and I knew Mama's condition would never improve. I was only thirteen, but it was time to make plans for the future.

PART II

NEW YORK

"Is That His Girlfriend?"

"I'm not interested in anything serious right now," I said, kicking off the bed sheet.

"I'm just asking where this is going. Does this mean anything to you? Do I mean anything to you?" Beth asked, annoyed, her head popping up from my chest.

"We've only known each other three months, I don't think we need to try and define our relationship at this point."

"So, you do consider us to be in a relationship?"

"Of course I consider us to be in a relationship. I really enjoy being with you; I mean this summer has been great. It's just with school starting in two weeks I don't want to make promises that I can't keep."

"Kevin, I just want to know what this is." Beth sighed heavily, sitting up in bed with an exasperated look on her face.

"This is two people, who enjoy each other's company, getting to know each other better, and having a good time," I said, caressing her neck, and kissing her. "This is a good thing."

Beth smiled, lying back down in the bed, her head once again resting on my chest. I had maneuvered my way out of danger without committing to anything. When it came to women, it was a skill I had mastered.

❋   ❋   ❋

I had never really been interested in girls, but after my thirteenth birthday I began to think about them constantly. Unfortunately, girls were not interested in me. It was a problem that St. Ann's Boarding School solved, because that's where I met Jeremy Kendall.

Ninth grade classes were sectioned off alphabetically at St. Ann's, and Jeremy was seated in front of me in Sister Poche's class. Over six feet tall, and weighing close to two hundred pounds, Jeremy was a star athlete at St. Ann's, a freshman starter on the football, basketball, and baseball varsity teams.

"You want to change seats, little man," Jeremy whispered to me the first day of class, as I struggled to look over his shoulder.

"You think we can?"

"Yeah, why not."

"Shouldn't we ask first?"

"Nah, she won't care."

"Okay then, thanks." I gathered my books, and stood to switch seats.

"What are you doing, Mr.…, Mr.…," Sister Poche called out, a ruler pointed in my direction as she flipped through her attendance log.

"Matthews, Kevin Matthews," I answered, feeling stranded.

"Mr. Matthews, what are you doing?"

"I was go'n change seats with this guy," I said, pointing to Jeremy.

"'Going to,' you were 'going to,' Mr. Matthews." Sister Poche glanced down at her log again. "Now, Mr. Kendall would be 'this guy,' correct?" Sister Poche asked, now directing the ruler at Jeremy.

"Yes ma'am, Jeremy Kendall."

"Whose idea was this?" Sister Poche asked, walking in our direction.

"Mine," I said, thinking there was no reason for both of us to get into trouble. "I can't see over him because he's so big, so I thought I'd ask him to change seats with me."

Sister Poche stopped a few feet in front of us, tapping the ruler in her palm as she considered my explanation. "That's a very valid reason Mr. Matthews, but in this class all requests will be directed to me. Would you mind switching seats with Mr. Matthews, Mr. Kendall?"

"No ma'am, I don't mind," Jeremy said, a huge grin on his face.

"Very well then," Sister Poche said, returning to the front of the classroom.

"You're all right, little man," Jeremy said to me.

"My name is Kevin."

"Right, Kevin, sorry about that. I'm Jeremy." We shook hands and he never referred to me as "little man" again.

Jeremy and I really hit it off, so a few weeks into the school year he requested a room change with Father Gable, the school's football coach, and we became roommates. I was amazed by what becoming friends with the right person meant socially. I went from being an outcast the year before at my old school in LaPlace, to becoming everyone's best friend at St. Ann's. I knew people only liked me because of Jeremy, but I didn't care, especially when it came to girls.

St. Ann's was an all boys' school, but Evangeline Academy, our sister school, was all girls. Jeremy proved to be an invaluable resource since he was not only a star athlete, but also a good-looking guy. Muscular, with dark brown skin and chiseled features, girls loved him. And to get to Jeremy, they had to go through me. At school dances or sporting events, all the girls wanted to talk to me; many even thought I was cute. It's just that at five feet four inches, most girls were taller than me. They treated me like a little brother, pinching me on the cheek or playing with my hair. I hated it. Then during my junior year of high school, something freakish happened, I grew six inches in less than six months. My growth spurt continued, and by the end of my senior year, I was six feet three inches, having bulked up to two hundred and ten pounds.

"What in the world have you been eating, Baby?" Ms. Bertha asked. "You growing like a weed in a rainstorm."

My larger physical stature, not to mention being best friends with the coolest guy in school, gave me an unshakable confidence, and I became very popular with girls. I knew they no longer only wanted to pinch me on the cheek, and I was determined to make up for lost time.

Although my social activities accelerated greatly during high school, I allowed nothing to interfere with my studies. I graduated from St. Ann's at the top of my class, and received a four-year academic scholarship to Tulane University in New Orleans, where I majored in Psychology; a science that I thought would aid me in unlocking the mysteries of my childhood. As my fascination with the field grew, I decided to pursue a PhD in Clinical Psychology after my undergraduate studies were completed.

I graduated Summa Cum Laude from Tulane, and posted off-the-chart scores on my Graduate Record Examination and GRE Psychology tests. My test scores assured my acceptance into any graduate program in the country. I chose Teacher's College at Columbia University in New York.

I arrived in New York on Saturday, May 21, 1983. My classes didn't begin until August, but I had landed a part-time research position with Dr. Albert Reyas, a professor at Columbia, that began the first week in June. Through the University I rented an apartment on 107th Street and Broadway, which was only a few blocks from campus. The place was tiny, one 14 x 16 room on the third floor, with two small windows facing out onto the street. One side of this room served as my kitchen. There was a mini refrigerator, and a stove more resembling a hot plate, with two small cabinets above it. I added a small bistro table with two chairs. I bought a black futon for the other side of the room, which doubled as my living room and bedroom. An eighteen-inch television, a radio/cassette tape player boom box, and an alarm clock, all placed on blue milk crates, were the only other furnishings. The apartment also had a bathroom the size of a closet, and a closet the size of a shoebox. Nonetheless, it was mine, and I was thrilled. This marked the first time I would be living alone. The rent was three hundred dollars, a steal if you asked New Yorkers, an astronomical amount in Da-dee's opinion.

"Three hundred dollars? A month? The place must be huge. Do you need a place that big, after all it's only go'n be you living there, right?" he questioned over the phone.

"Trust me, I'm the only one living here, there isn't room for anybody else."

I met Beth at the Laundromat my first week in town. After spotting her folding clothes, at five feet eleven inches she was hard to miss, I picked out a machine next to her.

"Excuse me, do you know where I'm supposed to put the detergent?" I asked.

"In the compartment on top," she said, turning to me with a smile and pointing out the location.

"Do I put it in now, or do I put my clothes in first?"

"You can put your clothes in first."

"Thanks." I began loading my clothes, whites, dark and bright colors, all into one machine.

"Wait a minute. What are you doing?"

"What do you mean?"

"You can't put all those in the same wash, the colors will bleed." Beth opened the door to another washer.

"Really?"

"Haven't you ever done laundry?"

"Yeah, I have." I smiled, and winked at Beth.

She thought for a moment. "Very cute, I can't believe I fell for that."

"Neither can I, but if it makes you feel better, I really didn't know where the detergent went," I said, both of us laughing.

Later that night over dinner, I discovered that Beth was a second year graduate student at Teachers College, also pursuing a PhD in Clinical Psychology. With an unending source of conversation, dinner flowed into coffee at a local café, which flowed into a quick look at my new apartment, which flowed into the two of us all over each other on my futon, with underwear being our only remaining clothes.

"I better be going," Beth announced at two a.m., just as things were heating up.

"Why? What's wrong?"

"What do you mean why?" she asked, standing to get dressed. "I just met you."

"I mean why is it you 'better' be going? Will something bad happen if you stay?"

"Well, I hope it wouldn't be bad, it certainly isn't bad the way I've imagined it, but it is too soon." Beth sat on the end of the bed, putting on her shoes.

"So you've imagined it, huh? When did you have time to do that? After all, you just met me, right?" I whispered, crawling up behind her, and nibbling her ear. I eased Beth back down on the bed, kissing her. She responded by passionately returning my kisses. *I've got her just where I want her, she won't be going anywhere tonight,* I thought.

Then, without warning, she pushed me back at arms length, and stood from the bed.

"I better be going, because you're convinced I'm going to stay," Beth said, smiling and heading for the door.

"What? Wait a minute," I said, jumping from the bed to stop her.

"Don't worry, Baby, you just met me too. When you get to know me better, you'll be a little more accurate in predicting my behavior, good night," she said, her right hand caressing my face as she backed out the door. I watched as Beth walked down the hallway, and stepped into the elevator, turning to blow me a kiss as the doors closed.

Beth and I spent a lot of time together after that, but although I enjoyed being with her, I was also dating other women I'd met. Beth knew about the other women, but she never said anything. What could she say? I had made no commitments to her. I did make it clear to these other women that Beth came first in my life.

"We can hang out, but I'm seeing someone right now, and I don't want to mess that up," I declared proudly, implying there was something noble in this egotistical pronouncement.

Surprisingly none of these women had a problem with what I told them. They were either convinced they could change my mind, or simply wanted from me the same thing I wanted from them. In my mind, it was the perfect situation.

After neatly tying up my "relationship" discussion with Beth, I glanced at the clock, which read *2:00 a.m.* I had to get up at seven for work, which meant I would get five hours sleep if I fell asleep right away; a feat never accomplished. I proceeded to lie in bed wide-awake watching the clock roll past *2:30 a.m.*, *3:00 a.m.*, *3:30 a.m.*, and *4:00 a.m.*, Beth lying next to me sound asleep. If there was one thing that annoyed me about Beth, it was her ability to fall asleep within minutes of her head hitting the pillow. Regardless of what kind of day she had, what kind of mood she was in, or how she felt physically, once Beth got into bed, she was going to sleep.

I eventually dozed off around four-thirty, but my sleep was short-lived. A far more sinister tormentor, New York City Sanitation trucks, had replaced Earl, my sleep nemesis as a child. At least Earl was consistent, he never woke me before the sun rose, but the garbage trucks had little regard for whether it was light out or not. Not more than an hour after I fell asleep, they rolled up beneath my window, engines roaring. Shortly thereafter, the loading of the garbage began. There was the sound of bags being tossed, cans being knocked over, the piercing sound of the machine that crushed the garbage once it was in the truck, the random honking of horns from cars whose paths were blocked by the truck, and the most pleasant of all New York City morning sounds, the obscenities exchanged between the drivers of the cars that were blocked and the sanitation workers.

"Get that truck out of the damn street! I got to get to work!"

"I'm just trying to do my job, okay; asshole."

Aggravated by my lack of sleep on yet another night, I let out a sigh of frustration that woke Beth, who was curled up in a ball next to me, reducing her long frame to that of a child.

"What's wrong? Can't sleep?"

"Do I ever?"

"What time is it?" she asked, snuggling up next to me.

"Ten minutes to five. I have to get up at seven; it doesn't even make sense to try and fall back to sleep now."

"I'm sorry, Baby, is there anything I can do?" she asked, crawling on top of me.

After sleeping little more than an hour, I was exhausted. Despite that fact, within seconds of Beth asking the question, she felt my erection stiffening against her body.

"I guess there is something I can do," she whispered, giggling.

I'm not sure if the sanitation workers completed their job downstairs, but I wasn't aware of a single sound outside of my apartment for the rest of the morning.

I made it into the office at seven forty-five. April was standing behind her desk when I stepped off the elevator.

"Hello, Mr. Matthews."

"Hey, April," I said, continuing toward Dr. Reyas' office.

"Wait a minute," April said, walking out from behind her desk and stopping me. "Weren't you supposed to call me last night?" April was the receptionist for all the offices on our floor. Tall and slim, with mocha skin and curly black hair, I asked her out my first day of work, and we continued to occasionally see each other over the summer.

"I was supposed to call you?"

"When you left yesterday, you said we could check out a movie and grab a bite to eat after I got off work," April said, folding her arms across her chest, and feigning anger.

"Oh damn, that's right. I'm sorry, I got tied up."

"I could have done that for you if you had called me," she said, leaning into me, her supposed anger turning to flirtation. "I had something special planned for you too."

"Oh really, and what was that?"

"Let's just say I know you're sorry you missed it."

"How about this weekend?"

"Okay."

"And by the way, I like being in control. That means I do the tying up, not you, remember that," I said, pointing and shaking a finger in her direction as I walked away.

I went into the office and began setting up the camera for a patient interview. Dr. Reyas was testing the Trauma Model of Recovery, which stated that once someone experiences a traumatic event, they are treated, but recovery includes integrating the trauma back into their life, effecting a change in one's schema, or the way a person views themselves. The research was slated as a seven-year project. Today I would be interviewing Amber Rodriguez, a nine-year old who had never known her father, and was orphaned after her mother, a street prostitute, died of a drug overdose. Amber had found her mother's body after returning home from school. The goal was to document how she viewed relationships. I would show Amber a set of cards, each illustrating adults and children in different settings. It was my job to ask one question, "What do you see?" I would videotape her answers for Dr. Reyas to review.

Amber arrived with her Aunt, Lydia Martinez, who was now her legal guardian, at eight o'clock.

"Somebody's right on time," I said.

"It's really early," Amber said, stretching and yawning as she walked into the office.

"Not as early as if you had to go to school today," I said. "Good morning, Ms. Martinez."

"Good morning, Kevin. How long do you think you'll need her?"

"No more than an hour."

"Okay then, I'll be in the waiting area when you finish. Amber, you be a good girl, okay?"

"Auntie, I'm hungry."

"Sweetie, you had breakfast," Ms. Martinez said, slicking down a piece of Amber's hair that had escaped her headband.

"But I'm hungry," Amber whined. "I want some doughnuts."

"You answer all of Kevin's questions, and I'll buy you doughnuts after we finish. Deal?" Ms. Martinez stuck out her hand for Amber to shake on it.

"Deal," Amber said, slapping her aunt's hand.

Ms. Martinez left, and we prepared to start the interview. Amber took a seat in front of the camera and stared directly into the lens; she had become very comfortable with these sessions. I sat in a chair next to the camera, and pressed the record button. The first picture I showed Amber was of a little girl staring into a mirror. Looking out from the mirror was a woman standing with her arms outstretched.

"Okay, Amber, what do you see?"

Amber studied the picture thoughtfully. "That little girl was outside playing, and when she came back into the house, her Mom had gone off to a place where only rich people could live, so the little girl couldn't be with her any longer."

Amber associated most things with not being rich. A pretty Puerto Rican girl, with smooth caramel skin, long shiny black hair that fell near the middle of her back, and big dark brown eyes that you knew would cause men to melt in years to come, she held a distorted self-image. "I wish I was pretty like them," she once said to me, pointing out models in a magazine.

"What are you talking about? You're beautiful," I assured her.

"No I'm not. You got to have plenty of jewelry and nice clothes to be beautiful."

Desires for material possessions aside, I also found Amber to be, and understandably so, wanting for something on a much deeper level. "I wish you were my Daddy," she always said to me at some point during her visits. She would look me directly in the eye, no fear of rejection. I thought back to the times as a child when I fantasized about Mr. Frank being my father; it was a fantasy I would have never dared verbalize.

Amber and I finished the interview a little after nine. When we walked into the waiting area, Ms. Martinez was seated reading a magazine.

"All done," I said.

"Oh my, that was fast. Were you a good girl?" Ms. Martinez asked Amber.

"Yes, now it's time to get some doughnuts. You want to come, Kevin?" Amber asked, taking my hand.

"I am a little hungry. I think I will join you two if you don't mind."

"Oh please, Kevin, of course not," Ms. Martinez said.

"Leaving for the day, Kevin?" April asked, as we stepped into the elevator.

"Just grabbing a bite to eat, I'll be back."

"Doughnuts are on me, what do you want, Missy?" I asked Amber, walking into the Dunkin Doughnuts shop across the street.

"A jelly doughnut," Amber said, pointing to them behind the counter.

"One jelly doughnut it is."

"And a chocolate doughnut too," Amber added, her focus switching as she pointed to that section.

"Okay, one jelly, and one chocolate doughnut."

"And a regular one too," Amber said.

"No no, two doughnuts are enough," Ms. Martinez said.

"Why, Auntie?"

"Tell you what, how about some milk to go with your doughnuts," I suggested.

"Okay, chocolate milk," Amber answered.

"How about you, Ms. Martinez, can I get you anything?"

"Oh no, no thanks, Kevin, and will you please call me Lydia," she said, reaching out to squeeze my arm. "You make me feel like an old maid, calling me Ms. Martinez all the time."

Lydia Martinez was no old maid, not by any stretch of the imagination. She couldn't have been older than thirty, and the striking features that were still being developed in young Amber had already come into fruition in her aunt. She was a short woman, five feet two inches at the most, with the same smooth caramel skin as Amber, hazel eyes, wavy brown hair with blonde highlights that she wore pulled back into a ponytail, and curves in all the right places. Were it not for Amber, I surely would have made a move on Lydia. But I was very careful when it came to getting involved with women who had children. Careful, meaning I didn't.

I paid for Amber's doughnuts and milk, as well as a few doughnuts for myself, and we took a seat in a booth, Amber pulling me in next to her.

"So where you guys headed after this?" I asked Lydia.

"I have to get to work. I'm going to drop off Amber with my mother, she watches her during the day," Lydia said, taking a seat on the opposite side of the booth.

"Remember, Kevin, I stay with my Granny during the day," Amber said, taking a huge bite of her doughnut, a glob of jelly falling onto her shirt.

"Amber, be careful," Lydia, said. "You don't have a change of clothes with you, and I don't have time to go back to the house."

"Oh-oh, there's a stain," Amber said, looking down at her shirt.

"Let's go in the bathroom, maybe I can get it off," Lydia said, standing.

"I can do it myself," Amber said quickly, motioning for Lydia to sit down. Amber grabbed a handful of napkins from the table and headed for the bathroom.

"She wants to be a big girl so badly," Lydia said, smiling and looking after Amber.

"They all do, Lydia, they all do."

"You called me Lydia, it's about time, Mr. Matthews," Lydia joked. "So, you're single, Kevin?"

"I am, school keeps me pretty busy, you know."

"What about that pretty young girl at the office, nothing going on there?"

"April, well, we've been out a couple of times, but it's nothing serious."

"That's what they all say."

"How about you?"

"I'm single as of Friday night," Lydia said, reaching over and taking a piece of Amber's doughnut.

"Damn, that recent huh? Sorry to hear that."

"Don't be, I'm better off this way," she said, eating the doughnut, and waving her hand like it was no big deal.

"What did he do?"

"Take a guess, Kevin," she said, with a chuckle.

"How did you find out?"

"Walked in as he was on the down stroke," she said, laughing through the pain. "The only thing I asked of that man was that he love and treat me right. That's not asking much, is it?"

"No, it's not."

"I guess it wasn't in him. That's okay though, if he won't, I know there's a man out there who will. A good woman is a blessing, Kevin. You find one, treat her right."

After thinking about Lydia's comment, I decided to give Beth a special evening. I called and invited her to dinner, enticing her with the promise of smothered chicken, collard greens, and sweet potatoes; knowing Beth loved southern dishes. After preparing the greens and potatoes first, I started cooking the chicken. I checked the clock, and it read *6:55 p.m.* Beth was due to arrive at seven. I ran into the bathroom and drew a hot bath, adding in some scented bubbles. I took a cue from a scene witnessed in countless romantic movies, and sprinkled rose petals atop the bubbles, after which I lit four candles, placing one on each corner of the bathtub. Music, I thought, I need the right music. I opened my tape case and pulled out the latest Michael Franks release,

Passion Fruit. I moved my boom box into the bathroom and popped in the tape playing the first track, *Alone at Night*. After dashing into the kitchen, I placed six strawberries around the edge of a small bowl, adding sugar in the middle, and then poured two glasses of champagne. I took the glasses, the strawberries, and the bottle of champagne back into the bathroom, placing them on a tray next to the bathtub.

"Whatever it is sure smells good," Beth yelled out, walking in the door.

"It'll be ready in a few minutes," I said, greeting her at the door.

"Okay. I need to take a quick shower. I just left the gym, which you can probably tell from my appearance." She was wearing black tights with a cut-off gray tank top, and her hair was pulled back in a pony-tail. She understandably wasn't wearing a drop of make-up, and was still sweating, as her body attempted to cool down from working out; but she looked beautiful. It felt like I was seeing her for the first time. "Why are you looking at me like that?" Beth asked, self-consciously adjusting her hair.

"You look beautiful," I said, wiping a bead of sweat from her forehead.

"Yeah right, I look beautiful, like this."

"You do."

"Thank you," she said. "Just let me jump in the shower, and I'll help you in the kitchen."

"No no, tonight, I'm going to take care of you."

"Kevin, what's going on?"

"Just what I said, I'm going to take care of you. I only have one request"

"Which is?"

"Absolutely no more questions. Agreed?" I asked, kissing Beth.

She thought for a moment, and then smiled. "Agreed." I sat her down on the bed, and then took off her socks and sneakers, giving her a quick foot massage before removing the rest of her clothes and leading her into the bathroom. "Kevin, what's—?"

"Shhh," I said, placing my finger to her lips. "No more questions." I helped Beth into the bath, and handed her the bowl of strawberries, Beth taking one, dipping it in the sugar, and offering me the first bite. I handed her a glass of champagne, raising mine for a toast. "This is going somewhere. It does mean a great deal to me. And you mean a great deal to me," I said, stopping to kiss her between each statement.

I wasn't sure if I loved Beth, but I was going to treat her right.

The phone rang at four a.m. the following morning. After falling asleep early that night, I was frustrated to be robbed of a good night's sleep. Beth didn't move until I got out of bed.

"Where are you going?" she mumbled.

"To answer the phone," I said, amused by her ability to sleep through anything. "Hello."

"Who is it?" Beth asked. I took a seat at the kitchen table, not answering her. After a minute or so passed without me speaking, Beth sat up in bed, becoming nervous.

"It's okay. I'm glad you called tonight. I'll talk to you tomorrow," I said, hanging up the phone.

"Who was it?"

"It was my grandfather."

"Your grandfather, what's wrong?"

"My mother died."

It was a call I dreaded receiving all of my life. After twelve years of being trapped in a body that allowed her to communicate with no other living soul, Mama was free. I wouldn't sleep another wink.

I called Da-dee the next morning and he explained that Mama passed quietly in her sleep. An orderly at the nursing home who knew him had been thoughtful enough to call and tell him the news.

"Sarah finally at rest, bless her soul," Da-dee said. "Yeah, God done called home an angel, and after the way she lived her life, I know her reward will be everlasting peace."

Da-dee rarely viewed death negatively. He believed that if you lived a good life, your transition into the afterlife was something to be celebrated, not mourned. We talked for about thirty minutes, both of us leery as to how the funeral arrangements would be handled.

"I'm coming down there, and I'm going to the funeral," I said angrily.

"That's your right, and I won't let anyone deny you it, I promise you that. You just get down here, I'll find out all the details on the services. You need money to get home?"

"No, I'll just charge the flight to my credit card."

"How is this go'n affect your schooling?"

"School doesn't start for another week and a half, I'll be back in time."

"What about your job?"

"Don't worry, that won't be a problem."

"Okay then, you give me a call when you work out your travel plans, let me know what time to pick you up from the airport and everything."

"Okay, I'll talk to you later, bye."

There was really nothing for me to take care of. Beth left the apartment that morning so I could spend some time alone, but she told me she would take care of my plane reservations, as well as speak with Dr. Reyas about my needing time off from work. Beth was one of his standout students the year before, and they shared a good relationship. She even arranged for me to have an additional week off, so I could spend more time at home following the funeral. She returned to my apartment that evening with an itinerary for the entire trip, one that she voluntarily paid for.

"Kevin, I'm just telling you this because I want to be there for you, I'm not trying to put any pressure on you," Beth said, taking a seat next to me on the bed.

"What?"

"I want you to know that if you would like me to come with you, I'd be more than happy to do so," she said, reaching out to hold my hand.

"You don't have to do that. School starts in less than two weeks. I know how hectic things are for me, and I imagine they're just as bad for you."

"It's no problem, really it isn't. If you need me to be there with you for support, for whatever, just let me know."

"I don't know, I don't think it's necessary, I'll be okay."

"Well, if you should get there and change your mind, just call me, okay?"

"Thanks," I said, kissing her hand.

"You probably want to be alone tonight. I'll give you a wake-up call tomorrow morning."

"No, I want you to stay."

We didn't talk much that night, and got into bed before eleven. Beth attempted to stay awake until I fell asleep, but it just wasn't in her. She was asleep less than ten minutes after we said goodnight. I didn't kid myself into believing there would be any sleep for me. I stayed in bed until Beth maneuvered into a fetal position, a sure sign that she was out cold, and then got up and sat in a chair watching her sleep. I never really gave serious thought to Beth accompanying me to the funeral, convincing myself that it was an inconvenience I didn't want to place on her. Deep down I knew that wasn't the reason. I didn't want Beth to go with me because she was white. I remembered the comments people in Louisiana made regarding my mother and father's relationship, and I didn't think I could handle such abuse.

"Is that his girlfriend?" white people would question. "Nigger thinks he's white now."

"Boy just like his daddy, love them white women," black people would say.

As I sat staring at Beth, Mama seemed to be a fixture in my mind. Then it dawned on me. *How could I have been so blind?* Beth bore a striking resemblance to my mother. She was the same height as Mama, five feet eleven inches, had the same olive complexion and curly black hair, and although her eyes were not as light, they were also blue.

There was a sad irony apparent to my situation. Here I was preparing to go home and say my final goodbyes to Mama, a woman who had loved me more than anyone else in the world, and I was ashamed to take Beth, someone who also cared deeply for me, based on the idiotic reason that the color of her skin was white, the same as Mama's. I realized that in spite of all of the things I had accomplished, at this point in my life I was a failure as a man.

THEY WANTED NO PART OF ME

I arrived in New Orleans on Thursday morning at eight o'clock. Da-dee met me at the airport gate.

"You look tired," he said, shaking my hand.

"Didn't sleep much last night."

"Yeah, I guess not. Well, it's good to see you, even if it is under trying circumstances."

"It's good to see you too."

We went downstairs and picked up my luggage, and then drove home in a familiar fashion, total silence except for the wind rushing through the windows.

Duke spotted the truck before we turned into the driveway, and even at his advanced age, he bolted down the road, running alongside my window, joyously barking at the sight of me. Ms. Bertha, alerted by Duke's response, was under the garage to greet us by the time we parked.

"Oh child, it is so good to see you," Ms. Bertha cried, grabbing me around the waist and squeezing me tightly, while Duke frantically jumped and circled around us to gain my attention. "Bend down here and give me a kiss."

"It's good to see you too, Ms. Bertha."

"I'm so sorry about your mama, but we should be thankful. She at rest with the Lord now."

"I guess so."

"How New York treating you?"

"Good, things are good," I answered, petting Duke to calm him down.

"You look like you lost weight," she said, patting my shoulders and chest. "Well, I don't like that one bit. You go put them bags in the house and then come get you some breakfast, you hear me. We got to get some meat back on your bones." Ms. Bertha hugged me tightly once more, before heading home. "Preacher, you make sure that boy come over here and get something to eat, you hear me. You come too if you hungry."

"Okay, Bertha," Da-dee said. "Kevin, I hope you didn't eat on the plane, cause that woman go'n give you enough food to feed an army."

I dropped off my bags, and Da-dee and I went over to Ms. Bertha's, who as expected, had cooked entirely too much food. There were pancakes, grits, eggs, potatoes, ham, bacon, sausage, toast, and grapefruit out on the table when we walked into the kitchen.

"Bertha, there ain't but two of us, how you expect us to eat all this food?" Da-dee asked, staring at the buffet.

"Never mind you, Preacher, this boy need to eat. He can't find this kind of cooking in New York," she said, loading my plate with food. "Ain't that right, Kevin?"

"No, they don't feed you like this, I have to be honest."

"Baby, I know they don't," she said, shaking her head, and piling my plate even higher with potatoes.

"You wanna be all agreeable, let's see you finish this mess a food she done give you," Da-dee whispered.

"Preacher, what that you saying? Don't you be starting no stuff in here this morning. I done invited you into my house, but man of God or not, you know I'll put you out just as quickly," Ms. Bertha said, laughing and slapping Da-dee on the back.

It was good to be home.

Da-dee left to run errands in town after we finished breakfast, and I went back to the house. It was mid August, and close to one hundred degrees outside; of course Da-dee didn't have the air conditioners running. I turned on both units, and then walked from room to room looking at the house. I had only been in New York four months, but that was the longest I had been away from home in my life. I went up to the attic and couldn't help but smile when I saw the twin bed next to the window. Da-dee left the place untouched after Johnny passed away. I would have been in for a marathon conversation had he still been alive. "Kevin, living in the Big Apple, plenty of people up there, yes sir! How tall them buildings?" I missed Johnny.

When I got back downstairs, I noticed something strange in the field behind the house. Most of the trees had been cut down. I then remembered Da-dee telling me that Manny Clement, the man who owned the property, had decided to turn the land into a subdivision. He split it up into one-acre lots, and contracted his construction company to build the houses. New Orleans was steadily growing, and as real estate ran low in the city, people were beginning to migrate out to LaPlace. Da-dee said Manny was going to make a fortune.

I took a three-hour nap that afternoon, my lack of sleep over the past few days catching up with me. Da-dee returned home around six and we had dinner. Ms. Bertha cooked for us again, but Da-dee insisted she bring the food over to our house so we could serve ourselves.

"That woman will feed a man until he burst, if you let her," Da-dee said.

Ms. Bertha cooked crawfish etouffee, knowing it was my favorite dish, with garlic bread and potato salad. For dessert, she made a chocolate pecan pie, which she instructed us to serve heated with vanilla ice cream.

"I don't mind ya'll serving yourselves, but my dishes have to be presented in the proper fashion, so you get the full enjoyment of the meal."

The food was great, and Da-dee and I stuffed ourselves without Ms. Bertha's help. Da-dee ended up in his recliner, barely able to move, with me on the couch in the same condition.

"So the wake on Saturday, the funeral on Sunday," Da-dee said. "Jesse say you welcome to attend."

"She's my mother, I don't need his invitation."

"I ain't saying you do, it's just I thought you should know how he felt."

"Since when do you talk to him?"

"Man's changed, God says we must forgive our enemies."

I respected Da-dee's religious beliefs, but I also knew he wasn't a stupid man, and must have known the only change in Mr. Boutte was his desire to be Mayor of LaPlace. Mayor Landry, who had held the office for the past twenty years, was retiring, and Mr. Boutte was in the middle of a heated campaign against Manny Clement, who was spearheading a population growth in LaPlace unlike any seen before. Mr. Boutte needed the black community's support, and Da-dee was one of its most respected leaders.

"I've said and done a lot of things I ain't proud of, Reverend, and I want you and your congregation to know that I came here today to ask for your forgiveness," Mr. Boutte had confessed from the DoRight Baptist Church pulpit, an image that sent chills up my spine.

"I don't know how you can talk to such a phony," I said to Da-dee. "I mean you have to know he's full of it."

"I don't know what in the man's heart, the Lord will be his judge, not me." I shook my head in disagreement. "Kevin, I'm the voice for a lot of people in this community, they depend on me to make sure their concerns are addressed by the politicians who run this town. My feelings ain't important, I got responsibilities." Da-dee was still playing the role of a hero.

Even though I'd taken a nap earlier, I found myself barely able to keep my eyes open by ten o'clock. I slept soundly that night, and didn't wake up until after nine the next morning. I knew Da-dee wouldn't wake me, he thought I needed the rest, but I couldn't figure out why Earl had been so considerate.

"What happened to Earl this morning?" I asked, joining Da-dee at the kitchen table.

"Got hit by a car about a month ago. Some kids was playing out in the street near the driveway, and Earl decided to chase them off. Benny was pulling out of Bertha driveway and hit him with his truck."

I couldn't believe it, but I almost became teary after hearing the news of Earl's demise. It was just another reminder that things would never be the same. This confused me even more, because I never considered things to be all that great.

I spent most of the morning catching up on local news with Da-dee. Ms. Bertha called and invited us over for lunch, but Da-dee declined, saying his stomach was still upset from eating too much the day before.

"Well, I'd love to sit and talk some more, but I done put this work off longer than I should have. Let me get out here and take care of it," Da-dee said at one o'clock.

"Okay, I'm going to take the truck and go for a ride."

"Alright, got plenty of gas in there," he said, walking out the front door.

I got dressed to leave. There was one more person I needed to visit, Mr. Frank.

When I pulled into the store's driveway, Mr. Frank was sweeping up the parking lot.

"Hey, big city boy!" he yelled, running over to shake my hand. "How you doing?"

"Pretty good, Mr. Frank, pretty good."

"Look like you lost weight, what, you can't get them girls to take care of you up there in New York?" Mr. Frank laughed, slapping me across the stomach.

"I'm trying, Mr. Frank."

"I bet you are. Come on in the store, get out of this heat." We walked into the store and Mr. Frank went into the storage room to put away the broom. "Hey, Kevin, get yourself an ICEE, got some new fangled peach flavor," he yelled out. I went over to the ICEE machine, and filled a large cup with Mr. Frank's latest experiment in cold refreshment. "You like it?" he asked, returning from the storage area anxious for my feedback.

"It's pretty good," I said, leaning on the counter next to the register.

"I don't know, I still don't think it's as good as the strawberry."

"Me neither," I said, both of us laughing.

"So you in town to pay respects to your mama, huh?"

"Yeah, Da-dee called me Wednesday morning, I took the first flight out yesterday."

"I tell you the truth, I'm go'n miss her. But I must admit, I'm glad she won't suffer any longer."

"I guess so."

"Oh it's for the best. When we cry over losing a loved one, those are selfish tears. A woman like your mama, I know she in a better place, ain't no doubt about that."

"Yeah, you're right," I sighed, shaking my head in agreement. "So what you think about Mr. Boutte's run for mayor?"

"Boutte ain't no good, you know that. Problem is that bastard he running against ain't no better than he is."

"He's trying to get Da-dee to help him with his campaign."

"Preacher a better man than I am," Mr. Frank said, walking from behind the counter to the ICEE machine. "I know what he trying to do, get some issues taken care of that will help the people around here, but I couldn't deal with no snake like Boutte, or Clement. You help them get elected, how you know they go'n keep they word?"

"So you're not going to vote for either one of them?"

"I was hoping somebody else put they name on the ballot," he said, filling his cup with the peach-flavored ICEE.

"Like who?"

"Don't matter, can't be no worse than them two," he said, laughing and sipping the ICEE. "You know this thing actually ain't half-bad."

"What if nobody else runs?"

"There ain't no 'if' in it, ain't nobody else running."

"So, you're not going to vote?"

"Oh, I'm go'n vote, too many people suffered so I could do that. I just hope Preacher get one of them devils to publicly commit to making some changes in this town that'll help the black folks around here."

"So you're going to vote for whoever Da-dee supports?"

"I guess so. But Lord knows I'm go'n be sick over it either way."

Mr. Frank and I discussed New York and school for the next couple of hours. When I made it home, Da-dee had cooked baked chicken with mashed potatoes for dinner.

"After all that food Bertha gave us yesterday, I don't know about you, but I need something bland," he said.

"I hate to admit it, but I feel the same way."

"So, they go'n have the viewing from eleven to five tomorrow at Benson's Funeral Home," Da-dee said, dishing up dinner.

I hated the whole concept of a viewing. I understood the purpose was for people to see their loved ones one last time, but I never felt I was looking at the person I once knew. Regardless of how many times I heard people tell morticians they had done a wonderful job, and the deceased looked beautiful, "just like they did when they were living," I always thought the bodies looked just like what they were, lifeless corpses. The image I possessed of my mother was that of a naturally beautiful woman. I held no desire to see her face painted like a ceramic doll in an attempt to make her look like she was still alive.

I hated the viewing aspect of funerals, but I felt the ceremonies themselves were of great importance. It was a time when people shared memories of their loved ones, and grieved together as a process of group healing. I remembered the warm feelings experienced at Johnny's funeral; it brought people closer together, causing them to appreciate each other more. I feared Mama's funeral would not create such a positive atmosphere.

"Who do you think will be there?" I asked.

"Oh, I don't know, not that many folks I guess. I know Bertha said she wanted to ride over with us to pay her respects, Frank probably go'n come."

"He is. I went to visit him today and he said he was going to stop by."

"I figured that's where you went. Outside of that, I guess just her people will be there. I mean that parlor room Benson got ain't that big anyway."

"So, you talk to Mr. Boutte about my being there, huh?"

"He stopped by on Wednesday to give me the news, I told him Miriam had already called me. He wanted to know if you was go'n be able to make it. Said he knew you was probably busy, but if you could make it, you was welcome to be there."

"What, he thought I wasn't going to come to my own mother's funeral, that man has a lot of nerve," I said, agitated, standing and pacing the room. "If he thinks,"

"Kevin, wait a minute."

"What?"

"I don't wanna tell you how to deal with this situation, but I think you looking at it the wrong way."

"All I'm saying is I'm not going to let that man, or anyone else for that matter, interfere with me saying goodbye to my mother."

"It seem to me like that's exactly what you doing." Da-dee's words stopped me in my tracks. "Sit down." I looked at him, not moving. "Kevin, sit down." I reluctantly sat back at the table. Da-dee took a seat next to me. "Your mama was a special woman, loved you like nobody ever will again in this life. You can live to be one hundred years old, and nothing will ever replace your mother's love. Now in one sense, Sarah left us a long time ago, and I know losing her the way you did back then was a painful thing, had to be, there was nothing about that situation to rejoice in. But tomorrow, Son, tomorrow is not a day for sadness; tomorrow is not a day for bitterness. It don't matter who's there tomorrow, and it don't matter how much wrong they done, even if you don't think they regret it. Dwelling on the past will never change it, just won't allow you to live in the here and now. When you walk into that funeral home tomorrow, you think about your mama. You think about how happy she is looking down at you, at all the things you done accomplished. You think about how she been freed from this earthly prison, and now lives in the graces of our Lord. You think about all of those things, and you rejoice in the blessing God granted you by making her a part of your life, because she will always be with you."

I knew Da-dee was right, but I was still upset. I thanked him for his advice, and said goodnight.

Da-dee, Ms. Bertha, and I arrived at Benson's Funeral Home at eleven o'clock the next morning.

"Good morning Reverend Matthews," Mr. Benson said, greeting us at the door. Mr. Benson was the funeral home director. He was a short, small-framed white man appearing to be in his late fifties, and was dressed in all black as usual for a mortician.

"Good morning, Mr. Benson," Da-dee said. "This is my grandson, Kevin, Sarah's boy."

"That's right, how you holding up, Son, my you have grown," Mr. Benson said, shaking my hand.

How the hell do you know I've grown, I've never seen you before in my life, I thought. "I'm doing okay," I said, forcing a smile.

"This here is——," Da-dee began to say.

"Oh, I know Ms. Bertha. How are you?" Mr. Benson said, shaking Ms. Bertha's hand.

"Doing okay, Mr. Benson."

Mr. Benson led us into the viewing parlor, and appeared to motion for us to have a seat near the back of the room.

"Why are we being seated way back here?" I asked.

"Oh no, I didn't mean to, I mean you can sit anywhere you like," Mr. Benson said, flustered.

"Being her only son, I would think so."

"Of course, of course, my apologies."

"No apologies necessary, Mr. Benson," Da-dee said, with Ms. Bertha looking on uncomfortably.

We walked to the front of the parlor, and I intentionally looked away from Mama's open casket. Mr. and Mrs. Boutte were seated in the first row on the right hand side of the church. It had only been a few years since I'd seen them, I still occasionally bumped into them when visiting Mama, but they looked much older. Mrs. Boutte's once dark brown hair was completely gray, and her skin now contained so many freckles, it was difficult to distinguish between them and her original skin color. Mr. Boutte was almost completely bald, although I didn't know if this was a new characteristic, since I had never seen the man without a hat. There were four other people seated next to them, two women and two men. I assumed these were two of my uncles and their wives. Having seen my mother's brothers only a few times growing up, I didn't remember what they looked like. Mrs. Boutte was crying and did not turn to greet us, but Mr. Boutte rose from his seat after spotting us. I quickly took a seat on the opposite isle.

"Good morning, Reverend Matthews, Ms. Bertha, thank you for coming," Mr. Boutte said, offering a handshake. Da-dee shook Mr. Boutte's hand, but Ms. Bertha just nodded. She was not as forgiving. Mr. Boutte then headed in my direction. That's not a good idea old man, I thought. "How are you, Kevin?"

"I'm fine," I said, not turning to look at him.

"I'm glad you could make it. "I know Sarah would have wanted you here."

"She was my mother."

The sharpness of my tone made him uneasy. "So ah, how New York treating you?" he asked. I couldn't believe the nerve of this man. After ignoring me for twenty-two years, he suddenly wanted to discuss how my life was going. He's got to be kidding, I thought. "Reverend Matthews say you doing real well up there."

"I'm sorry, Mr. Boutte, I'm just not in the mood to talk right now."

He stood silently for a moment, and then reached out to touch my shoulder. I quickly leaned out of reach.

"How your wife holding up?" Da-dee asked, distracting Mr. Boutte from my unfriendly actions.

"She having a tough time, you know, it's hard to lose a child."

"Not so hard to turn your back on one though," I said, the words escaping before I could sensor them.

"I don't think that was necessary, Kevin," Da-dee said.

"It's okay, it's okay," Mr. Boutte said.

"No, it ain't okay," Da-dee, said. "It's disrespectful, that's what it is."

"Disrespectful? You think I should respect this man?" I asked.

"It's disrespectful to your mama," Da-dee said.

The truth of his statement stung me. I felt trapped. "Excuse me, I need some air," I said. I made my way to the front of the building, and burst through the front doors, almost knocking down two men who were entering.

"Kevin Matthews," one of them said, as I walked past. I turned and took a closer look. It was James and Josh Boutte, my cousins. "What's up, cuz?" James said. It wasn't even twelve o'clock, but I could smell the alcohol on his breath. I stared at both of them, not saying a word, and then turned to walk away. "Come on man, you ain't go'n say hello, we blood, Blood," James said, laughing and following me.

Josh realized I was in no mood for jokes, and grabbed James by the arm. "James, let Kevin be on his way. Let's go on in and pay our respects."

"I'm just trying to say hello to our cousin," James yelled, pulling away from Josh. "What's up, cuz?" James stuck out his right hand for me to slap him five.

"Let's go, James," Josh said.

James and Josh both stood about five feet eight inches, and couldn't have weighed more than one hundred and fifty pounds each. They posed little threat to someone my size, but I knew James would give me a reason to look past that. I didn't have to wait long.

"Can you believe this," James said to Josh. "I come to pay my respects, and this nigger——,"

As had happened nine years earlier, he never finished his statement, my right fist substituting for the lead pipe. James crumbled to the ground and Josh turned to retaliate, but after taking a good look at me, he decided against it.

Hearing the commotion from inside, one of the men, possibly James's father, ran out from the funeral home. He looked at James, and angrily headed in my direction.

"What the hell is wrong with you, boy?"

I turned to face him, my stare freezing him in his footsteps. I didn't say a word, but the fierceness of my expression made him think better of his actions. Instead, he retreated to the spot where James was lying, blood still oozing from his nose. I looked at all three, daring them to speak. They didn't say anything; they wanted no part of me.

I Pulled The Shades Down

"James, I done warned you plenty of times about your drinking, this here is the last one I'm go'n give you," Chief Brady said, furious that James would show up in such condition at a funeral. "The next time, I'm go'n lock you up, that's a promise. And ain't nobody go'n be able to save you," he said, looking in Mr. Boutte's direction.

"Chief, that ain't fair, James ain't lay a hand on Kevin," Josh said.

"If I was you, I'd just shut up, cause you go'n be locked in the cell next to him if you ain't careful. Now, do ya'll understand me?" James and Josh didn't answer. "I said, do ya'll understand me?" Chief Brady slowly repeated, removing his sunglasses for emphasis.

"They understand you, Chief," Mr. Boutte said.

"But, Daddy," said the man who had rushed out to aid James.

"I don't wanna hear nothing from you boy," Mr. Boutte said. "You take that drunk of a son you done raised and you get him home, you hear me. I'll be over there directly to deal with him."

The man did as he was told without delay. He, along with his wife, the other couple, James, and Josh all went to their cars and left.

"I done about all needs to be done here, Preacher," Chief Brady said.

"Thanks, Chief," Da-dee said.

"Son, once again, my condolences," Chief Brady said to me, tipping his hat. He then walked over to his patrol car, and left.

"James ain't had no business being here in that condition, and I wanna apologize," Mr. Boutte said to me. "James, Josh, or nobody else from my family for that matter won't be causing you no more problems, I can promise you that."

"We appreciate that Mr. Boutte," Da-dee said.

"Kevin, the parlor is go'n be open until five. My wife probably go'n be here the whole day, she can't bring herself to leave Sarah's side, but you go on back in and be with your mama when you get ready," Mr. Boutte said. He then walked to his pick-up truck and left.

"Lord, they won't give the poor woman no peace even after she gone," Ms. Bertha said, still upset.

"Kevin, I'm go'n drive Bertha home, you take the time now to go and pay your respects to your mama," Da-dee said. I knew from his tone that he was not happy with my behavior.

Da-dee walked Ms. Bertha to the car and they left. I went back into the funeral home.

"I'm so sorry, Son, can I get you anything, a cold drink, maybe?" Mr. Benson asked. I looked at him, recognizing his concern was genuine.

"No thank you, sir."

"Okay then, you let me know if you need anything, you hear."

I walked to the front of the parlor, and for the first time looked at my mother in her casket. To my surprise, she looked lovely. She was wearing a black dress with sheer sleeves, the opal pendant Nicholle had given her, and her favorite gold hoop earrings. Her fingernails were well manicured, but had no polish. Mama never wore fingernail polish. Her hair was laid out beneath her, providing a frame for her face, which looked absolutely beautiful. Mr. Benson had placed a minimal amount of make-up on her, a little lipstick and rouge being his only additions, allowing Mama's natural beauty to shine through. Staring down at her, I could hear her voice.

"Who's the luckiest woman in the world?"

"You are," I whispered aloud.

"And why is that?"

"Because you got me."

I closed my eyes, leaned in the casket, and kissed her; completing a ritual we practiced each night when she tucked me into bed. For a moment, I was ten years old again, transported back to a time when my mother's love defined my world, and made me feel safe and protected. I opened my eyes, almost expecting her to return my gaze, but the crystal blue eyes that could comfort me with a glance, were shut to the world forever. I walked back to my chair and took a seat, realizing that I was crying.

I sat silently for the next two hours. Twenty people at most came in to pay their respects, all friends of Mr. & Mrs. Boutte. Around three, Mr. Frank arrived. He walked to the front of the room, and kneeled in front of the casket saying a prayer. He then stood, looked at Mama, smiled, and walked over taking a seat next to me.

"How you holding up?" he asked, placing his arm around my shoulder.

"I'm okay."

"I already done heard about what happened. You put that out of your mind, think about your mama."

"That's what I'm trying to do."

"I'll be honest with you, I don't normally like to look at folks in them coffins, bad way to remember somebody if you ask me. But your mama, nothing can dim her beauty, not even death. I tell you the sight of her brought a smile to my face."

"I thought the same thing."

"Well, I'm go'n let you be alone," he said, shaking my hand and hugging me.

"Thanks for coming, Mr. Frank."

"You was blessed to have that woman as a mother, truly blessed."

"Mr. Benson go'n be closing the place in a bit, I'll be waiting in the car," Da-dee said, after coming to pick me up later that day.

"Okay, thanks."

I sat looking at Mama, knowing this would be the last time I would see her face. She hadn't spoken a word to me in over twelve years, but I felt like I was losing her for the first time. I suddenly found it difficult to catch my breath, and the room temperature seemed to balloon to what felt like a hundred degrees. I began to sweat, and couldn't get comfortable in my seat. I stood removing my jacket and tie, but that didn't help. I sat back down, feeling trapped once again.

"You look like her you know," a voice said, startling me. It was Mrs. Boutte. She was standing next to the coffin looking down at Mama. "Folks said you only had her skin color and hair, but I can see it, you look like her. Got the same mouth, cheekbones, even the eyes, may not be the same color, but they the same size and shape." She turned and looked at me for the first time, at least the first time I noticed. "Yeah, you look like her." I didn't know what to say. I just sat silently, diverting my eyes from her stare. "Sarah told me when you was born, she said, 'people will say he looks like his daddy, but I see me in him when he smiles.' Of course, I didn't really listen to her then." I remained silent. Mrs. Boutte turned and looked at Mama, and then walked out, leaving me alone in the room.

I stood and went over to Mama's casket. "I have to go, Mama, but I want you to know I love you. You were a blessing, just like Mr. Frank said. Good-bye, I'm going to miss you," I said, leaning into the casket and kissing Mama one last time, before turning to leave.

"Everything okay?" Mr. Benson asked, as I walked out of the parlor.

"Yes Sir, you did a wonderful job. She looked beautiful."

I spent the next week locked in the house, not wanting to see or talk to anyone. Mr. Frank called and asked if I would be stopping by the store, and also invited me to his house for dinner, but I declined both invitations.

"That's okay, you don't worry about coming to see me, you got to heal this thing within yourself in your own time," he said. That was the thing I loved about Mr. Frank, he never pressured you into anything.

Da-dee spent most of the time working in his shed during the day, but we had dinner together every night, and then watched TV, Da-dee in his recliner, and me on the sofa. This was where we were on Friday night when the phone rang.

"I got it," Da-dee said, jumping from his chair. "Hello. Yes operator, I will accept the charges." It was my father calling from prison. "Hey, how you doing? I figured that, it was kind of hectic here over the weekend with the wake and the funeral, plus regular church services." I went into the kitchen to get a glass of water, pretending not to be interested in the conversation. "Like I said, they held it over at Benson's Funeral Home, he always do a nice job for folks. Okay then, yeah, I'm pretty tired, so I'm go'n turn in. I'll talk to you later." Da-dee hung up the phone, and sat back in his recliner.

"So that was my father?'

"Yeah, he just wanted to call and see how things went."

"We buried Mama a week ago, and he's just calling to check on how things went?"

"Said he been trying every day, but ain't nobody been answering the phone."

"That's a flat out lie; I've been in this house all day, every day. If he had called, I would have answered the phone."

"Maybe it's best he didn't call."

"All I'm saying is he didn't call." Da-dee didn't respond. I walked back over to the sofa and took a seat. "He didn't ask if I was here?"

"He knows you here."

"But he didn't ask just now, did he?"

"No, he didn't."

I was livid. I didn't want to speak to the man, so I couldn't understand why I was so mad that he didn't ask about me. Screw this, I thought. I have enough to deal with; I can't let that bastard affect me. I decided the best thing for me was to get some rest, so I said goodnight to Da-dee, and went to bed.

As I lay in bed, my thoughts shifted to Mr. and Mrs. Boutte's behavior the week before at the funeral. Mr. Boutte showed genuine concern for my feelings, even after I reacted with scorn to his attempts at communication. Mrs. Boutte looked at me for the first time through the eyes of a grandmother, something I didn't think possible. I wondered if in death, Mama had convinced them that love was colorblind.

Not being able to sleep, I got up and started packing. I wasn't flying back to New York until Sunday evening, but I planned on spending Saturday night in New Orleans with some friends. At least that's what I told Da-dee. In truth, I was going to spend Saturday with one specific friend, Megan Waters.

I first saw Megan during registration my freshman year at Tulane. Standing five feet eight inches tall, with cocoa brown skin, high cheekbones, big almond-shaped green eyes, and an ass so round and firm that it appeared to be sculpted; I quickly became obsessed with her.

Megan worked in the campus bookstore, and I would stand in line for hours, sometimes purchasing nothing more than a pen, just to hear her speak. She had a deep voice, and spoke in a whisper, requiring you to lean in close to hear her. It had a paralyzing effect on me during our first encounter.

"That's all you need?" she asked.

"Yeah, unless you can ah, ah," I stuttered, every clever line I knew escaping my memory.

"Unless I can what?"

"Oh sorry, nothing, I was just thinking out loud."

I gathered my nerves, but then noticed she was wearing a heart pendant with the words *Megan & Steve, Forever* engraved on it. Great, she already has a boyfriend, I thought. This limited our interaction to me buying supplies, and I bought a lot of supplies. Many times I made Jeremy come with me. Jeremy's athletic career had ended his senior year in high school when he tore ligaments in both knees, but his hard work academically paid off, and he was accepted into Tulane. We of course became roommates.

"Didn't I tell you, she's the finest thing on campus," I said to Jeremy, after pointing Megan out in the bookstore.

"Damn, she is fine, but do we have to buy something? I can see her from right here, and that line will take forever."

"No man, you've got to hear her voice, it'll give you chills."

I made at least one trip per week into the bookstore, always standing in Megan's line. Then one evening, after completing semester finals, Jeremy, Monica Franklin (Jeremy's girlfriend), and I were all headed out to *The Wave*, our favorite campus bar, to celebrate. I asked Jeremy to drive over to the bookstore.

"You're not even going to say anything to her, this is a waste of time," he complained.

"I don't know, man, you know with all the Christmas parties that are going to be happening over the next few weeks, maybe I could invite her to one."

"You could, but you won't."

"Just stop by there, you let me worry about what I'm going to say."

"Who are you guys talking about?" Monica asked.

"I'm just going to see a friend before I go home for the holidays," I said.

"A friend?" Jeremy asked sarcastically.

"That's right, a friend, now pull the damn car over," I said, slapping him on the back of his head.

Jeremy parked on a side street next to the bookstore. As I pulled myself out of the car from the backseat, I whispered to him, "You don't need to be telling this girl all of my business."

"Just hurry up," he said, pushing me from the car.

I went into the store and to my surprise it was completely empty. There was only one cashier working, and it was Megan. Now's the perfect time, I thought. I walked over to the register and picked up a pack of gum.

"That's all?" she asked.

"Yeah, but I was wondering if, ah…," I said, stopping mid-sentence, overwhelmed by what I saw. I couldn't believe it, she wasn't wearing the *Megan & Steve, Forever* pin.

"You were wondering what?"

"Ah, I was wondering if the bookstore is going to be opened over the holidays?" I said, rattled by the possibilities presented.

"Nope, last exam is tomorrow, and our last day open is tomorrow."

"Okay, thanks, thanks." I rushed back to the car. "She's not wearing the pin!" Jeremy didn't say anything. "Did you hear me, she's not wearing the pin."

"Get in the car," he said.

I crawled into the backseat, my mind racing. Surely they must have broken up, I thought. "Man, I have to do something."

"Tell him," Jeremy calmly said to Monica.

"Tell me what?"

"Well, Kevin, I know Megan. We went to high school together," Monica said.

"What?" I asked, jumping toward Monica from the back seat, bringing us nose to nose, and frightening her in the process. "Do you know Steve?"

"Yeah, Steve Mason, that was her boyfriend," Monica said.

"Was? You said was, what happened?"

"I don't know what happened, but they broke up a few weeks ago," she said, leaning back in her seat to put some distance between us.

"Monica, you have to invite her out," I said.

"Okay, I'll go do it now."

"No, not now, wait a minute!" I yelled.

"Man, will you stop acting like a bitch!" Jeremy said. "You want to meet the damn girl, don't you?"

"Well, yeah."

"Then just relax. Monica, go in, and tell her to meet us later at the *The Wave*."

"Okay," Monica said, shooting me a strange look as she got out of the car.

"Man, can you believe this? I'm finally going to meet her," I said to Jeremy.

"Thank God."

Megan met us at the bar around eight that night, and Monica introduced us. "You're the pen guy," Megan said, shaking my hand.

"What?"

"The pen guy, you come in and buy pens all the time," she said, with a smile.

"Oh, yeah, well that was the only way I got to see you."

"That's sweet."

"So, what happened to Steve?"

"We broke up."

"I know that, the pendant is gone."

"What are you talking about?"

"The pin you wore all the time, *Megan & Steve, Forever*."

"Oh, yeah."

"So what happened?"

"I don't want to talk about Steve."

"Come on, you can tell me."

"Give me a Stoli Gimlet," Megan said to the bartender. "Look, Kevin, we can hang out, but I don't want to talk about Steve."

"Okay. So, what's a Stoli Gimlet?"

"Stoli Vodka and Roses Lime Juice."

"Sounds like a strong drink."

"Don't worry, I can handle it."

Megan proceeded to handle at least five gimlets over the next four hours. Jeremy and Monica were drinking Long Island Ice Teas, and by the time we left the bar I was the only one in any condition to drive. I didn't drink. Monica lived on campus, so I dropped her off first, after which I planned on dropping Jeremy off at our dorm, before driving Megan home.

"Are you going to be okay, Jeremy?" I asked, pulling into a parking spot in front of the dorm.

"I'm cool." Jeremy stumbled from the car, tripping and falling onto the pavement.

"I better walk him upstairs," I said to Megan.

"Okay, I'll come with you."

"Maybe you should wait here."

"No no, I can help."

I got out of the car and lifted Jeremy off of the pavement, placing his arm around my shoulder to steady his balance. As I guided him through the doors of the dormitory, Megan grabbed Jeremy's other arm in an attempt to help, but her staggering, combined with Jeremy's, caused both of them to fall.

"We fell, Kevin," Jeremy said.

Megan began laughing hysterically.

"Come on guys, you have to get up," I said.

"Kind of late for visitors, isn't it, Kevin?" a voice asked.

It was Manny, the dorm RA. School regulations didn't permit female visitors after eleven o'clock, although this rule was never enforced.

"She's just helping me get Jeremy up to the room. Once we get him up there, we'll be right back down," I said to Manny.

"She's helping you," Manny said, looking down at Megan. "Maybe I should help you."

Manny pulled Jeremy from the floor, and I helped Megan. After a few mishaps, we made it to the elevator and up to our floor. Manny led

Jeremy into our room, dropping him on the bed. Jeremy passed out as soon as his head hit the pillow.

"He's going to pay for this tomorrow morning," Manny said.

"Yeah, guess he can't handle it," Megan said, falling on my bed, passing out also.

"Guess she can't handle it either," Manny said, laughing. "Hey, Kevin, that's the chick from the bookstore, isn't it?"

"That's her."

"The one you been buying all the pens from. Oh shit! I can't believe this, damn she's fine," he said, taking a closer look at Megan. "You been trying to get with her all semester."

"I know."

"How long you been hooking up with her?"

"Tonight's the first time."

"Well my brother, looks like tonight is the night," he said, reaching his hand out to give me a pound.

"Man, I'm not going to do anything with the girl, she's passed out," I said, pushing his hand away.

"Whatever you say. Tell you what, I'm just going to leave you two alone, you do whatever you feel you have to. Damn, some brothers got all the luck," Manny said, leaving the room.

"Come on, Megan, let's get you home," I said, pulling her from the bed.

"Home, I don't want to go home. I want to stay here with you. You don't want me to stay?" she asked, draping her arms around my shoulder.

"You're drunk, Megan."

"No, I'm not. Why don't you take off your clothes, and I'll prove it to you," she said, slurring her words.

"Megan, you're drunk. Now you don't have to go home, you're more than welcome to sleep here, but nothing is going to happen tonight."

Megan didn't argue. In fact, she was asleep before I finished my statement.

The next morning when I woke up, Megan was already awake.

"Nothing happened," I said.

"I know."

Megan leaned in and began kissing me. She glanced over at Jeremy's bed, and after seeing he was still out cold, took off her jeans and crawled on top of me.

"Megan, what's going on?" She didn't answer.

I had dreamed about this woman from the first day I saw her, and now she was mine. This could be the one, I thought.

"Kevin, I think you should know that, well, I had a great time with you last night, and an even better time with you this morning, but after what I just went through, I'm not looking for a boyfriend," Megan said, climbing out of the bed later that morning.

Not looking for a boyfriend? She could have at least waited a few days before blowing me off, she must have hated it, I thought. I played it cool though and said, "No problem, I mean, I had a great time too, but I'm not interested in anything serious right now either. I am interested in something else though." Megan smiled, and crawled back into bed. We would be together, or I should say we would sleep together, for the next four years.

❋   ❋   ❋

Megan picked me up early Saturday evening. She was wearing a tank top that stopped beneath her breasts, exposing her stomach, a pair of jean shorts, flip flops, blue sunglasses, and a blue bandana tied on her head. She looked unbelievably sexy. Da-dee had met Megan during my college days, and was happy to see her.

"How are you, darling?" he said, hugging her.

"I'm good, Reverend Matthews, I'm good," Megan said, self-consciously folding her arms to conceal her bare stomach.

"Why did you wear that outfit if you're embarrassed by it?" I whispered to her.

"I wore it for you, and I won't be taking it off if you don't shut up."

Da-dee thought my friendship with Megan was more serious than I let on, although he would not have approved of our true relationship.

Before leaving, I walked over to Ms. Bertha's house to say good-bye.

"It sure was good seeing you, Baby," Ms. Bertha said. "You do good up there in New York, okay, make us all proud."

"I'll do my best."

"I know you will," she said, kissing me goodbye and running her hand through my hair. "Still got that good hair, don't you?"

"I'll see you for Christmas, Ms. Bertha," I said, laughing, and walking away.

"Who's that pretty young lady over there picking you up?" Ms. Bertha asked, leaning forward on her porch to get a better look at Megan.

"That's Megan, you've met her before, she went to college with me at Tulane."

"Oh yeah, now I remember. Beautiful girl, could use a little weight on her though. You bring her back out here when you come for Christmas, I'll take good care of her for you."

"Maybe I will, Ms. Bertha, maybe I will."

I went back to the house, and said good-bye to Da-dee, then loaded my luggage into Megan's new silver convertible Porsche. After graduating with a degree in Political Science, Megan had been accepted into Yale Law School, her father's Alma Mater. And although her father was tough on her at Tulane, always requiring her to have a job, he was quite proud of her acceptance into his Alma Mater, and rewarded her justly.

"Kevin, I'll see you for Christmas, Baby," Ms. Bertha yelled, as we backed out of the driveway. "Take care."

I waved good-bye to her and Da-dee, both of them disappearing in a cloud of dust as Megan sped away, Duke chasing behind the car.

"Where are we going?" I asked, thirty minutes later as Megan exited Interstate 10 onto Elysian Fields.

"Just relax, Baby, Megan's going to take care of you." Megan drove down Elysian Fields, crossing over to Esplanade Avenue and pulling into a parking spot in front of Port of Call. "Burgers and Huma Humas, welcome home, Baby," she said jumping from the car. Port of Call was a neighborhood restaurant famous for its massive burgers and huge rum punch drink concoctions called Huma Humas. I loved the hamburgers, but not being a drinker, *Huma Humas* were off limits.

"Megan, I don't drink."

"I'm starving," she said, ignoring me. When we walked in the restaurant, every table was taken. "You want to eat at the bar?"

"Better take what we can get."

"Don't need a menu, we'll have two burgers with everything, medium rare, and two Huma Humas," Megan said to the bartender, as we took a seat.

"Megan, I'm not drinking one of those things."

"Kevin, you've got to loosen up, man. He'll have one," she said, overruling me with the bartender. "So, is Jeremy going to marry Monica or what?"

"You know Jeremy, Mr. Straight Arrow."

Jeremy and Monica continued to date through college. After graduation, Jeremy, like Megan and I, kept up a family tradition by going to both his parents' Alma Mater, when he was accepted into Stanford University's medical program, specializing in Sports Medicine. Monica followed Jeremy out west, taking a job with IBM in San Jose. The two were living together, and I knew it was only a matter of time before they announced their engagement.

Our order arrived, and Megan and I both stuffed ourselves. Two hours later, and after a second *Huma Huma*, I had loosened up to the point of wanting nothing more than to get Megan in bed.

"Megan, where are we staying?"

"I don't know, pick a place."

"What do you mean, 'pick a place?'"

"Just what I said, pick a place, any place you want to stay."

"Oh, you got it like that now?"

"I did say any place," Megan said, pulling out a stack of credit cards, and waving them in front of me.

We left Port of Call, and drove to the Riverside Hilton, checking into a room on the fifteenth floor.

"Lay down," Megan said, pushing me onto the bed, and pulling off my shorts and underwear. She kicked off her flip-flops, and pulled down her jean shorts, standing before me wearing only light blue lace panties and her tank top. After turning her back to me, and slowly bending over to remove her panties, teasing me with every move, she crawled onto the foot of the bed. "Let's see if that white girl has taught you anything," Megan said, straddling my body.

I would like to say that Megan and I spent the evening making love, but that would be an inaccurate way to describe it, since there was nothing tender about the way we had sex. We rarely kissed, there was no foreplay, and we never said anything to each other during the act. It was as if our bodies were taken over by two strangers, purely in search of sexual satisfaction.

After exhausting ourselves physically over the next few hours, Megan got out of bed, and started getting dressed.

"Where are you going?"

"Home, but don't worry, all the room charges will go on my credit card."

"Why are you going home?" I asked, getting out of bed. "How am I supposed to get to the airport tomorrow?"

"I'll pick you up at eleven; I think that's check-out time. We can grab some lunch and hang out until your flight leaves."

"But why can't you stay the night?"

"I need some sleep, and I sleep best in my own bed," she said, heading for the door.

"What about me? Damn, my mother died last week, you can't talk to me for a while?" I asked, plopping down on the bed like a spoiled child.

"Whoa, Kevin, just hold back, man."

"What?"

"Look, we don't do this to each other, okay."

"Do what?"

"Lay guilt trips on each other. I mean that's why this works so well. We see each other, we have a good time, but we don't bring the outside world into it, and that includes our personal problems."

"Personal problems, I just lost my mother! What kind of heartless bitch are you?"

"Look, when we met I had just...," Megan said, stopping to compose herself. I could tell she was upset. She walked to the window, and even though her back was to me, I could tell she was crying. I had never seen Megan cry.

"You had just what? What's wrong with you?"

"Kevin, we've all got things we have to deal with," she said, wiping her eyes and turning to face me. "You're a grown man. You better learn to take care of yourself, because trust me, no one else will, and I certainly won't. I don't ask you to do it for me, and I won't let you try and guilt me into doing it for you. Now I'll be by tomorrow at eleven to pick you up, is that cool?"

"That's fine."

Megan left without saying another word. I was confused by her reaction, but was too upset to examine what caused it. I sat in a chair next to the window and stared out at the Mississippi, the lights of the city flickering off of its wide belly of muddy water. I was angry. I was angry that Mama had been taken from me. I was angry that my father never wanted me. Megan's right, I thought; in the end, you really have no one but yourself to depend on. I walked over to the mini bar and pulled out two bottles of vodka, pouring them in a glass with orange juice. I took my drink, along with every other bottle of alcohol in the bar, and sat back next to the window. I remained in that position drinking, until I passed out. It was as if I pulled the shades down on the rest of the world.

"This Could Ruin Everything"

I woke up with a massive hangover the next morning. My head was pounding, my throat was so sore I couldn't swallow, and my stomach felt like someone had beaten my insides with a wire hanger. I could barely make it to the door when Megan arrived to pick me up.

"Do you know what time it is?" she asked, barging into the room.

"I'm not feeling very well," I said, stumbling back to the bed, empty bottles of every alcohol imaginable littered across the floor.

"I bet you're not, you emptied the mini bar," she said, laughing. "It's an hour past checkout, you've got to get ready or they're going to charge a late check-out fee, and I think you've already run up the bill more than enough."

"I don't think I can leave right now, my head is killing me, and my stomach feels like there's a tornado in there," I said, lying back in the bed, arms outstretched on both sides.

"Did you throw up?"

"No, I hope I don't do that. I hate it when I throw up."

"Right now, that's the best thing that could happen to you." Megan pulled me from the bed, and led me to the bathroom, telling me to shove my finger down my throat in order to throw up.

"I can't do this, it's going to make me gag," I said, kneeling in front of the toilet bowl.

"It's supposed to make you gag, moron, you're trying to throw up."

Annoyed by my squeamish behavior, Megan grabbed a stick from her hair, which held it in a bun, and shoved it down my throat, causing me to unburden the contents of my stomach with four heaves. I collapsed next to the toilet.

"I feel like I'm going to die," I whined.

"Oh, quit being a baby."

I didn't eat anything for the rest of the day, and looked near death when I got off the plane that night in New York.

"What happened to you?" Beth asked, meeting me at the airport gate.

"I don't know, I think I might have gotten food poisoning," I lied.

I couldn't sleep Sunday night, and still felt nauseous Monday morning, as I got dressed for my first day of school. I had two classes scheduled, a nine o'clock *Substance Abuse Issues & Treatment*, the irony of this being my first class painfully apparent, and a twelve o'clock *Survey of Child Development*. Both classes were two hours long.

"Lord, get me through this day, and I promise I'll never touch another drop of alcohol as long as I live," I prayed.

There were about twenty people in my first class. Our professor, Dr. Feldman, began class by introducing himself, detailing his experience in the field of *Substance Abuse*. He then proceeded to entertain both the class and himself by using his attendance log to guess each student's name. The next fifteen minutes were spent reviewing our class syllabus for the semester. I was exhausted, and barely able to concentrate when Dr. Feldman finally began his lecture on: *What is addiction?* You've made it all the way to Columbia, and you're about to blow it, I thought. That fear of possible failure was all I needed to jumpstart my body. I was able to not only zone in for Dr. Feldman's lecture, but sustained that focus through my next class. For me, nonperformance when it came to academics was unacceptable, regardless of the circumstances.

After class, I rushed home in hopes of taking a nap. I had been assigned to write a paper for my *Substance Abuse* class, and not wanting to fall behind, I planned on getting my first Field Assignment completed that evening. I was required to attend an Alcoholics Anonymous Meeting, which the paper would be based on. I located an open AA meeting at seven in Chelsea, a neighborhood about ninety blocks south of my apartment. It was only two-thirty when I made it home, so I figured I could get at least three hours sleep before I went to the meeting. After wolfing down a slice of pizza, I got into bed, setting the alarm for five forty-five. I was just dozing off when a bead of sweat rolled into my right eye, stinging it. I can't catch a break, I thought. It was late August, and the temperature in my apartment was in the nineties. "Just turn up the fan," Da-dee told me when I complained about the heat, so I got up, and positioned my white three-speed box fan on a chair next to the bed. I flipped the switch to high, and crawled back in bed, falling asleep instantly. I slept soundly until the alarm woke me. I then hopped in the shower, dressed quickly, and was headed out the door when the phone rang.

"Hello."

"Hey, Baby, how are you feeling?" Beth asked.

"Great, I was able to take a nap after class, finally got some sleep."

"Look, if you're feeling better, I'd like to come over tonight. I need to talk to you about something."

"I don't know. I've got this meeting to go to at seven, and then I really need to start work on my paper when I get back."

"Kevin, it's important. I really need to talk to you tonight."

"Okay, I'll stop by around nine."

"No, I'll come there."

"Beth, are you okay?"

"Yeah, yeah, I just want to talk about us. Look, it's six twenty, you better leave, I'll see you tonight, bye."

I knew Beth wanted to discuss our relationship. She didn't buy my story about having food poisoning, and I knew she suspected something. I felt ashamed. I had slept with another woman the first time I needed comforting and Beth wasn't around. I had to make things right.

I took the train downtown to Chelsea, and walked up from the subway onto 23rd Street at six fifty-five. After getting confused as to which way was east or west, not to mention uptown or downtown, a directional problem that would plague me my first six months in New York, I found the building where the meeting was being held. I ran up the stairs to the second floor, taking a seat at the end of a horseshoe of chairs, moments after the meeting began.

"It's a patient disease, one that will stalk you for the rest of your life," a middle-aged man said, standing in front of the room, while those seated nodded their heads in agreement. "After twenty years of sobriety, I recently came close to taking a drink after merely inhaling the scent of a glass of scotch. I began imagining how it would feel to take a slow sip, feel it slide down my throat, warming me on the inside in a way I once thought nothing else in this world ever could. I was powerless over the desire to have that feeling, which in turn made me powerless over the alcohol."

The man's name was Bill, and he was the guest speaker for the evening. After Bill's speech, others discussed their experiences and struggles. I sat listening as the group shared intimate details from their life without fear of judgment. I realized these meetings were a safe house for them. I was most impressed by the group's ability to look at themselves truthfully in order to help in their recoveries. It was a lesson that would have served me well.

The meeting ended at eight-thirty. Due to construction delays on the subway, it took me an hour to get home. I ran from the station, and spotted Beth pacing back and forth in front of my building.

"Sorry, I'm late, subway delays," I said, out of breath. "How long have you been waiting?"

"I just got here," she said, re-directing the nervous energy of her pacing into a manic massaging of both arms as if she were cold, even though the temperature was in the eighties. "I would have gone up, but I forgot my key."

"What's wrong with you? You can't be cold."

"No no, I'm not. Let's just go upstairs, okay?"

As we rode up in the elevator, I silently rehearsed a speech to profess my feelings for Beth. One that would let her know I was ready to commit to a serious relationship.

"I know what you want to talk about, and I want to talk about it also. Just take a seat and hear me out," I said, as soon as we walked into the apartment.

"Kevin, I don't think——,"

"No, just let me say this while I have it straight in my mind," I said, ushering her over to the bed to sit down. "I know you wanted to come home with me for the funeral, and I should have let you. I was thrown by Mama's death, and just wanted to be alone, but that wasn't fair to you. Being in a relationship means that we go through things together, that we both allow the other to be there in difficult times; I realize that now, and I'm sorry. Before I left I told you that this, what we have, this relationship, was going somewhere, I want you to know I meant that. I don't want to lose you, Beth." My words had been perfectly chosen, I thought. I looked at Beth expecting her unbridled gratitude; instead, she raised her hands to her lips in a prayer-like fashion and began to cry. "What's wrong, what did I say?"

"Kevin, I'm pregnant."

"You're pregnant?"

We sat staring at each other. This could ruin everything, I thought.

"What do you think we should do?" Beth asked.

"What should we do? There's only one thing we can do," I said, my composure deserting me.

"Kevin, I don't know if I can handle going through that."

"Beth, you're not thinking about all the consequences that will come along with having a baby," I said, standing and pacing the room, her words chasing me.

"Yes I am. I mean, I think we can handle it. Think about it, money wouldn't be a problem; I mean I'm sure my parents will help us out. The baby wouldn't be born until May, so it's possible I might not even have to miss any school."

"You might be able to handle it, but I can't."

Beth was silent for a moment. "Okay, fine, I don't need you to help me," she said, standing and heading for the door.

Realizing that my current approach was backfiring, I decided, in the most calculating of fashions, to deal with the situation from a different angle.

"I'm sorry," I said, gently grabbing her by the arm to stop her from leaving. "I didn't mean what I said, I just panicked. I saw everything we've been working toward being taken from us, but you're right, we do have options. I really care for you, Beth, and like I said earlier, I don't want to lose you. We just have to decide what's best for us, not what's best for me, not what's best for you, but what's best for us."

I spent the rest of the night convincing Beth that even though I one day wanted us to start a family, now was not the time. She listened, but was still struggling with the idea when I walked her home the next morning.

"I feel it's the right thing for us, at least right now," I said to Beth, standing in front of her building, which was on the same block as my apartment.

"I just need to think about it, okay?"

"Of course, and I want you to know, I'll support whatever decision you make."

"Thank you," she said, kissing me goodbye.

I couldn't look myself in the mirror when I got back to my apartment, fearful of the disgust I might feel. I tried to convince myself that I'd done the right thing, and that having a baby would ruin both our lives. But I knew what I had done was wrong. I knew it was cruel. That knowledge would change nothing.

The following Tuesday at eight a.m., Beth and I were seated in the waiting area of an abortion clinic on West 60th Street. The room was filled with nervous faces, no one wanting to make eye contact. Beth attempted to put up a brave front, but the tightness with which she gripped my hand alerted me to her fear.

"It's going to be okay," I said, kissing her hand.

"I know, I know," she said, shaking her head to convince herself it would be.

It had been an awful week. Beth spent every night at my apartment crying, and was too upset to go to class. I knew she wanted to keep the baby. In her mind there was no reason not to. She knew her family would support her both emotionally and financially, she eventually wanted to have children anyway, and she was in love with me, the father of her child. A baby was the last thing I wanted. I cared for Beth, but we had only known each other for three months, far too short a time to know if we would have a future together. We were both in school, and one of us would probably have to put our education on hold, something I was not willing to do. Above all else, I wasn't certain I wanted to have kids. Parents defined a child's existence for its entire life, and I didn't know if I wanted that responsibility. All of these were valid issues, so if I had pointed them out to Beth, I would have been justified in doing so. It was the deception used in my arguments that was reprehensible. I wasn't willing to take a chance on Beth not agreeing with me, so I dangled the idea of us having a family together later in life. "Five, six years from now, we'll be out of school, we'll have jobs, we'll be ready to start our family the right way," I had lied. I even hinted that having a baby at this point could destroy our relationship. "The pressure, the sacrifices, even with the way we feel about each other, they could cause us to grow apart, not give us the time we need to build the life we want, the way we want it," I told her.

Sunday night, after discussing our options, of which I secretly felt only one to be viable, Beth decided to go through with the abortion. "Thank you for being here for me," she told me. "A lot of guys wouldn't know how to deal with this, but you've been here supporting me every step of the way. I love you, Kevin." I felt my insides being squeezed, the pressure coming from my own guilt. I had used Beth's love as a weapon, manipulating her into a decision she might regret for the rest of her life. One of my greatest fears was to become the type of man my father was. If I had been brave enough to look in the mirror, I would have already seen his image.

"Elizabeth Harris," the nurse called out. Beth held my hand tightly, as if hoping I wouldn't allow her to stand. I squeezed her hand, kissed her, and told her that everything would be okay. She stood and walked over to the nurse, who was holding the door open to the back of the clinic. Beth looked back at me one last time before walking through the door. She looked frightened, like a child being sent off with strangers. I wanted to yell out to her that she didn't have to go through with the abortion. I wanted to tell her she was right, and we could handle having the baby together. Instead, I said nothing.

EMPTY

"I'm sorry, but I just can't stop crying," Beth said, her eyes puffy and red.

"It's okay, it's okay, it's been a rough day, it's going to take time," I said weakly, busying myself around the apartment with meaningless tasks.

"Come lie down with me."

"I have to go and get your prescription filled before the drugstore closes," I said, grabbing my keys and heading for the door.

"Do that later, I need you to come and lie next to me for a while." I sat on the bed, and Beth laid her head on my lap. "Do you think God will punish me for what I did?"

"What are you talking about?"

"I don't know, I mean, I really think it was the right thing for us, but was it the right thing?"

"Beth, why are you doing this? This serves no purpose. We did what we thought was best. We weren't ready for a baby; we both agreed that we weren't ready. I mean, we can't change it now, we just have to accept it and move on."

"I'm sorry, I'm just not certain in my heart that it was the right thing," she said, sitting up in bed, the movement causing her to wince in pain.

"Are you okay?"

"Yeah," she said, lying back down. "Look, why don't you go and get the prescription filled. I'm going to try and get some sleep."

Beth turned her back to me, curling up in a fetal position. This move was normally a preamble to her falling asleep, but I knew nothing would allow her rest on this day.

After being an emotional wreck on Tuesday, Beth pulled herself together the next day and made it to all of her classes. She stayed at my apartment for the rest of the week, before leaving on Friday to spend the weekend with her parents. I rode the subway with her to Grand Central Station, where she was catching a train to her parents' home in Westchester.

"Thanks for being there for me this week," Beth said, hugging me. "I don't think I could have gotten through it without you."

"Yeah, yeah, of course, I mean, you're welcome," I stammered.

"What are you going to do tonight?"

"Not much, I'm pretty tired."

"I know what you mean. Okay then, I'll give you a call later?"

"Alright, yeah."

Beth kissed me goodbye, and boarded the train. I watched as the train pulled out, then hopped back on the subway, and headed home.

When I walked up from the subway at my stop, it was pouring rain. I didn't have an umbrella, so I decided to wait out the rain under a store awning.

"Kevin, hey Kevin," a voice yelled from across the street. I turned to see who was calling me, squinting to bring the shadowy figure into focus as it approached me. "Kevin, it's Lynn." It was Lynn Edwards, an aerobics instructor at my gym. We had been out on a couple of dates over the summer, enjoying what was a strictly sexual relationship, but stopped seeing each other when she decided to get back together with her old boyfriend.

"Hey, Lynn," I said, kissing her hello.

"What are you doing out on a night like this?"

"Waiting out the rain; no umbrella. Where are you headed?"

"Home. You want to grab a drink somewhere?"

"Yeah, why not."

"There's this cool little bar, *The Emporium*, right around the corner from my apartment, we can go there."

"That's cool."

"Come on, get under my umbrella." Lynn pulled me in close, her arm around my waist.

The bar was only a few blocks away, but Lynn's umbrella was not big enough for both of us, and we were soaked by the time we walked in. Lynn was wearing blue jeans and a white t-shirt, which clung to her body because of the rain. I found myself distracted by the visual.

"You've seen them before, so I don't know why you're staring," Lynn said, closing her umbrella.

"I don't think my memory did them justice." Lynn had an out-of-this-world body. She was five feet seven inches tall, eighty percent of that seemingly legs, and weighed about one hundred and fifteen pounds, an exquisite balance between cut muscle and feminine softness.

"What can I get you?" a waitress asked, moments after we were seated.

"A glass of Pinot Grigio, please," Lynn said.

"And for you?"

"He'll have a coke," Lynn answered.

"Actually, I think I'll have a Stoli Gimlet."

"A Stoli Gimlet? Kevin Matthews wants a vodka drink?" Lynn asked sarcastically.

"Pinot Grigio for her, a Stoli Gimlet for me," I said to the waitress, who laughed as she left to get our drinks.

"Since when do you drink, Kevin?"

"You haven't seen me in two months, a lot can happen in two months."

"Really? So, how's Beth?"

"She's good, how's MC T-thug?"

"He's good, and his name is T-Ray, no MC, no thug," she said, laughing.

"His name is Raymond, and he might not be an MC, but he is a thug."

"Why you talking about my man? I didn't say anything about Marsha Brady."

"Why do black women always have to go there?"

"No, the question is, why do black men always have to go there."

"You got me, I give, let's move on."

"Of course you and Beth are about the same color so I guess I should let you pass, excuse the pun."

"Damn, I give, let's move on," I said, raising my hands in surrender and laughing, as the waitress placed our drinks on the table.

"So really, when did you start drinking?"

"I always drank."

"You never had a drink with me?"

"I thought I had to maintain my full senses with you, never knew when that criminal you were dating might show up."

"I thought you said we were going to move on."

"True, true. Tell you what, here's to our first night out drinking together. May the focus of the night be on just us." I raised my glass for a toast.

"I don't know if I should drink to that or not, that toast sounds like it's carrying some hidden implications," Lynn said, smiling seductively, and raising her glass.

"None that you're not aware of."

Two hours later, I was holding Lynn against her living room wall, with her legs wrapped around me, and her t-shirt being the only article of clothing worn by either of us.

"You have a condom?" she asked.

I ignored her question, thrusting inside her body, her legs clamping around my waist pulling me in further. We both climaxed in this position, with me deep inside Lynn. I carried her over to the sofa, and collapsed next to her, with my head falling onto her chest.

"You missed me, didn't you?" she asked, playing with my hair. I didn't answer. "You know, I'm not on the pill."

I have no explanation for what happened next, but her statement aroused me. "Let's go in the bedroom," I said, lifting her from the sofa; her legs once again locking around my body. I carried her into the bedroom, entering her as we fell onto the bed.

I knew Lynn had condoms in the apartment, but I didn't want to put one on. We would have sex all night, the recklessness of our actions proving to be a turn-on for me. I had no idea why.

I didn't make it home until after noon the next day. After grabbing a bite to eat, I went to sleep, not waking up until the phone rang later that night.

"Hello," I answered groggily.

"Hey," Beth said softly. "I'm sorry, you were sleeping?"

"No no, well, I just dozed off, but it's no problem. How are you?"

"I'm okay, I just wanted to call and see how you were doing."

"Yeah, I was going to call you, but I just thought you needed the time alone," I lied, embarrassed that I had not been the one to make this call.

"I tried you last night too, but you didn't answer."

"I'm sorry. I was so tired that I fell asleep as soon as I got home last night. I must have not heard the phone."

"Yeah, that's what I figured. I really did exhaust you this past week, huh?"

"Don't worry about me, how are you feeling?"

"Pretty good. I told my mother."

"You did?" I asked, the news fully waking me. "What did she say?"

"She said she wished I had come to her, but that I was an adult, and it was my decision to make. I told her how supportive you were, and that you really had been there for me. She was happy that I hadn't gone through it by myself."

"Yeah."

"Well, I'm pretty tired, so I'm going to go to bed. I just wanted to call and see how you were doing."

"I'm fine, but the important thing is that you're okay."

"I am. I'm going to stay here tomorrow night. Mom wants us to spend some more time together. I'll be back for classes on Monday, okay?"

"Yeah, yeah, that's a good idea."

"Maybe we can get together Monday night."

"Definitely, I'll see you Monday night. Bye."

I felt physically ill. Seconds later the phone rang again. "Yeah," I answered, thinking it was Beth calling back.

"Yeah? What kind of a way is that to answer the phone?" April asked.

"Oh, sorry. I thought you were someone else."

"Who?"

"Don't worry about that. What's up?"

"No need to get snotty. What are you doing tonight?"

"Why?"

"Some friends and I are going to the *Latin Quarter*, you want to come?"

"I don't think so, I'm pretty tired."

"Kevin, I know you're going through a rough time right now, but you can't just shut down. I mean, you've been in a funk the past two weeks. You have to get out, have some fun. A few drinks, a little dancing, a little me; might help take your mind off things, and trust me that's what you need to do."

April was referring to my mother's death, but she was right nonetheless. I needed to take my mind off things, and I was willing to try anything in doing so.

I met April at the *Latin Quarter*, and after a few hours of drinking, we couldn't keep our hands off of each other. She had come with two friends, Pam and Lisa, but Pam had disappeared with some guy, and Lisa seemed miserable being a third wheel.

"Your friend doesn't look like she's having much fun," I whispered to April.

"She's fine," April insisted.

"Well I'm not. I'm ready to get out of here, why don't we go back to my place?"

"You got stuff to drink there?"

"No, but we can pick up something."

"Everything's closed by now."

"I'm ready to leave too. You guys can stop by my place and have a drink if you like," Lisa said, overhearing our conversation.

"Cool. Let's go have a few more. Lisa lives really close by. We can stop in, have a few drinks, and then go home. I promise I'll be worth the wait, Baby," April said, hugging and kissing me.

"That's cool."

"Get me a drink, I want a Kamikaze," April said, stretching out on the sofa and pulling me on top of her, as soon as we walked into Lisa's apartment.

"What do you want, Kevin?" Lisa asked.

"Vodka and orange juice is cool, thanks."

Lisa left to get the drinks, and April and I started making out on the sofa. I was a little uncomfortable since we were in someone else's apartment, but that didn't bother April. Lisa walked back in with the drinks, right as she unzipped my pants.

"Okay, I'll leave you two alone," Lisa said.

"You don't have to leave," April said, motioning for Lisa to sit next to her. I looked closely at Lisa for the first time all night. Short, skinny, kind of pale, with blonde hair and blue eyes, she wasn't really my type, but at the moment she looked very sexy.

"Why don't we go in my room, I don't want to wake up my room-mate," Lisa said, smiling at us, before exiting down the hall.

"Come on, Kevin. Lisa wants us to go to her room," April said, giggling, and pulling me up from the couch.

"April, what's going on?" I asked.

"I told you I had something special planned for you, remember," she said, leading me to the bedroom. "And by the way, tonight, I'm going to be in control."

I woke the next morning with a nasty hangover. Lisa and April were asleep next to me. Some men would have considered what happened to be a fantasy come true, but now sober, I felt no great satisfaction. I felt empty.

"Parlez-Vous Anglais?"

"For the last time, get up, Megan. Beth will be here in less than an hour."

"What time is it?" Megan asked, not moving from her position in bed, a pillow across her face to block out any hint of light.

"It's six o'clock."

"I need some water. Can you get me some water?"

"I'll get you some water, but you have to get up."

"I heard you the first time. I'm going to get up, just get me some water, please."

"Water isn't going to help you, trust me."

It was Saturday, December 10, 1983. The day before had been the last day of finals, and Megan and I had spent the previous night celebrating. Having taken five classes: *Statistics I, Physiological Psychology, Survey of Child Development, Substance Abuse and Treatment, and Psychology of Trauma*, my schedule had been a full one, but carrying an A average into each exam, I had pulled through with flying colors. My personal life was another story.

Beth and I remained together, but our relationship was never the same. I felt uncomfortable in her presence and avoided spending time with her. I started drinking and partying a lot, two things in which I knew Beth had no interest. We came close to breaking up several times, but strangely I always found myself convincing her to stay, convincing her I would make things right.

Megan and I were also spending a lot more time together, although the sexual aspect of our relationship ended after our last encounter in New Orleans. She had also completed her first semester at Yale with stellar grades; unfortunately, her life was just as chaotic.

"Megan, are you going to get up or not?" I yelled.

"No, I'm going to lie here all evening, and you and Beth will have dinner while I do so. Of course I'm going to get up, asshole, just give me some water," Megan said, throwing the pillow in my direction. "Why are you cooking dinner anyway, is she mad at you?"

"Yeah, she's mad, she's mad because I was supposed to meet her and her parents for brunch and I didn't show up because I was out all night with you, and couldn't wake up this morning."

"Hey, I didn't make you stay out, you're a grown man."

"Oh really, you had nothing to do with it. I guess you don't remember this, 'Oh come on, Kevin, you're not going to let me go to this party all by myself, are you? You know I hate to drink alone, and what if something happens to me, you'd never forgive yourself,'" I said, stumbling across the room, mimicking Megan's words and behavior from the night before.

"Damn, I really was wasted, wasn't I?"

"Yeah, you were, and I had to take care of you, which is the reason I didn't get home until eight this morning, which is the reason I over-slept, which is the reason I'm cooking dinner tonight."

"Had to take care of me?"

"Yes, Megan, I had to take care of you."

"Look, I may have been a little tipsy, but I can take care of myself."

"Whatever."

"I'm serious, Kevin, I can take care of myself. I don't need you to watch over me."

Megan hated the idea of needing anyone, even her parents. She seemed to have a very loving family, but although she spoke kindly of them, there was little emotion in her words. "Your mom and dad really take care of you, don't they?" I had asked a week earlier, after Megan opened a letter containing a check for three thousand dollars. The check was an early Christmas present, a reward for her excellent schoolwork. "They make sure I have everything I need, but I didn't ask them for the money," she said, placing the check in her wallet, and dropping the letter on the table without even reading it.

Megan finally got dressed and left around six forty-five; Beth arrived minutes later.

"Hey, Baby," I said, leaning in to kiss Beth, who turned her head so I would find her cheek.

"Hey."

"Did you apologize to your parents for me? I'm really sorry I couldn't make it, but I just wasn't feeling well."

"Staying out all night drinking can do that to you."

"Staying out all night, what are you talking about?"

"Kevin, don't lie to me. Who were you out with?"

"Beth, don't start. I wasn't out with another woman, and I'm not sleeping with anybody else. I was out with Dave." Dave Mills lived in the apartment across the hall. We were friends and occasionally hung out together. Dave was my scapegoat for anything that went wrong. Beth hated him.

"You were out with Dave?"

"He knew this after hours spot, and one thing led to another. Look, I'm sorry, okay?" I said, rubbing her shoulders. "I had a little too much to drink, and before I knew it, it was eight o'clock."

"Eight o'clock, so you're telling me that's when you and Dave came home?" she asked, knocking my hands away.

"Yeah, that's when I came home, and don't tell me I wasn't home after eight, because I was. If you don't believe me you can ask Dave."

"Okay, let's go ask Dave." Beth made a beeline for the door.

"What?"

"You said if I don't believe you, I can ask Dave, so I'm going to ask Dave," she said, yanking the door open.

"Beth, what is wrong with you? Damn, I thought we were supposed to be having dinner. Is that why you came over here, to fight? I made a mistake, okay? I'm sorry I missed brunch with you and your parents. I'm sorry I stayed out all night. Are you happy now?"

"No, I'm not happy, Kevin," she said, slamming the door, and beginning to cry. She walked over and looked out the window, and after unsuccessfully attempting to regain her composure, turned to face me. "I'm not happy about you not showing up for brunch, I'm not happy about you being out until eight in the morning, and I'm not happy that you're lying to me about who you were with."

"Lying?"

"I was outside your apartment when you and Megan came home this morning." I had introduced Megan to Beth months before. "Well? Aren't you going to say anything?" she demanded.

I didn't answer. Beth let out a sigh of frustration, then walked over to the sofa and took a seat, wrapping her arms around her stomach and rocking back and forth, while tears lined her eyelids. She had faced her parents at brunch knowing full well why I was not there. She had waited all day before confronting me, and even given me the opportunity to be truthful about what had happened. I honestly believe she would have forgiven me had I done so. The day had taken a toll on her. She now looked helpless. I searched for words that I thought would make everything okay.

"I love you," I said.

"You what? You love me? You choose now to say that to me," she said, standing from the sofa, her helplessness turning into rage. "How dare you? I catch you cheating on me with another woman, a woman you introduced to me as your friend, and you think you can make it all better by telling me you love me."

"I didn't have sex with Megan last night."

"Oh, you didn't have sex with her last night? Go to hell, Kevin!" Beth stormed toward the door.

"Wait," I said, grabbing her by the arm. "Look I didn't have sex with Megan, we went out, we go out all the time, but we don't sleep together. And I didn't say 'I love you' to make it all better, I didn't even know I was going to say it. It just came out. It's how I feel."

"Kevin, you don't love me. You've never loved me, you never will love me, and it's my fault for not realizing that sooner."

"Look, Beth it's just—,"

"I don't care what Megan is to you, I never have. The only thing that mattered to me was who I was to you, and now I know. I'm somebody you can lie to, somebody you can cheat on, and I'm even somebody you can convince yourself you love when you need to. And I'm also someone you know deserves better."

"Beth, I mean it, I love you."

"Please don't do this, Kevin. There is no doubt in my mind that you don't love me, even if you honestly believe you do at the moment, so let me leave, let me find somebody who will."

I released her arm, and she walked out the door. I watched her walk down the hall and press the elevator button, hoping she would turn to look back at me. She never did. The elevator doors opened, and she stepped in. My first instinct was to run after her, but I just shut the door, and walked back into my apartment. I felt numb. Beth's words were echoing in my head, "Kevin, you don't love me, you've never loved me, you never will." I had dismissed the idea that I couldn't love Beth because she was white, but I could no longer ignore that possibility. Could I have slept with this woman, allowed her to fall in love with me, while the whole time feeling she wasn't good enough for me because of the color of her skin, I thought. Was I no better than the people who had shunned my mother for loving my father, for loving me? I remembered Mama's words, "Racism by anyone is nothing if not morally unjust." Embarrassed and ashamed, I fell to my knees in prayer:

Our Father, Who Art In Heaven,

I stopped after the first line, unable to continue. I didn't feel worthy of asking God for guidance. He had blessed me with the love of a good woman, and I responded by abusing that woman. I never struck Beth, but I lied to her, cheated on her, convinced her to have an abortion, and rejected her love because the society I grew up in told me that such a love was wrong, and I was too weak to think otherwise. I thought back on my other relationships. I realized that for the past five years my life had consisted of nothing but lying, cheating, and countless other acts of selfishness toward any woman who had the misfortune of meeting me. "You and me, we one and the same," my father said. I could no longer run from the truth of this statement.

The phone rang at eleven o'clock the next morning. I was still asleep, after spending most of the night drinking alone in my apartment.

"Hello."

"So, did it work?" Megan asked.

"Not exactly."

"What, is she still mad at you?"

"Nope, she broke up with me."

"What? She broke up with you? Because you missed a brunch date?"

"No, she broke up with me because she saw the two of us come back to my apartment on Saturday morning, and when she asked me about it, I lied and said I was out with Dave."

"Well did you tell her nothing happened?"

"She didn't believe me."

"God, this is all my fault."

"It has nothing to do with you, Megan. I don't deserve Beth, she's better off without me."

"What are you talking about?"

"I treated Beth like shit; you know that better than anyone."

"I'm so sorry, Kevin."

"There's nothing to be sorry about."

"You don't realize what you've lost."

"Yeah, I do."

"You may never find it again."

"I'm not sure I deserve it."

"Everyone does, Kevin. Hey, are you going to be okay?"

"I'll be fine, I always am."

"Pick a place," Megan said, her tone abruptly changing.

"What?"

"Pick a place, any place you want to go?"

"I'm not sure I'm ready for what you were offering the last time you gave me that option."

"Don't be an idiot. Just pick a place."

"What kind of place, a place to eat, a place to drink?"

"No, a place to go."

"What do you mean a place to go?"

"Look, you're off from work this week until after the New Year, right?"

"Yeah."

"And you don't fly home for Christmas until when?"

"A week from Tuesday, the twentieth. Why?"

"That gives us eight days. I've got three thousand dollars to burn, so pick a place, any place you want to go."

"Any place I want to go?"

"That's what I said."

"Okay, Montmartre."

"Ma-what?"

"Montmartre, it's a section of Paris," I said, laughing.

Megan thought for a moment. "You got a passport?"

"Yeah."

"I'll be there in a couple of hours."

"Excuse me, but I said it's a section of Paris, that's in France, darling."

"I know where Paris is, and I'll be there in a couple of hours. Bye."

She's nuts, I thought, after hanging up the phone. I then remembered that Megan was a little nuts. I quickly called her back, only to get a busy signal. I thought about our conversation, but figured even Megan wouldn't try to pull this off. I decided to get some more sleep. When my apartment buzzer rang later that afternoon, I knew who it was.

"Megan, I'm sleeping," I said into the intercom.

"Buzz me up, now!"

I buzzed her into the building and unlocked the door, then stumbled back into bed. Megan burst through the door moments later.

"You've got about an hour to pack and get ready, the car is coming at five, our flight leaves at eight," Megan said, pulling me from the bed.

"Megan, I'm tired. I don't have time for this nonsense."

"You picked Paris, we're going to Paris," she said, opening my closet door. "Now put some clothes in a bag, and pack warm, it's probably cold in France this time of year."

"Very funny, will you please leave me alone? I got dumped last night, remember?"

"Kevin, I just charged two tickets for the eight o'clock American Airlines flight from Kennedy to Charles DeGaulle airport in Paris; they're non-refundable, so get dressed, and let's go."

I waited for Megan to start laughing; she never did.

Megan and I arrived in France at nine a.m. on Monday morning. We were booked on a return flight the following Sunday evening, which meant we would have seven full days in Paris. Megan didn't have time to book a hotel, so the first order of business was finding a place to stay.

"How do you pronounce the name again?" Megan asked, pulling out a subway map as we walked from the airport.

"Montmartre," I said, bundling up in my jacket. The temperature was in the thirties, and there was a fierce wind whipping any body part left exposed.

"I think we had it right, if we take this blue line train from the air-port to the Gare du Nord stop, we'll be in Montmartre or at least close to it," Megan said, tracing our journey with her finger on the map.

"Where are we going to stay once we get there?"

"I don't know, but it's Paris, how hard can it be to find a hotel?" I agreed, and we headed over to the Metro booth. "Well, go ahead," Megan said.

"Go ahead where?"

"Go ahead and get the train tickets, you speak French, I don't," Megan said, handing me the French francs we had exchanged our American currency for at the airport.

"I don't speak French," I said, pushing the money away.

"You said your mother taught you French when you were little, and I know you took it in college."

"You took Spanish in college, do you speak it?"

"Hablo español, pero no estamos en España, estamos en Francia."

"Okay, you speak Spanish, what else did you say?"

"I said I speak Spanish, but we are not in Spain, we are in France." Megan slapped the money in my hand, and pushed me toward the ticket booth. "Now go and buy the tickets."

I walked up to the window, staring at the ticket agent. "Est-ce que je peux vous aider?" the agent asked.

"Oui, je voudrais deux billets pour le train s'il vous plait," I said, handing the agent a hundred-franc note. The agent gave me two tickets and some change. "Merci," I said. I turned and walked toward Megan, purposely wearing a confused expression and hiding the tickets.

"What happened? Did you get them?" Megan asked.

"Not bad, not bad, if I have to say so myself," I said, pulling out the tickets, and waving them in the air.

Megan swiped the tickets from my hand. "Calm down, Kevin, you bought some train tickets; I'm waiting to see you check us into a hotel."

We boarded the train, and thirty minutes later, arrived at the Gare du Nord stop. When we walked out of the station, the sights and sounds of the city transfixed me with excitement. The streets were teeming with traffic, and the massive façade of the train station, whose roof was decorated with nine statues of what I assumed to be French royalty peering out over the city, shadowed our surroundings. Piercing horn honks, which rang out from the smallest cars imaginable, and sidewalks bustling with pedestrians making their morning commute created a symphony of sound, causing my head to dart frantically in all directions, fearful I might miss something. Glass-fronted cafes dressed in holiday attire and filled with Parisians sipping their morning coffee brought to life countless paintings and postcards I'd seen of the city. I couldn't believe it. I was in Paris.

"Well, we're here. I guess the easiest thing to do is ask someone where the nearest hotel is," Megan suggested.

"Okay." After searching out a friendly face, I stopped an elderly woman walking her dog. "Excusez moi, vous pouvez nous dire ou est l'hotel le plus proche?" I asked, slowly enunciating each syllable.

"Hôtel de la Gare du Nord; l'hotel est tout proche. Il se trouve Rue de Dunkerque. Remontez la rue et au prochain croisement allez à droite. L'hotel se trouve du coté gauche à cent mètres," the woman said, smiling and pointing out directions, before being pulled away by her dog.

"Merci, Merci."

"What did she say?" Megan asked.

"She said the hotel Gare du Norde is close by."

"Isn't that the name of the train station?" Megan asked, pointing to the name, which was etched in stone on the station facade.

"Yeah."

"So, was she saying there's a hotel close to the station; what did she mean?"

"She said it was on Rue de Dunkerque."

"What's on Rue de Dunkerque?"

"Gare du Norde is."

"This is Gare du Norde, Kevin. What are you talking about? What did she say was on Rue de Dunkerque?"

"I don't know, there's probably a hotel named Gare du Norde on Rue de Dunkerque," I said, obviously confused. "Look, whatever she's talking about is only a few blocks away, so let's just go and find it."

"A few blocks in which direction?"

"Well, she pointed that way. Let me see the map?" I said, pulling it from her pocket. "Okay, if we walk this way we should hit Rue de Dunkerque. All we have to do is make a right and walk down that street."

"That's all we have to do, huh?"

We headed out, and my directions were perfect. In less than ten minutes we spotted the Gare du Norde Hotel.

"The hotel is named Gare du Norde also, well, how about that?" I said. "Now if you'll follow me, I'll get us checked in."

We went into the hotel, and up to the registration desk. "Bonjour et Bienvenus, comment puis-je vous aider?" the hotel clerk greeted us.

"Bonjour, nous voudrons une chambre," I said, stumbling over my words.

"No, Kevin," Megan interrupted, pushing me aside. "Parlez-vous anglais?"

"Yes I do speak English, Mademoiselle," the clerk answered, with a smile.

"Thank you. We need a room," Megan said.

"Of course, we have single, twin, and double rooms available. The room rate is four hundred ten francs, approximately seventy dollars US, per night for two people, which includes tax and services," the clerk said.

"Would it be possible for us to check in now?" Megan asked.

"One moment, please." The clerk picked up a clipboard, flipping through some pages. "Yes, I have a double room that is ready."

"Okay, we'll take it. And we'll be checking out on Sunday," Megan said, handing the clerk her credit card.

"I could have——," I began to say.

"Kevin, don't say anything. Just be happy we've got a room, and you've got me."

After dropping our bags off in the room, we grabbed our map, and hit the streets of Paris.

"Where should we go first, Eiffel Tower, the Louvre, no, I know, let's check out the stores on the Champs Elysées?" Megan said, looking at the map.

"Sacré Coeur," I said.

"Sacré Coeur, what's that? Another museum?"

"It's a church."

"A church, if you want to go to a church, why don't we go to Notre Dame?"

"Nope, we're going to Sacré Coeur," I said, taking the map from her hands.

We located the church on the map, and realizing that it was only blocks away from the hotel, set out on foot. The midday sun had raised the temperature, making for pleasant conditions. After walking about fifteen minutes, we spotted Sacré Coeur, sitting majestically atop Montmartre.

"I think we can go up those to get to the church," Megan said, pointing to a steep incline of stairs. We walked up the stairs, and after catching her breath from the climb, Megan was captivated by the view of the city below. "Oh my God, this is incredible. What a great place to start sightseeing, you finally got something right," she said, turning to find me staring straight ahead at the church, uninterested in the view. "Kevin, what are you doing? Come and look at this."

"In a minute," I said, unable to take my eyes off of the church.

It was the whitest building I had ever seen. Everything looked just as Mama had described it. The top of the church contained three oblong domes, two smaller ones to the right and left, and a larger one in the middle that rose into the heavens. At the church's entrance were three grand archways, with two bronze statues positioned on opposite ends above them, one of St. Joan of Arc, the other of St. Louis, both seated on horses. High above the statues, and centered beneath the middle dome, was a statue of Christ, his hand raised in a blessing.

"Kevin, will you come look at this view. I mean what the hell?" Megan said, an elderly woman shooting her a dirty look. "Shit, look what you made me say."

"Try and watch your mouth when we get in the church," I said.

We went inside and took a seat on a pew near the back. There were very few people inside, and the silence permeating the building was hypnotic. The walls of the church were covered with beautiful mosaics, one depicting Christ with outstretched arms. As I sat in the church, I became lost in the image, and felt a presence enveloping my body. I closed my eyes, succumbing to the spirit, as tears rolled down my cheek. I knew it was Mama. Less than two days before, I felt myself unworthy to ask God for guidance, I now knew why. "Before you ask for guidance, you must ask for forgiveness," she whispered to me. I kneeled and began to pray:

Father, lately I've not lived my life in a manner deserving of your love. I humbly ask for your forgiveness.

When I returned to my seat, Megan was staring at me. "Are you okay?" she asked.

"I will be."

Megan and I explored every inch of Paris over the next five days, from sunup to sundown. We hit every tourist attraction, including two days inside the Louvre. Our second visit was prompted after I dreamt about one of the paintings. The painting was by the French Artist Marie-Guillemine Benoist, and entitled *Portrait of Negress*. It portrays a beautiful black woman with deep chocolate skin, pouty full lips, and dark haunting eyes, seated in a chair, boldly staring out at anyone who dares return her gaze. Half-draped in what appears to be a white sheet, exposing her right breast, and gathered at the waist by a red sash, she is wearing a white head wrap, and gold hoop earrings, much like the ones Mama wore. There was a combination of strength, pain, honesty, and vulnerability in the woman's stare that captured my imagination. The night after seeing the painting, I dreamt I was chasing this woman.

I was in my apartment working on a paper, when I looked out the window and saw *The Negress* standing in front of my building. I ran downstairs and spotted her turning the corner at the end of my block. I ran after her, with my chase persisting all over the City, until I lost her in Times Square. I returned to my apartment distraught, convinced my life would be empty until I found her.

The next morning I woke up obsessed with the painting. I told Megan about the dream, and asked if we could go back to the museum. After seeing the painting a second time, its affect on me was magnified. I'll never forget that face, I thought. I spent hours staring at the picture, and wouldn't leave until Megan insisted we do so, saying she wanted to get in some more shopping.

We left the museum and walked to the Champs Elysées, stopping at a café for a bite to eat before we hit the stores.

"Bonjour," the waiter greeted us.

"Bonjour, je voudrais," I said slowly.

"No no, English is good," the waiter blurted out.

"Merci," Megan said to the waiter, laughing. "I've spent six days listening to him torture people with his French, maybe he'll give up now."

We ordered and sat looking out the window, watching as people hurried about doing their Christmas shopping. It was Saturday evening at seven o'clock. We had less than twenty-four hours left in Paris.

"Thank you," I said to Megan.

"For what?"

"For this trip. I needed it, thanks."

"You know Megan will always take care of you, you're my best friend, Kevin." Megan smiled, taking my hand and squeezing it. "So, how are you doing with that whole thing?"

"The break-up, I'm okay with it, I mean it was definitely for the best. It's just, I don't know."

"What?"

"Beth didn't deserve the way I treated her."

"Kevin, look, relationships sometimes don't work out. Your mother just died, and you were going through your own stuff. You're a great guy, Kevin. Beth knows that. Who knows, you guys might get back together. I mean, maybe the timing wasn't right."

"I convinced her to have an abortion." Megan released my hand, taking a sip of water to digest what she had heard.

"Beth had an abortion?"

"She didn't want to, I talked her into it. Still think I'm such a great guy?"

"When did this happen?"

"I found out she was pregnant the Monday after I came back from Mama's funeral. She had the abortion the following Tuesday."

"How's she handling it?"

"Surprisingly well, at least that's how it seems. I mean we really never talked much about it after it happened."

The waiter returned with our food, and we ate in silence, Megan needing time to process the information I'd shared. I began to think about Beth. I had convinced her to have an abortion, but didn't have the decency to be there for her afterwards. We hadn't had a drink of alcohol the entire week, but I suddenly felt the need for one.

"You want to get a bottle of wine, it is our last night," I said.

"Good idea," Megan agreed.

We finished off two bottles, and a few hours later, ended up in a crowded bar a few blocks down from the restaurant.

"Roses lime juice, do you have Roses lime juice?" Megan slowly yelled to the bartender, thinking a slower pace and higher volume would help translate her request.

"Elle voudrait un jus de citron que s'appelle Roses avec la vodka Stoli sur la glace," a guy next to us said to the bartender.

"No," the bartender said.

"No Roses, but I'm sure he has lime juice," the guy said to Megan with no hint of a French accent.

"No, I'll just have Stoli with orange juice; O.J.," Megan mouthed to the bartender. "Thanks," she said to the guy.

"My name is Richard," the guy said to Megan.

"I'm Megan, nice to meet you. This is my friend Kevin."

"Kevin, nice to meet you," Richard said, shaking my hand. He was a good-looking guy, white with blonde hair, well dressed, and appearing to be in his late twenties. "Where are you guys from?"

"New York," I said.

"I'm from Connecticut," he said.

"Connecticut, I go to school in Connecticut, Yale," Megan said.

"I did my undergraduate work at Yale," Richard said.

"You're on vacation?" I asked.

"No, I live here now. You're at Yale too, Kevin?"

"No, Columbia," I said.

"Small world, I went to Columbia Business School," Richard said, all of us laughing at the coincidence.

We found an empty table, and ended up talking and drinking for the next couple of hours. Around midnight, I got tired.

"We better get going," I said, as Megan chatted Richard's ear off.

"Why don't you come back to the hotel, have a drink with us?" Megan said to Richard.

"You mind, Kevin?" Richard asked.

"No, Kevin doesn't mind," Megan said.

Richard was a nice guy, but I was in no mood to continue drinking. "Megan, I don't think the hotel has a bar," I said.

"Where are you staying?" Richard asked.

"The Gare du Nord," I said.

"Oh, I know where that is, there's a cute little bar right around the block, we can grab a drink there," Richard said.

We walked out of the bar, and hailed a cab. Richard gave the driver instructions, and as the cab pulled off, Megan's head fell over onto my shoulder.

"Is she out?" Richard asked.

"She's out alright," I said, tapping Megan's face and getting no response.

"But she was wide awake just seconds ago."

"She crashes quicker than anyone I know, sorry about this."

"No problem. I should probably be getting home also. I never know when to call it a night; Megan may be doing me a favor." It was a short ride to the hotel; Richard and I exchanged numbers on the way. "She's going to be pretty much dead weight; do you need some help getting her to the room?" Richard asked.

I was pretty tipsy myself, and considering Megan's condition, thought it was a good idea. Richard asked the cab driver to wait for him, and we both carried Megan into the hotel, one of her arms around each of our shoulders. We stumbled through the lobby and onto the elevator, with the night clerk looking on suspiciously. When we made it to the room, I handed Megan off to Richard, so I could find the key.

"Where are we?" Megan mumbled.

"Don't worry, Megan, we're going to take care of you," Richard said.

"Here it is," I said, pulling the key from my pocket. I opened the door, and Richard carried Megan into the room, laying her in bed.

"What are you doing?" Megan asked, as Richard removed her coat.

"Just getting you out of your coat, so you can get comfortable in bed. Just lay still, we're going to take care of you," Richard said.

Without warning, Megan swung and hit Richard across the face. She then rolled off the other end of the bed, crawling into the corner. "Kevin, why are you doing this to me?" she yelled, looking up at me.

"What are you talking about, Megan?" I asked.

"Don't touch me, don't either of you touch me," she said, crying.

"Megan, what are you talking about, we're just trying to get you in bed," I said, kneeling next to her on the floor. Megan looked at me, and after regaining her bearings, rushed into my arms.

"I'm sorry, I'm sorry," she cried, burying her head in my chest.

"It's okay, calm down," I said.

"Is she okay?" Richard asked.

"I think so," I said, with Megan still clinging to me.

"I'm sorry I hit you, Richard," Megan said.

"It's okay, it's okay," Richard said.

I stood Megan up and sat her on the bed, and then walked Richard to the door.

"What was that all about?" he asked.

"Man, I have no idea. I'm really sorry, but thanks for the drinks, and definitely give me a call the next time you're in New York," I said, shaking his hand.

"I'm sorry, Richard," Megan said.

"It's okay, Megan, really it is," Richard said, before leaving.

When I walked back into the room, Megan had crawled into a ball atop the covers on her bed. "I don't want to talk about it," she said.

"Okay." I undressed and crawled into bed. "Goodnight, Megan," I said, turning off the light.

"Goodnight."

I forgot to set the alarm clock that night, but woke up at six the next morning, my body having adjusted to our weeklong schedule. Megan was seated on the edge of her bed staring out the window.

"How do you feel?" I asked.

"I had an abortion too, you know, six weeks before I met you."

"No, I didn't know," I said, moving to sit next to her.

"No, just stay there, let me get this out."

"Okay."

"I know you're probably already thinking that's what happened between me and Steve, that's the reason we broke up, right?" I nodded. "Well, that's only part of the story. You see Steve, the man I loved, the man I thought I would marry, well he didn't love me; only I didn't know it. Oh, he liked dating me, taking me out and showing me off to his friends, and he liked having sex with me. He's the only guy I've ever been with besides you, bet you didn't know that either; I mean, who would have guessed it?" Megan smiled, as she began to cry. "We had only been dating for about four months, but I loved him, and I was certain he loved me. I remember I was so excited when he gave me that pin, *Megan & Steve, Forever*; I know, stupid, right? Love can have that effect on people. Well, one night, we're out drinking: me, Steve, and his friend Carlos. I didn't drink much back then. I know, also hard to believe, but I didn't. Anyway, I've only had two drinks and my head is already spinning, so I tell Steve I've had enough, I'm feeling a little tipsy, and maybe I should just drink water. Steve says, 'Oh, come on Meg, have some more, don't worry, I'm here to take care of you.' I remember he kissed me and said, 'I love you, and I'll always be here to take care of you.' That was all I needed to hear. We drank until the bar closed, and then drove back to Steve's apartment. I don't know how we made it; I mean we were all wasted. When we got home, Carlos crashed on the couch. Steve and I went into the bedroom, and were all over each other. So, we start having sex, and Steve whispers in my ear, 'I love you, Baby, you make me so hot.' I said, 'I love you too, Baby.' 'Will you do anything for me?' he asked. 'Anything,' I told him. 'I want to watch you,' he said. I thought he wanted me to touch myself. He pulled out of me, and began kissing me, watching as I touched myself. I was really drunk and could feel myself going in and out of consciousness, but I kept touching myself. Steve stood next to the bed, and put his dick in my mouth, talking to me the whole time. 'That's it, Baby; I love it when you do it like that. I want to watch you get fucked.' I heard what he said, but didn't really understand what he was talking about, so I just closed my eyes and kept touching myself. Then I felt another body pushing my legs open; I opened my eyes, and saw Carlos climbing on top of me. I tried to sit up, but Steve, the man who loved me, forced his dick further in my mouth, holding me down with his weight, and said, 'don't worry, Baby, we're going to take care of you.' Before I knew it, Carlos was inside me. I don't know how long it lasted, but when he finished, he rolled over in the bed, laughing. I jumped up, ran into the bathroom, locking the door behind me, and then got in the shower, trying to wash Carlos out of me. After that, I just fell in the tub crying. Steve managed to get the door open, and walked over to the shower looking down at me. You know what he said, 'what's wrong, Baby? That was hot.'"

Megan never made eye contact while telling the story. After she finished, I walked over and sat on the bed hugging her. Her only response was to lay her head on my shoulder. A few seconds later, she broke the embrace, standing and heading to the bathroom.

"Did you tell anyone?" I asked.

"My parents."

"What did they say?"

Megan stopped, but did not turn to look at me. "My father said I was drunk when it happened, and no one would believe me if I went to the police. He said that I had lied to him, and put myself in a position for it to happen. He said the best thing for me to do was to get rid of the baby, put what happened behind me, and move on with my life. And that's what I did."

"Maybe we should just take it easy today," I suggested to Megan later that morning while packing. "You know, stay at the hotel, check out late, grab something to eat, and then head to the airport."

"Kevin, I've been living with this for the past three years, I'll be fine."

"Okay."

We finished packing and went downstairs to check out. Our flight didn't leave until six, but we planned on getting in some last-minute shopping. We also wanted to make one more visit to Sacré Coeur. After taking in the city at sunset every evening from this location, Megan had also fallen in love with the church.

"Cette rue intersecte Rue Muller," I overheard the desk clerk say to a woman when we arrived in the lobby.

Rue Muller, I thought, recognizing the street name. "That's it," I said loudly, startling Megan. "Twenty-five Rue Muller, that's it!"

"That's what?" Megan asked, the clerk and the woman looking back at us, confused by my outburst.

"That's the address, that's the Gautreauxes' address."

I had told Megan about my mother's stay in Paris with the Gautreaux family on our flight over, and she suggested we look them up, but I couldn't remember the street address, or even the name of the street. We had left New York in such a rush there was no time to try and locate the information, even though I'm not sure who I could have contacted that would have known anything. I didn't know Nicholle's parents' first names, so with nothing more than the last name Gautreaux to go on, I gave up on trying to find them. It wasn't until the clerk said the street name that my memory was jogged.

"Are you sure?" Megan asked.

"I'm positive, twenty-five Rue Muller, that's definitely the address. Mama would always repeat the complete address when she talked about the Gautreauxes."

"Is that close by?" Megan asked, pulling out the map.

"Mama told me it was blocks from Sacré Coeur."

"Can I help you?" the clerk asked.

"Yes, we need to check out, but also, would you know where twenty-five Rue Muller is located?" Megan asked the clerk.

"Yes, it should be a few blocks from the Montmartre stairs" he said, pointing out a location on the map.

We couldn't believe it. We checked out, leaving our bags at the hotel, and headed to the Gautreauxes' house. I could hardly breathe from anticipation.

"I don't know if these people still live here, or if they will even remember Mama if they do," I said to Megan, becoming more nervous with each step.

"That's it, twenty-five Rue Muller," Megan said, pointing to the address.

It was a buttery yellow two-story home, with neatly manicured hedges in front. The shutters on the second floor were open, each window decorated with detailed black iron-wrought framework, and interiorly dressed with sheer white curtains. We walked to the front door, and after gathering my nerves I rang the bell. Moments later the door opened.

"Bonjour," said an elegantly dressed black woman, appearing to be in her late sixties.

This can't be the right house, I thought. "Bonjour, je m'appelle Kevin Matthews. Parlez-vous anglais?"

"Yes, I do," the woman answered warily.

"Oh, thank you, my French is not very good. This is my friend Megan Waters." The two nodded hello. "Sorry to disturb you, I think we probably have the wrong house, but we're looking for Nicholle Gautreaux."

"Nicholle is my daughter. Are you friends of hers from America?" the woman asked, smiling, her defenses dropping at the mention of her daughter's name.

"Nicholle is your daughter? But you're black," I said, my confusion causing my voice to register a few octaves higher than normal. "I'm sorry, I didn't mean that the way it sounded, it's just I didn't expect you to be black." Megan elbowed me in the side.

"Are you friends of Nicholle?" the woman asked again.

"No ma'am, we're not friends of Nicholle, we've never actually met Nicholle, but my mother was a friend of hers. You actually knew my mother also, although it was a long time ago, I mean you might not even remember her. You see, my mother spent time with your family when she studied here. She was from Louisiana, although she was going to school in New York when she visited."

The woman sighed deeply, her hand going to her chest as if the wind had been knocked from her. "Mon Dieu, you're Sarah's son," she said, wide-eyed. "I am Celeste Gautreaux, Nicholle's mother. Please, please, come," she said, motioning for us to come into the house. I couldn't believe what was happening. "Gérard, venez vite," she shouted to the back of the house.

She led us into a large living room with high ceilings and glossy hardwood floors. The room was furnished with two huge creamy white sofas, a mixture of pale blue and turquoise throw pillows on each, a Maplewood French Provencal armchair, a crystal vase containing a multicolored arrangement of flowers sitting atop a glass coffee table, and a Persian rug. There were leafy green potted plants strategically placed by the windows, and a framed print of The Visitor by Romare Bearden hung on the wall.

"This room looks like a page out of a magazine," Megan whispered to me.

Soon after entering the room, we were met by a distinguished looking black man with glasses, also appearing to be in his late sixties, with salt and pepper hair, and a mustache to match. Nicholle's mother rushed to the man's side.

"Gérard, do you know who this is?" The man removed his glasses to study Megan and me. "This is Kevin Matthews, Sarah's son."

"Sarah, from America?"

"Yes, can you believe it? Kevin, this is my husband, Nicholle's father, Gérard."

"Very nice to meet you, Kevin," the man said, shaking my hand. "Very nice indeed."

The Gautreauxes were thrilled with our visit. I apologized to Mrs. Gautreaux for my reaction at the door, but explained that my mother's parents were not the most racially tolerant people in the world, and I was surprised they would allow Mama to stay with a black family. Mrs. Gautreaux told me that Mama, with help from Nicholle, hid Mr. and Mrs. Boutte's views about race from them, while simultaneously hiding the Gautreauxes' race from Mr. and Mrs. Boutte. Mrs. Gautreaux said they spoke to Mr. and Mrs. Boutte on the phone a few times, but the subject of race never came up. I reasoned that Mr. and Mrs. Boutte heard the Gautreauxes' accent and assumed they were white, never thinking to question their race, and never learning otherwise. The Gautreauxes eventually found out about Mama's deception after I was born, when Nicholle told them that Mr. and Mrs. Boutte had disowned Mama due to the race of my father.

"Kevin, I was so sorry to hear news of your mother's death," Mrs. Gautreaux said.

"Excuse me?"

"To lose your mother at such a young age, it must have been really hard on you."

"How did you find out about Mama?"

"After not hearing from your mother, and not being able to reach her, Nicholle phoned your mother's parents. They told her about the car accident, and your mother being killed. Nicholle tried to get information on how she could get in touch with you, but your mother's parents said they were not in contact with your father."

I considered telling the Gautreauxes the truth about Mama, but didn't want to deal with the ugliness of what really happened. When they asked about my father, I said he died of a heart attack months after Mama's accident, and I was raised by my grandfather. I felt bad lying to them.

"Your mother and Nicholle, they were inseparable," Mrs. Gautreaux fondly remembered, handing Megan and me a framed picture of the two. The picture showed Mama and Nicholle standing atop the Eiffel Tower, with the city as their backdrop. I became choked up at the sight of my mother. She looked so happy. She was wearing a white button-up shirt, black mini skirt, black beret, and of course her opal pendant and gold hoop earrings.

"Oh my God, Kevin, your mother looks just like Beth," Megan whispered to me. I had never shown Megan a picture of my mother. "We have got to talk," she said, pinching my arm.

Nicholle was dressed in the same outfit as Mama, minus the beret. She was not the race I expected, but was more beautiful than I ever imagined. She had smooth dark skin, with big brown eyes, high cheekbones, and full lips. She had a short Afro, and was wearing an opal pendant just like the one she had given Mama.

"So, how long will you be in Paris?" Mr. Gautreaux asked.

"Today is our last day," I said. I explained to the Gautreauxes that I didn't have any of their information when I arrived in Paris, and it was only by pure chance that I was able to remember their street address.

"Nicholle will be so sorry she missed your visit. I know she would have been thrilled to meet you," Mrs. Gautreaux said.

"I was hoping maybe we would have time to go and visit her."

"Nicholle will not be home for the holidays until the end of the week," Mr. Gautreaux explained.

"Oh, so she doesn't live in Paris."

"No, she lives in New York," Mr. Gautreaux said. The news left me speechless.

"What is it?" Mrs. Gautreaux asked, as I stood with my mouth agape.

"Oh, nothing, it's just that I'm currently going to school in New York. Nicholle and I live in the same city."

"So the two of you will have the opportunity to meet," Mrs. Gautreaux said.

"I really would like that," I said. "More than anything, I really would like that."

SHE LAUGHED

"Christmas is a day of great joy," Da-dee said to the congregation. "For God's love found supreme expression in the unspeakable gift of a Savior. God loved us so much, so dearly, that he gave us the gift of his only begotten son. We, then, must accept this gift with gratitude. Now family gathering and gift giving have their places, but we must never let these things take the place of the real meaning of Christmas, which is celebration in the birth of our Savior."

"Yes Lord," said the congregation.

"And as we look back over our life, and think about what God has done for us, realizing that he looked beyond all our faults, and saw only our needs, we must bear witness to Isaiah's Prophecy that Jesus Christ is wonderful. He is a counselor in time of need. He is a mighty God, who can move mountains. He is the Prince of Peace. Just as the Heavenly host praised him, we too must continue to praise and echo the words, 'Joy to the World, the Lord has come; Let Earth receive her King.' Merry Christmas, and God bless you all."

"Your grandfather is an excellent speaker, so eloquent," Megan said, as we stood to leave. It was her first visit to DoRight Baptist Church.

"Yeah, he's pretty good," I agreed.

"Good to see you, Brother Matthews," a deep baritone voice chimed in my ear, as two massive paws grabbed me by the shoulder spinning me around. "What, you don't know nobody no more?" It was Melvin Lawes, or I should say Deacon Lawes, my neighborhood bully as a child. Melvin was now a man of God. He was born again during a five-year stint in prison for robbery. Melvin had been incarcerated at Angola State Penitentiary, the same facility that housed my father, and Da-dee seized the opportunity to save another soul. He spent time with Melvin whenever he visited my father, counseling him on the

forgiveness of God, and telling him that there was a better life awaiting him, all he had to do was ask God to grant it. I'm told Melvin's
conversion was a swift one, and after his release from prison, only two
months prior, his sole desire was to do God's work. Melvin was now
on the Deacon board at DoRight Baptist Church.

"Hey, Melvin, how are you?" I asked, as Melvin grabbed me in a
bear hug that nearly cut off my circulation. He was a huge man, about
six feet two inches, and well over three hundred pounds.

"I'm blessed, I'm blessed," he said.

"It must be six years since we've seen each other. You look great,
man."

"Well, what can I tell you, Kevin? God is good, God is good."

"Kevin, ya'll come straight over to the house, you hear," Ms. Bertha
said, easing in between Melvin and me, and eyeing Megan from head
to toe. "The food's ready, I just got to warm it."

"Okay," I said.

"Melvin, you coming over?" Ms. Bertha asked.

"Oh, you know I don't ever say no to what the Lord lays out before
me," Melvin said.

"Well, I'm go'n be laying it out before you, not the Lord, so you
make sure you come over there directly, don't hang around here talking all day, and have folks waiting on you. You see Kevin got company
for Christmas dinner, and I know this child is ready to eat, ain't you,
Baby?" Ms. Bertha asked Megan.

"Yes ma'am, I am really looking forward to it. Kevin tells me you
are an amazing cook."

"Oh ain't that nice, well let me go get Preacher, and get home so I
can have this food ready for when ya'll get there." Ms. Bertha squeezed
Megan's forearm, smiling, before walking away. "Melvin, I ain't playing with you, you get to the house on time today, don't be around here
talking all day," she said, looking back.

"Yes ma'am," Melvin said.

"Oh, I'm sorry, Melvin, this is my friend Megan," I said.

"Nice to meet you, Melvin." Megan shook Melvin's hand.

"Oh, the pleasure's all mine, I done heard all about you from
Ms. Bertha."

"From Ms. Bertha?" I asked. "She's only met Megan a few times, what could she possibly tell you?"

"Now, Kevin, you know Ms. Bertha, all you need to do is give her a little information, and she'll take care of the rest. You hear her tell it, ya'll already halfway down the isle," Melvin said, laughing. "Bless her heart though, bless her heart. And I tell you something else, ain't nothing wrong with what she saying, no sir, ain't nothing wrong with it. A good woman is a blessing."

"I just love when Christmas falls on a Sunday, Jesus' birthday celebrated on his Father's day. And Preacher, you laid it out for them today," Ms. Bertha said, piling everyone's plate with fried turkey, ham, cornbread dressing, string beans, cranberry sauce, macaroni and cheese, and hot buttered rolls. "Folks get so tied up in that gift-buying silliness, they forget what this day is all about. You got enough food, Baby?" Ms. Bertha asked Megan.

"I could use some more of that dressing," Melvin said.

"Melvin, I ain't talking to you, I'm asking our guest," Ms. Bertha snapped, ignoring Melvin's request.

"Yes ma'am, this is plenty," Megan said.

"See how she doing us, Melvin, every other Sunday she feeding us 'till we so stuffed, we got to loosen our belts, now she got a guest over, and she done forgot all about us," Da-dee said, teasing Ms. Bertha, who was beside herself with excitement at Megan's visit.

"Yes sir, I got to agree with you there, yes sir," Melvin said.

"Now, Preacher, I'm standing here complimenting you on what a beautiful sermon you gave. I done cooked all this good food for you, and you got nerve to talk about me. Now what kind of mess is that?" Ms. Bertha asked, standing over Da-dee's shoulder.

"I'm just calling them how I see them, Bertha," Da-dee said, barely able to contain his laughter.

"Calling them how you see them, huh? Well, I don't know what you been looking at, cause Melvin ain't never stuffed." Ms. Bertha began loading Melvin's plate with more cornbread dressing. "I ain't cook for nobody eat like Melvin since Johnny was alive."

"Who was Johnny?" Megan asked.

"Johnny was a friend of ours," I said.

"Johnny Mo' was his name, Baby, and let me tell you, that was somebody you wish you had met," Ms. Bertha said, taking a seat at the table.

"Johnny Mo?" Megan asked.

"His name was Jonathan Morgan," Da-dee said.

"One of the most beautiful souls ever to walk this earth, and, Lord, did he ever walk it," Ms. Bertha said, causing everyone at the table except Megan to burst into laughter.

"I don't get it," Megan whispered to me.

"I'll explain later."

We spent the entire afternoon with Ms. Bertha, Megan endearing herself further by finishing off her entire plate of food, and sampling two desserts. After dinner, we sat on the porch talking, Duke cozying up next to my chair so I could massage his big head. Davey, Ms. Bertha's eldest son, arrived at five o'clock to pick her up. She was going to spend the week with his family and her grandchildren.

"You come back and see me, you hear, Baby," Ms. Bertha said to Megan, hugging her goodbye.

"Yes ma'am, I certainly will, and thanks for dinner, everything was delicious," Megan said.

"Oh, you're welcome, Baby, it was my pleasure, it really was," Ms. Bertha said, squeezing Megan's hand. "Kevin, when you leaving?" she asked, not taking her eyes off Megan.

"I leave on Saturday, Ms. Bertha."

"Well, I'll be back here on Thursday. You make sure you stop by here, cause we got some things to discuss, you hear me."

"Okay, Ms. Bertha."

"Melvin, you got all the food you want?" Ms. Bertha asked.

"Yes ma'am, I do," Melvin said, lifting a bag containing six pieces of Tupperware filled with leftovers.

"Preacher, you keep an eye on the place till I get back," Ms. Bertha said, climbing into her son's car.

We stood waving goodbye as the car pulled out of the driveway.

"Well, I better be heading home," Melvin said.

"Come on over to the house for a while, Melvin," Da-dee suggested.

"No, I better be going, got to be at work early tomorrow," Melvin said.

"Melvin, it ain't but six o'clock, come on to the house, talk a while longer," Da-dee insisted.

Melvin agreed to join us. I was happy he did. Melvin and I had never been friends growing up, but for some reason I was enjoying his company immensely. I felt a strange connection with him that I could not fully grasp.

"Who wants coffee?" Da-dee asked, as we walked into the house.

"I'll have some, thank you," Megan said.

"I'll have a little also, Pastor," Melvin said.

"None for me," I said.

Da-dee started preparing the coffee, and Megan and I took a seat on the sofa.

"I guess I better take a chair from the table. I know Pastor don't allow nobody to sit in his throne," Melvin said, referring to Da-dee's recliner. Melvin grabbed a chair from the kitchen table, and brought it into the living room. "So, Megan, you go to school up there at Columbia with Kevin?" he asked, taking a seat.

"No, I'm at Yale, I'm in Law School," Megan answered.

"Yale, hot dawg!" Melvin squealed. "Even an old country boy like me done heard of Yale. That's in New York too?"

"No, it's in New Haven, Connecticut. It's only about ninety miles from Manhattan though," Megan said.

"Manhattan, how you like it up there in the Big Apple, Kevin?" Melvin asked, leaning forward in his chair. "Plenty of people up there I bet. How tall them buildings?" Melvin's words caused me to start laughing uncontrollably. "What, what I said?" Melvin asked, as I doubled over on the sofa.

"Boy, what's wrong with you?" Da-dee asked from the kitchen.

"I'm sorry, Melvin, but you remind me of someone, and I just realized who it is."

"Who?" Melvin asked.

"Don't take this the wrong way, but you remind me of Johnny."

"Man, go on away from here with that nonsense."

"No, I'm serious."

"Sure enough look like him," Da-dee said. It was true. Melvin was the same size, had the same skin color, and wore a beard and mustache like Johnny.

"What? Now, Pastor, don't be egging this boy on," Melvin said.

"Not only look like him, but talk just as much as Johnny too, and that's saying quite a bit," Da-dee said, joining us in the living room. "Coffee be ready in a minute," he said to Megan.

"Megan, you see how they do me," Melvin said.

"I'm sorry, but who was Johnny again?" Megan asked.

"Friendliest guy you ever could meet, but he was a little slow," Melvin said.

"Had a brain injury when he was young, never was the same after that, but he was a good soul. This is him right here," Da-dee said, handing Megan a picture. The picture was of Johnny at his Baptism, right after Da-dee dipped him in the water.

"He sure does look happy," Megan said. Da-dee and I made eye contact, both smiling at the memory of our friend. "Melvin, I have to say, he does look a little like you."

"Oh, now you against me too, ain't no hope for me tonight, no sir," Melvin said.

"Melvin, man, you even talk like Johnny," I said, laughing.

Melvin stayed for a few hours, and we talked about the transformation he had gone through in prison.

"Pastor saved my soul, Kevin. I'm as sure of that, as I am that I'm sitting here," Melvin said. "I knew I wasn't living right, but I couldn't change my ways. Yes sir, Pastor saved my soul."

After Melvin left, Da-dee talked with Megan and me a while longer, before saying goodnight.

"You're going to bed? It's only eight-thirty," I said.

"Eighty-three years old now, can't stay up like I used to," Da-dee said. "It was a pleasure seeing you again, Megan."

"Oh, you too, Mr. Matthews, I really enjoyed the sermon this morning." Megan hugged Da-dee goodbye. "Thanks for having me."

"You come and see us again, you hear. And don't worry, I won't let Bertha corner you," Da-dee said, laughing, as he left the room.

Eighty-three years old? It didn't seem possible. Da-dee was the only family I had left, at least the only family that meant anything to me. At eighty-three years old, I knew time was not on our side. I was suddenly panic-stricken.

"Kevin, are you listening to me?" Megan asked, elbowing me in the side.

"What? Oh, I'm sorry."

"What were you thinking about?"

"Nothing, nothing. What did you say?"

"I said I really enjoyed spending the day with your family, and I wanted to thank you," Megan said, leaning over and kissing me.

"You're welcome."

We sat in silence for a few seconds, neither of us knowing how to deal with the thoughts and emotions I knew we were both entertaining. We chose to ignore them. Instead, the rest of the evening was spent mapping out in great detail our plans for New Year's Eve. We were both flying back to New York on Saturday, and had decided to bring in the New Year together in Times Square. Time flew by, and it was two a.m. before Megan left.

"So, thanks again for inviting me. I really had a good time," Megan said, as we walked to her car, Duke joining us, though uninvited.

"I'm glad you came."

We were both nervous. It was a weird feeling. More than anyone else in the world, I felt comfortable around Megan. I knew she felt the same about me, but there was now an uncertainty in our actions doing something as simple as saying good night.

"Well, I guess I better be going," she said.

"Yeah, okay, I'll give you a call before Saturday."

"Okay," she said, bending down and rubbing Duke's head. "What are you going to do for the rest of the week?"

"Probably just hang around here. Monica and Jeremy didn't come home this year, so there's really nobody to visit."

"Can you believe she's pregnant?"

"Yeah, I can."

"Me too," Megan said. "I guess Jeremy's going to be popping the question sooner than planned."

"Did it last night."

"Are you serious?"

"Well, he told me he was planning on doing it Christmas Eve. What are you doing for the rest of the week?"

"Not much. I'm sure my mother will demand I spend every waking moment with her, since I, in her words, 'deserted the family' on Christmas."

"You are going to have to pay for that," I said, laughing. "Okay, then I'll give you a call. Goodnight." I leaned in and kissed Megan.

"You know this is crazy," she said, with a chuckle.

"Yeah, it probably is. You'll call and let me know you made it home safe?"

"Okay," she said, smiling, and getting into her car.

Duke and I watched as she pulled out of the driveway. I would spend the rest of the night trying to convince myself it wasn't crazy.

I slept in the next morning, not waking up until almost eleven. Da-dee was already at work in the backyard. A few weeks earlier, his woodshed had been damaged by a storm, and he was making repairs. I looked out the window watching him work. He didn't look eighty-three years old. He was still solidly built, and his movements were fluid, and steady. He's going to be around for a long time, I thought.

Da-dee had left me a plate of grits, bacon, and eggs on the stove for breakfast. I was warming the food in the oven, when the phone rang. "Hello."

"Hey, I just wanted to call and say good morning," Megan said.

"Weren't you supposed to call me when you got home last night?"

"It was late, and I didn't want to wake up your grandfather. Besides, I figured you were asleep."

"No, I wasn't asleep. I didn't sleep much at all last night."

"I was up for most of the night too. I don't know about you, but I couldn't make sense of anything that was going on last night," Megan said, laughing to hide her nervousness. I didn't answer. "I mean, maybe we should just forget about it."

"No, we shouldn't. It's just strange, after all this time. I mean we've known each other for four years, hell we've slept together for four years. What changed? You were never interested in me before?"

"Oh, and like you were interested in me?"

"Megan, I wanted a relationship with you from the first time I saw you, but you always wanted to keep things casual."

"And you seem to have no problem with that. I mean, come on Kevin, it's not like you weren't screwing everything else you could. I, on the other hand, haven't slept with anyone other than you for the past four years."

"Yeah, why is that?"

Megan thought for a moment. "I don't know. I never felt comfortable with anyone else. I'm not even sure I felt comfortable with you, considering the way we had sex. And after what happened last time...,"

"What happened? I asked you to stay, and you wouldn't. That's what happened if I remember correctly."

"Yeah, but why did you want me to stay?"

"I wanted you to stay because I was hurting, and I didn't want to be alone. The question is why didn't you stay?" Megan was silent. "Look, I don't want to argue. I'm not sure what we were feeling last night, but I don't think we can just ignore it, whatever it was."

"I didn't stay because I didn't like the idea of you needing me, and I definitely didn't like the idea of me possibly needing you. I'm a little damaged, Kevin. God, that sounds so dramatic."

"Megan, we're all a little damaged."

"You know when your friend, what was his name, Melvin?"

"Yeah."

"When Melvin was talking about feeling trapped when he was younger, about not enjoying the way he was living then, I feel the same way now, Kevin." Megan's voice started quivering as she began to cry. "I don't like shutting myself off emotionally to everyone around me. I don't like drinking night after night so I won't have to be sober with my own thoughts. You know why I do so well in school? Because focusing all my energies on school allows me not to deal with my personal life. Hell, I don't have a personal life. I hate my father, I don't trust men, I don't have any girlfriends...I'm all alone."

"Megan, calm down, it's alright. I feel the same way sometimes. I mean we're basically the same person. I don't have much of a personal life either. I hate my father too. I'm frightened by relationships, so instead I use women, which in turn causes me to hate myself. My grandfather's the only family I have in this world, and I'm scared to death I'm going to lose him. I feel alone too."

"You think that's what this is, two people scared of being alone?"

"I don't know. I mean, we've been friends for four years, and I know our friendship has been real, at least for me it has."

"It's been real for me too."

"So, maybe we've just looked past the obvious."

"The obvious being that two damaged people can repair each other."

"No, Smart Ass, the obvious being that what we've both been looking for has been right in front of us. I think we have to at least give it a shot."

"So, you want to date me, Kevin? Is that what you're saying?" Megan laughed at her own question. "I'm sorry, but the whole thing just sounds so ridiculous."

"It does, but I think that's precisely what I want to do."

"You realize you won't be able to cheat on me. I know all of your lies."

"Good, I don't want to cheat on you."

"I guess this is going to be a New Year's Eve to remember."

"I guess it is."

"Okay, Mr. Matthews, I'll see you Saturday," Megan said, a childlike playfulness in her voice.

"I'll see you Saturday, Ms. Waters." I hung up the phone excited, but also nervous. It was a combination of feelings that I hadn't felt since I first met Megan.

"I'm going to take the truck, and go visit Mr. Frank," I yelled to Dadee, after finishing breakfast.

"You sure Frank there? He told me he was going to visit his grandbaby for Christmas."

"I talked to him on Saturday. He told me he was going, but said he'd be back today. He asked me to stop by the house." Mr. Frank closed the store every year during the week of Christmas. It was the only vacation he took.

"Alright then, keys in the truck," Da-dee said, lifting a couple of two by four pieces of lumber from the ground.

"I'll be back for supper."

"Okay, I'll be here. I ain't going nowhere."

As I watched him working, lumber hefted across his shoulders, he looked indestructible. I was instantly put at ease. Eighty-three years old or not, Da-dee was right, he wasn't going anywhere.

When I pulled into Mr. Frank's driveway, the sight of my old house caught me off-guard. Seeing it always made me sad. I got out of the car and rang the doorbell. When no one answered, I made my way to the backyard, where I found Mr. Frank busy at work in his garden.

"Hey, Mr. Frank."

"Big city boy! How you doing? Merry Christmas," Mr. Frank said, hugging me hello.

"Merry Christmas. How's your grandson? Mary had a boy, right?"

"Yeah, yeah, had a boy. Guess what his name is?" Mr. Frank said, with a huge grin plastered across his face.

"I don't know? What?" I asked, granting Mr. Frank the opportunity to speak what his expression had already announced.

"Maurice Frank Patin," he said proudly. "Now you know that boy ain't go'n want nobody to call him Maurice, so I guess we go'n have two Franks in the family."

"I guess so," I said, laughing.

"Here, take a look." Mr. Frank pulled a picture from his wallet.

"Wow, he's a big kid, huh."

"Ten pounds when he come out his mama. Mary talking about quitting her job to stay home and raise him, I told her from the looks of this boy, it's go'n take two incomes to feed him," Mr. Frank said, laughing and slapping me on the back.

"How's Mary doing?"

"Oh, doing good, real good, was up and around the first day she come home. Come on in the house, tell me how your Christmas was."

We went inside, and I told Mr. Frank about Megan spending the day with us, and how Ms. Bertha doted on her. I also mentioned how much I enjoyed spending time with Melvin, pointing out the similarities I saw between him and Johnny, which caused Mr. Frank to almost choke from laughter.

"Oh, wait 'til I see him, I ain't go'n never let him live this one down. It's true, I don't know how I missed it, but Melvin sure do look like Johnny, talk just as much as Johnny too," Mr. Frank said. "I will say though, I'm proud of him, that boy really turned his life around. Ain't had no kind of a man for a daddy. His mama, she wasn't much better, but Melvin done made something out of his life. I tell you, that boy can be proud when he look in the mirror." I nodded my head in agreement. "So, how you doing?"

"I'm doing good."

"How was them grades?"

"I got all A's during the semester, didn't get back my final exam scores yet, but I'm pretty sure I did okay."

"All A's, huh? You ain't messin' around up there, are you?"

"I'm trying to stay focused."

"That's the key. You do the work now, it'll pay off in your future, I can promise you that," Mr. Frank said, shaking his finger at me. "So, who's this Megan? Is this the one or not?"

"Oh, come on, Mr. Frank. You know Megan. She went to Tulane with me. You've met her before; she's been to the store with me."

"Oh, I remember her, pretty brown skin girl, right?"

"That's her."

"So, you still didn't answer my question. Is this the one or not?"

"I don't know, we've been friends for years, but we really never dated. I think we're both kind of considering it right now though. It's weird, it's like yesterday, out of nowhere, we looked at each other differently, you know, like we all of a sudden saw each other as possibly being more than just friends."

"It can happen that way. They say it's better to be friends first anyway."

"I don't know, I guess we'll just have to see where it goes."

"Ain't no harm in that. Besides, you'll know if it's real."

"I always hear people say that, but how do you know if it's real?"

"It's one of those things that words can't explain, but believe me, Son, when you meet the right woman, you'll know. There won't be any doubt in your mind, I can promise you that." Mr. Frank patted me on the shoulder for reassurance. "You want some gumbo, Mary pack me some to bring home. I tell you if I didn't teach that girl nothing, I taught her how to make a good gumbo."

Mr. Frank made us both a bowl of gumbo. He had taught Mary well, the food was delicious. While eating, we talked about New York, and I told him about my trip to Paris.

"Paris, France, boy you done been some places; I tell you the truth, you just like your mama. Hey, you remember that show we went to?"

"Yeah, *Purlie.*"

"I ain't been back to another one since I went with you and your mama. That's a shame, I mean, I really enjoyed the thing." Mr. Frank stood, handing me a picture from his mantle. The picture was of Mama, Mr. Frank, and me standing under the theatre marquee.

"You know I don't have any pictures of Mama, well at least none before she was hurt."

"What?"

"I don't. Mr. and Mrs. Boutte took all the pictures from the house. I never got any of them back."

"Now that's a damn shame, all them pictures your mama took, they couldn't leave you with none of them? Here, you take this one."

"No, you keep it."

"Tell you what, I'll get you a copy made. They can do that, right?"

"Yeah, that's a good idea. Thanks."

Mr. Frank replaced the picture on the mantle. "Now how they go'n keep all the pictures from you, the woman's own child. I tell you, I don't care what people say, Boutte ain't no good, never has been, never will, you ask me," Mr. Frank said, agitated. "Now, he go'n be running this town." Mr. Boutte had won the election for mayor. "What you need to do is call him, and ask for those pictures. No, what you need to do is go over there, and ask for them in person. That don't make no damn sense."

I thought about Mr. Frank's suggestion. "You know what, you're right."

"What?"

"You're right, I should go over there, and ask for them. They're rightfully my pictures."

"Well, I got your back, Youngblood. If you wanna go, let's ride." Mr. Frank grabbed his car keys, and headed for the door. "I'll drive."

We hopped into Mr. Frank's old Lincoln, and headed to the Bouttes' house. It may not have seemed like a big deal to many, but for two black men to ride over to a white man's house, not to mention a white man who was the mayor, and demand the return of property rightfully theirs, was a major act of rebellion in our town. I felt like a rancher in the old west, who after having his land robbed by the local cattle baron, rides into town demanding justice. It was an unbelievable adrenaline rush, one I'm certain Mr. Frank was experiencing.

"Let's go," Mr. Frank said, after parking in the Bouttes' driveway.

"No, you wait here. I should take care of this myself."

Mr. Frank agreed. I got out of the car, and as I walked up the driveway to the front door, I could hear the music from *The Good, The Bad, &The Ugly* (a classic western starring Clint Eastwood) playing in my head, *DaDa-Dahhhh, Dah, Dah, Dah*! I paused for a moment, collecting my thoughts as to what I wanted to say, and how I wanted to say it, then pressed the doorbell. Moments later the door opened.

"Kevin, hello," Mrs. Boutte said, curiously.

"Hello, Mrs. Boutte. I'm sorry to disturb you, especially during the holidays, but I was wondering if you had any pictures of me and my mother that you might be willing to give to me," I blurted out, wanting to be as direct as possible.

"Uh, uh, yes, yes, I do," she said, flustered. "Would you like to come in?"

"No ma'am, I don't want to bother you. If you need time to get them together, I can stop by later and pick them up."

"No need, they already together, just a minute." Mrs. Boutte walked away, disappearing into the back of the house. I could feel my nerves getting the best of me, so I took a deep breath to calm myself. Seconds later, Mrs. Boutte came back to the door. "Here you go," she said, handing me a leather-bound photo album. "It's got pictures from the time you were born in there. Your mama had them in a bunch of older albums, but I put them all together in this here one. It was big enough to hold them all, and it's a lot nicer."

"Well, thank you, I appreciate it."

"Kevin," she said, her right hand grabbing my arm, stopping me before I could turn to leave. "We had no business keeping those pictures from you all these years. We had no business doing a lot of things, and now, losing Sarah and all, well, I want you to know, I'm sorry." She squeezed my arm, nodding her head to underlie the weight of her statement. I thanked her again, and said goodbye.

"What she give you?" Mr. Frank asked, when I got back to the car.

"A photo album."

"Just like that? What did you say to her?"

"I just asked if she had any pictures of Mama and me that I could have," I said, opening the album to look at the pictures. I never made it past the first page. It was a picture of me in Mama's arms in the hospital. The words: *Kevin and Sarah—June 17, 1961* (my birth date), were written beneath the picture. Mr. Frank didn't ask any more questions. We just drove back to his house in silence.

I offered to share the album with Mr. Frank, but he thought it better I look at it alone first. He said I could stop by later in the week, and we would look at the pictures together. I thanked him for his support, and left.

My anticipation wouldn't allow me to wait until I was home, so I pulled into an empty parking lot to look at the pictures. It was unbelievable. Mama had pictures of everybody: Da-dee, Big-Ma (my grandmother), Mr. Frank, Mr. Frank's wife Betty, Mary, and several pictures of Nicholle with what I assumed were her husband and little girl. The pictures were in chronological order, so it was like looking at a photographic journey of my childhood from birth to age ten. Christmas was over, but I had just received the most precious gift imaginable.

When I arrived home, it was after seven o'clock.

"What you and Frank been talking about all day long?" Da-dee asked.

"You're not going to believe this," I said, showing him the album.

Da-dee was thrilled that I had asked the Bouttes for the pictures. "Those pictures are rightfully yours, we should have ask for them years ago," he said. We spent the rest of the evening looking at the pictures. Looking through the album again, I realized there wasn't a single picture of my father. I knew Mama had taken pictures of him, so I assumed they had been purposely excluded, Mrs. Boutte not able to abide keeping pictures of the man who had hurt her daughter. I didn't mind that there were no pictures of my father; in fact, I preferred it.

I spent the rest of the week helping Da-dee with various projects around the house. We finished repairing the woodshed on Tuesday, and Mr. Frank and Melvin stopped by on Wednesday to help us paint, with Melvin doing more talking than painting. Ms. Bertha returned home on Thursday as planned and invited Da-dee and me over for dinner, although I knew she had ulterior motives.

"I ain't go'n beat around the bush. Kevin, you getting old, you need to find a wife," Ms. Bertha said. "Tell him, Preacher."

"No no, Bertha, don't involve me in this."

"What you mean don't involve you, he's your grandson? Boy need a good woman to take care of him, and that's a nice girl he done found in Megan. We ain't go'n be here forever to take care of him."

"I don't know about you, Bertha, but I ain't planning on going nowhere anytime soon," Da-dee said.

"Well, I ain't planning it anytime soon either," Ms. Bertha agreed, laughing. "But that boy need himself a wife. Lord knows a good woman is a blessing."

On Friday, I visited Mama's grave to say goodbye. She was buried in the cemetery at St. Paul Catholic Church, the same church that had shunned us when I was younger. I had been angered when I found out she would be buried there, but then I remembered her words: "This is God's house, and God is always welcoming of his children. Don't ever allow ignorance to come between you and your beliefs." Mama was buried next to her paternal grandmother, a Cajun woman named Juliet, whom Mama called Nana. Mama told me stories of how Nana doted on her when she was a little girl, and I took solace knowing she was near someone who loved her.

"Well, Mama, I'll be going back to New York tomorrow. I just wanted to come and say goodbye," I said, sitting on the ground next to the grave. "I know you're excited about Nicholle and me meeting, and I'm sure you're the one who arranged for me to find the Gautreauxes. Megan can't understand how it happened, but I know it was you."

I sat and talked to Mama for over an hour, telling her about my plans for the new semester, and discussing what happened between Megan and me.

"Before I leave, I want to tell you something, not that you haven't been watching and don't already know, but, I haven't been behaving like the man you would have wanted me to become. I'm not going to go into detail; like I said, I know you've been watching, so there's really no reason to. I just want you to know that I'm going to make some changes in my life, I promise."

I stood and placed a kiss on Mama's grave, then said goodbye. Walking back to the car, it dawned on me that I hadn't talked with Mama like this since I was a little boy. She was no longer alive, but I felt she was once again a part of my life.

Megan and I arrived back in New York at three o'clock on New Year's Eve. LaGuardia, the airport we flew into, was a madhouse, and it took us two hours to get our bags. I wanted to take public transportation back into the city, but Megan insisted we take a cab. We got stuck in traffic, and didn't make it to the house until after six o'clock.

Megan had spent many nights at my apartment, but our relationship during that time dictated nothing would happen. We were both a little nervous about this night.

"So, we'll have dinner, and then we'll make our way down to Times Square, and just hang out until the ball drops at midnight?" I asked, while unpacking.

"That sounds good."

"I guess we can just come back here after that, unless you maybe want to go dancing somewhere."

"No, we'll probably be tired, so we might as well just come home. Besides, it's pretty cold out."

"That's true. You want to take a shower first?"

"What time are our reservations?"

"Seven."

"Seven? We'll never make it."

"Don't worry, it's only about twenty blocks to the restaurant."

We had made reservations at Sylvia's, a Harlem restaurant famous for its Southern Style cooking. Megan and I figured just because we weren't at home, there was no reason we couldn't eat like we were.

We arrived at the restaurant a few minutes late, but the place was empty, and we were seated immediately. Megan ordered the fried catfish, and I had the smothered pork chops. We both got black eye peas as a side dish, which Southern tradition deemed good luck for the new year.

"This is pretty good, but I don't think Ms. Bertha has anything to worry about," Megan joked.

"She would kill to hear you say that," I laughed. "She would kill to see us here together."

"Why?"

"Let's just say Ms. Bertha, how should I put it, she took a liking to you, a very strong liking."

"A liking?"

"Ms. Bertha loves to feed people, you love to eat; you two are a match made in heaven."

"What about us two?"

"What?"

"This is just so weird. I mean, I sleep with you for four years, and I don't feel anything."

"Thanks."

"You know what I mean. Then, I stop sleeping with you and we become great friends, and now, this."

"I think we were always friends."

"We were friends, but we were never as close as we have been over the last few months. I know I've opened up to you a lot more."

"Why?"

"I don't know, and don't put this all on me. Why do you think?"

"You know what I think."

"No, I don't, that's why I asked you."

"I think we should finish dinner."

"You know what, Kevin, you suck," she said, laughing.

We finished dinner without broaching the subject again. Instead we discussed when I should contact Nicholle. Mrs. Gautreaux had given me her phone number, but told me that Nicholle would not be returning from Paris until the second week in January. Megan thought it best that I wait an additional week before calling her.

"What's the first thing you're going to ask her?" Megan asked.

"How the hell they got away with hiding she was black from Mr. Boutte."

"No really, what do you want to know the most?"

"There's so much. I mean I want to know what her favorite book was. I want to know what made her laugh. I want to know who my mother was."

When Megan and I left the restaurant, the temperature was in the teens.

"So, you want to hop on the train, that's probably the quickest way to get to Times Square," I said, my teeth chattering.

"I don't know if I can handle this cold, Kevin," Megan said, nuzzling up next to me, using my body as a shield from the wind.

"We can just go back to my place until eleven, head downtown after that."

"Okay, that's a good idea."

We caught a cab back to my apartment, Megan curling up on the sofa under a blanket when we walked in. I knew the chances of us leaving again that night were slim.

"You want something to drink? I can run down to the liquor store and pick something up," I said.

"No, I think I'll start my New Year's Resolution a few hours early."

"New Year's Resolution? You're going to stop drinking?"

"Don't you think it's about time?"

"Yeah, yeah, I think it's a good idea. Tell you what, I'll make us some hot chocolate."

Megan and I sat talking and drinking hot chocolate for the next three hours. When the clock hit eleven, we both conceded that we had no intention of braving the cold, and going to Times Square. We continued talking, discussing the upcoming semester, and our plans after graduation. At eleven fifty-five we flipped on the television to bring in the New Year the way millions of other people would, with Dick Clark.

"Not the most exciting way to spend New Year's Eve," I said.

"I don't think I've ever enjoyed a New Year's Eve more." Megan raised her cup for a toast. "To a great New Year."

"To a great New Year," I said, toasting her cup. "Here we go."

We began to countdown together. "Ten, nine, eight, seven, six, five, four, three, two, one, Happy New Year!"

My entire block erupted. There was yelling, horns honking, and firecrackers going off. In my apartment it became deadly quiet.

"Well, I'd like to start my year off by kissing you if you don't mind," I said.

"No, I don't mind at all."

I leaned in, passionately kissing Megan. Then something strange happened, she laughed. I would have been insulted, but I felt the urge to laugh also.

"What's wrong with you?" I asked, pretending to be upset.

"I'm sorry, Kevin. I don't know what came over me. Come on, let's try again," Megan said, still fighting the giggles.

"Try again, the moment's been ruined. I can't believe you would do this, I mean, I'm really hurt," I said, before giving in to my own laughter.

"Can you explain to me what's going on?"

"No, I can't."

"We are freaks, that's all it is to it, we're both freaks."

As we sat on the sofa laughing hysterically, it became clear to us that we were meant to be friends, and nothing more. We also realized the friendship we shared would never allow us to be alone.

KIND OF BLUE

"Hi, I'm Kevin."

"Kevin, it is so nice to meet you," Nicholle said, her eyes beginning to tear as she hugged me. She looked as I remembered her from pictures, except her hair was now worn in long braids falling near the middle of her back. She was dressed casually, in a t-shirt, jeans, sneakers, and a light gray cardigan. "I cannot believe you are really here, let me look at you. Oh, it is so nice to meet you," Nicholle said, hugging me once more. "Come in, come in."

I walked into the apartment, a spacious duplex on East 36th Street, and was greeted by a tall dark-skinned black man. "Kevin, hello. I'm Ronald Simmons, Nicholle's husband," the man said, in a thick accent, which sounded both British and Jamaican.

"Hello, it's nice to meet you," I said, shaking Ronald's hand. "I actually recognize you from pictures that my mother had of you and Nicholle."

"I was never fortunate enough to meet your mother, but Nicholle tells me she was a very special woman."

"Kevin, please have a seat," Nicholle said, motioning toward the living room. The room was painted a rich ivory, and was tastefully decorated with a minimal amount of furnishings: a sofa, chair, and coffee table.

"Baby, do you need anything before I leave?" Ronald asked Nicholle.

"No no, have a good game."

"Okay, enjoy your visit," Ronald said to Nicholle, kissing her good-bye. "Kevin, I'm sorry I have to run."

"Tennis?" I asked, referring to the racket hanging over Ronald's shoulder.

"Squash. Do you play?"

"Squash? No, I've actually never heard of it."

"Great game, a little like racquetball. Maybe we can play sometime."

"Sure, sounds good."

"I'll give you a call. It was nice meeting you, Kevin." Ronald shook my hand again before leaving.

"Can I get you anything?" Nicholle asked.

"No, thanks."

"I cannot believe you are really here," Nicholle said, taking a seat next to me on the sofa. "I almost fainted when Maman told me that you had visited."

"Yeah, it's pretty amazing how I found them."

"I know, you overhearing the street name, and then remembering the address. After speaking with you on the phone, I told Ronald the story. He said it was destiny, the two of us meeting."

"I guess so."

"So, Maman also tells me your French needs work."

"I didn't realize how much until I visited Paris."

"Kevin, you mean my lessons over the phone were in vain?"

"I'm sorry to say they were," I said, both of us laughing.

"Is that it?" Nicholle asked, pointing to the photo album I was carrying.

"Oh, yeah, it is," I said, handing it to her. Nicholle and I had spoken at length on the phone before meeting, and I promised to bring the album with me. I also explained to Nicholle what really happened to Mama, apologizing for not being honest with her parents. I was glad we had unburdened ourselves of that conversation by phone.

"I have this one," Nicholle said, pointing to the picture of Mama and me in the hospital.

We spent the next few hours perusing the photo album, each page generating a new anecdote. Nicholle shared countless stories about Mama from their summers spent together in Paris, and we caught up on each other's lives.

Nicholle told me she had graduated from the Sorbonne in Paris. One year later, she met Ronald. They dated for two years, married, and had one child, Jolie. In 1972 (one year after Mama was attacked), the family relocated to New York, where Ronald was assigned to open an office for his father's publishing company, Simmons & Cahill. Nicholle later decided to go back to school, and earned a Master's degree in Comparative Literature from New York University. She now worked as an editor with Ronald's company.

I told Nicholle all about Da-dee, Ms. Bertha, Mr. Frank, and Johnny. "Is he the man who walked everywhere?" Nicholle asked. I also filled her in on my academic career, and how my being granted scholarships to St. Ann's, Tulane, and Columbia afforded me an education I never dreamed possible.

"Sarah always spoke of how bright you were," Nicholle said, smiling, a sense of pride in her voice causing me to blush. "So, you never told me, how did you like Paris?"

"I loved it. I always wanted to visit. Mama talked about it so much when I was little."

"Then I'm sure you visited Sacré Coeur. Sarah so loved the church."

"It was actually the first place we went."

"That reminds me, who was the young lady you visited with? 'Megan', I think Maman said was her name."

"She's a friend from New Orleans; she's in Law School at Yale."

"Yale Law, impressive, and she's just a friend?"

"Yes, just a friend," I said, with a chuckle, amused by her curiosity.

The day was going just as I hoped. It felt like our friendship was picking up right where Nicholle and Mama's left off. I knew there was only one topic that could spoil things. My father's name had not come up during the entire conversation, but there was one thing I needed to know.

"Nicholle, can I ask you a question?"

"Certainly, Kevin, anything."

"Why did Mama stay with my father?"

"I've thought about that a lot over the past few weeks, Kevin," Nicholle said, sighing heavily. "But it's very hard for me to answer. I never met your father, and the man Sarah described seemed to be two different men: one selfish, controlling, and volatile, the other thoughtful, kind, and loving."

"My father? Thoughtful, kind, and loving?"

"You never saw that side of him, did you? Sarah told me of the problems between you and your father," Nicholle said, diverting her eyes, uncomfortable with the conversation.

"Look, I'm sorry. I mean we don't have to talk about this."

"No no, it's not that."

"Then what?"

"Kevin, I'm going to share something that I'm sure your mother would have discussed with you once you were older." My stomach tightened in knots. "You see, Sarah was separated from your father the year before you were born. They lived apart for over a year, although they continued to see each other."

"I know. I heard them arguing about it one night, but I didn't know they were apart for that long."

"It was really a rough time for her. She was estranged from her family, and found herself all alone, except for her friend Linda. She was working in New Orleans teaching at a high school, so she decided to take an apartment in the city."

"I know," I said, fidgeting on the couch, becoming impatient with facts I was already aware of.

"Well, at the prompting of Linda, and I have to admit, me also, your mother started dating someone, Austin, I think was his name," Nicholle said, revealing information that was news to me. "The relationship was becoming somewhat serious. It wasn't until your mother found out she was pregnant that she and your father got back together."

"Nicholle, I don't think I'm clear as to what this has to do with me."

"Kevin, your father wasn't aware of Sarah's relationship with Austin until after you were born. One night he overheard her and Linda talking about him. He accused Sarah of cheating, and forced her to explain who Austin was. Once she told him, he questioned whether or not you were his child." My mind felt like a helium balloon that is popped with a pin, and then rockets off in every direction before crashing to the ground. "His ego won't allow him to find peace or accept love," Mama had said when I asked why my father hit her. Her meaning was now clear. "Kevin, there was no doubt in Sarah's mind as to who your father was, she would have told me otherwise," Nicholle assured me.

"But what you're saying is, my father doubted that I was his son?"

"I don't know, Kevin. I do know Sarah would have never lied to you about such a thing. The only reason she came back to your father was because of you."

I knew Nicholle meant well, but her statement made me physically ill. "May I use your bathroom?" I asked, shakily standing next to the couch, a sick and dizzying feeling taking over my body.

"Of course, down the hall to the right," Nicholle said, pointing out the direction.

I quickly made my way to the bathroom, and after turning on the faucets in hopes of drowning out the noise, fell to my knees puking. My head felt like a pinball machine, as guilt ricocheted through my brain. *My mother sacrificed her happiness for me. She had gone back to a man she didn't love so I would have a father. I was ultimately responsible for what happened to her.*

"Kevin, are you okay?" Nicholle asked.

"Yeah, I'm alright. I'll be out in a second." I pulled myself from the floor, and rinsed my face with cold water. After rinsing my mouth out with some toothpaste and mouthwash I found in the medicine cabinet, I opened the door to find Nicholle nervously waiting.

"Kevin, please forgive me. I didn't mean that the way it sounded."

"It's okay. I don't know what came over me," I said, still a little woozy.

"Come, sit down. I poured you a glass of ginger ale, it will settle your stomach," she said, leading me to the couch.

"Thanks."

"Kevin, you are not responsible for what happened to your mother, don't ever think that. When Sarah found out she was pregnant, she thought it would bring your father and her closer, that's why she went back to him. She loved your father."

"Why? That's what I don't understand, why she loved him?"

"Who among us can define our choice in falling in love? It's an emotion that justifies itself to no one."

"So, my father doubted that I was his son. It's funny, when I was little I often fantasized that he wasn't my father."

"I'm sorry that I upset you," Nicholle said, placing her arm around me for support.

"No, please, don't be. I asked a question, and you were honest with me. That's what friends do for each other."

"Yes, and I do hope you will consider me a friend. Sarah and I spent only four summers together, but I connected with her unlike anyone I've ever met," Nicholle said, smiling, while gently rubbing the opal pendant hanging around her neck.

"Mama never took hers off," I said, pointing to the pendant. "She was even buried wearing it."

"We would tell people that we were sisters separated as children, and the only clue we had in finding each other were these pendants. As strange as it sounds, some people actually believed us, or at least pretended to," Nicholle said, laughing at the memory. "Sarah's friendship was a blessing. Her spirit was, and remains, like a rare gem, its brilliance brightening the lives of those who knew her. I loved her, and I love you. It means a great deal to me, you becoming a part of my life."

"I feel the same way," I said, a childlike grin creeping across my face.

"What? What is it?"

"Mama, she's enjoying this."

"Yes, I think she is."

Nicholle invited me to stay for dinner, and shared more memories of Mama, painting a picture of someone who enjoyed life, reveling in its adventures. She recounted the summer the two backpacked across Europe, and detailed the time she spent visiting Mama in New York.

"Sarah and I didn't sleep for two straight weeks. We ate at every restaurant, saw every show, heard every band, and danced every night."

Nicholle even gave me a few dance lessons, teaching me the *Lindy Hop* in her living room. By the time I got ready to leave, it was after two a.m.

"I'm sorry to have kept you up so late," I said to Ronald, while putting on my coat.

"No worries, it was a pleasure talking with you," Ronald said, shaking my hand.

"I've had such a wonderful time. I hate to see you leave," Nicholle said, hugging me tightly.

"I had a great time too."

"Oh, I almost forgot. Wait one second," she said, running up the stairs. Moments later, she returned with an album in one hand, and a cassette tape in the other. "Sarah loved this recording. She phoned me when it was released, saying it was the most wonderful piece of music she had ever heard. I didn't know if you had a phonograph or cassette player."

"*Kind of Blue*," I said, reading the album title. "I only have a tape player."

"Well, you keep them both. *Flamenco Sketches* was her favorite," Nicholle said, pointing out the song title on back of the album cover. "She said it made her cry because it reminded her of everything beautiful that life has to offer."

"Thanks, thanks for everything," I said, hugging Nicholle, and kissing her before leaving.

It was snowing when I stepped outside, but the temperature had actually risen from earlier in the day. It was a beautiful night, the streets shrouded in silence, with the snow serving as a blanket for the city while it slept. As I walked across town to catch the subway, my mind drifted back to the stories Nicholle shared about Mama. I had always thought my mother's life was not a happy one. I was wrong. It had been a good life, one filled with adventure. Mama sipped wine while sailing down the Seine River in Paris, picnicked in London's Hyde Park, and danced into the wee hours of the night at *The Savoy Ballroom* in Harlem. She married the man of her choosing, had friends who adored her, and a son who worshipped her. Mama lived life on her own terms, making apologies to no one for her choices.

When I made it back to my apartment, I played the tape Nicholle had given me, rewinding side two so I could hear *Flamenco Sketches* first. Upon hearing the first deep bass notes, I could see Mama's smile. I listened as the song painted a picture of immeasurable beauty, allowing me to see the world as my mother did for the first time. I realized that Mama had defined her life in accordance with the blessings she was granted, rather than the hardships she endured. I promised myself to never again look back on Mama's life with pity, realizing that to do so would be a disservice to her memory.

A Fudgesicle On A Hot Day

"Done so quickly?" Dr. Starkes asked, after I handed in my *Statistics II* exam.

"Yes sir, all the answers were so clear to me, it was a little strange."

"There's nothing strange about it, answers are always clear to someone who is prepared. Enjoy spring break."

It was Friday, April 20, 1984. Academically, my second semester was proving to be just as successful as the first. My life outside of the classroom was also creeping back on track. My heart was finally at peace when it came to Mama, the knowledge of her happiness allowing me to welcome her back into every facet of my life. My friendship with Megan, who successfully stopped drinking, became one of mutual love and support, rather than dependence. And Nicholle and I grew closer, developing a bond of our own, while sharing the ones we experienced with Mama. I even mustered the discipline to end the sexual aspects of all my relationships. This decision came from no great moral awakening, but the realization that I used sex as a way of desensitizing myself. It seemed for me the most intimate of acts eliminated all possibilities of true emotional intimacy. The guilt I harbored from my relationship with Beth was my only burden, but it was one that was well earned.

Later that night I became engrossed in the misadventures of Ignatius J. Reilly, the anti-heroic main character in *A Confederacy of Dunces*, a novel Nicholle recommended, and stayed up until five o'clock that morning reading. The next morning I was scheduled to play squash with Ronald at nine (I had become addicted to the game), but considered turning around and going home when I arrived at the New York Sports Club on East 86th Street. Ronald claimed to be an average player, but the disparity in skill between an average squash player and a beginner was monumental. I normally spent the game frantically chasing down balls in every corner, while Ronald remained firmly planted at the T (the center point on the court), calmly returning my shots with a casual flick of his wrist. I loved the game, and my play was improving quickly, but after waking up with a headache from lack of sleep, the physical exertion I normally relished loomed as a death sentence. After deciding it would be ungracious to not show up for our match, I reluctantly went into the club.

"Good morning, my name is Kevin Matthews. I have a squash game with Ronald Simmons," I said to the desk clerk.

"Are you a member?"

"No I'm not, but Mr. Simmons should have left a guest pass for me."

"Oh, I'm sorry, Mr. Matthews, I just remembered that Mr. Simmons called and left a message for you," the clerk said, pulling out a note. "Mr. Simmons said that he can't make it this morning, but he would try and arrange a game for you with someone else."

"He would try? Well, do you know if he was able to do that?"

"You'll need to check at the squash desk. Oh, and don't worry about the guest pass, Mr. Simmons said he would take care of that later today."

I walked over to the squash desk. "Hi, my name is Kevin Matthews. I was supposed to play with Ronald Simmons this morning, but he couldn't make it. He was going to try and schedule a game with someone else for me. Do you know anything about that?" I asked the young lady manning the squash desk.

"Yes sir, your partner's already on the court. And Mr. Simmons wanted to let you know you'll be playing an A player, so you should bring your best game," she said, with a smile.

"My best game, that's not bringing much," I said, thinking aloud.

"Well, good luck anyway," she said, laughing, and handing me a towel. "You guys will be playing on Court Five. It's on the third floor."

"Thanks." This is just great, I thought. Being a beginner, I was considered a D player. Ronald was a B player. He arranged a game for me with an A player. Translation, I was going to be killed. It was bad enough the manner in which Ronald ran me ragged around the court, now that honor would go to a complete stranger.

I trudged up the stairs to the third floor, and headed down the hall to Court Five. As I approached the court, I could hear the ball being pounded against the walls as my opponent warmed up. I'll just have to take my medicine like a man, I thought. I knocked on the door to alert my executioner that I had arrived.

"Come on in," a feminine voice yelled out.

A girl? He arranged to have a girl beat me? I opened the door, and was rendered speechless by the face that greeted me.

"Hi, I'm Jolie," a young woman said. I was silent. "You are Kevin, right?"

"Yeah, yeah, I'm Kevin, Kevin Matthews," I said, staring at the woman.

"It's nice to meet you. Maman and Papa have told me so much about you," she said, extending her hand, but having to reach out and grab mine to shake it. "I'm Jolie Simmons, Ronald and Nicholle are my parents," she said slowly.

"Jolie? You're Jolie?"

"I'm Jolie," she said, forcing a smile, uncomfortable with my actions, or lack thereof. "Papa had to go into the office this morning, and Maman thought it would be a good idea for me to come. She's been wanting us to meet for a while."

I knew Nicholle and Ronald's daughter was named Jolie; they spoke of her often, and had even shown me pictures. But seeing her in person for the first time, I was paralyzed by her image. Jolie was a dead ringer for the woman depicted on canvas in *Portrait of Negress*, the painting by Marie-Guillemine Benoist that I'd seen in the Louvre. She was wearing a light blue tank top that accentuated her athletic frame, and stood about five feet ten inches, with long willowy legs that seductively escaped her baggy gray gym shorts. She had tight, well-maintained black dreadlocks, which fell near her shoulders, and were held in place by a light blue scrunchie.

"Kevin, are you okay?"

"I'm sorry, it's just that, well, you see, the girl at the desk said 'you guys are on court five', so I was expecting a guy, and you're certainly not a guy, and, well, your mother, she did tell me she wanted us to meet, but she said you were going to Florida on spring break, and we would have to meet another time, so when you said your name was Jolie, I didn't think you could be that Jolie, and so I was a little confused for a moment."

"Okay, so, ah, maybe you'd like to warm up. I'm going to go and fill my water bottle," Jolie said, leaving the court.

I had made a complete idiot of myself. As I warmed up, I realized things would only get worse once we began to play. Frustration with my moronic behavior produced greater power in my swing, but unfortunately it wasn't helping my game. With every second or third stroke attempted, the ball ended up slamming into the tin, the out of bounds area on the lower end of the front wall. I didn't even have a competitor, and I couldn't keep the ball in play. This was going to be down right embarrassing.

Jolie returned, and I explained that I was only a beginner, so she shouldn't expect much in the way of competition. She suggested we handicap the game in order to make things more interesting. In squash, within the marked boundaries, you are allowed to hit all four walls when returning the ball, the front wall being the only one required in constituting a legal stroke. Jolie proposed that she be allowed to use only the front wall when returning my shots. Taking into consideration the angles on a squash court, this would give me a decisive advantage. The sidewalls are crucial in recovering from well-placed shots by your opponent, and in creating difficult return shots for them. But even with the handicap, I knew I would pose no challenge. Aside from being a far superior player, I knew I would be too distracted to focus on the game.

After being demolished in the first game, my only three points being the result of pity from Jolie, my male ego got the best of me, and I began to play the best squash of my brief career. I was competing on only a few hours of sleep, but I felt re-energized. I chased down impossible shots, making each point a long and drawn-out battle. Despite my efforts, I lost the remaining seven games we played, and never scored more than the three points I'd managed in the first game. Squash is a sport where the slightest difference in skill level can result in lopsided scores. I knew Jolie was a much better player, so I held no illusions that I might steal a victory. But as strange as it sounds, the games were very competitive.

"Great match," Jolie said, shaking my hand after our final game.

Crippled by my exhaustion, I collapsed against the back wall of the court, gasping for air as I attempted to catch my breath. "Thought I had you for a second that game, didn't you?" I said, winded.

"You really played well. I never have to run that much when I play Papa."

"I'll make sure to point that fact out to him."

"It's true, you really made me work for every point," she said, dabbing her face with a towel, beads of sweat coruscating across her brow. In describing her attraction to my father, Mama had said, "Man reminded me of a fudgesicle on a hot day, mouth watering." Looking at Jolie, I knew exactly what she meant. "How long did you say you've been playing?" Jolie asked, taking a seat on the floor next to me.

"I've only been playing about three months, but I've never played this well."

"Guess I bring out the best in your game. The right person can do that."

"Well, I guess I found the right person."

After our match, Jolie suggested we grab a bite to eat at the diner across the street from the club. The place was packed when we arrived, and we had to wait over fifteen minutes for a table, but I would have waited an hour if necessary. Jolie explained that her plans for spring break fell through when her roommate came down with the flu. She decided to surprise her parents by coming home instead.

"So you go to Bennington; great school. What's your major?" I asked.

"English."

"No surprise there."

"Huh? Oh, my parents, yeah, I guess so," she laughed.

"You're a freshman, right?"

"Yeah, hope that doesn't scare you off."

"No no, it doesn't. And hopefully my behavior earlier won't scare you off. I was just caught a little off-guard."

"Maman wanted to surprise you. I didn't want to come at first, but when she described you again, I figured why not. I'll have to thank her when I get home," Jolie said, flirting.

"After the beating you gave me, I won't be thanking her."

"Only way to get better, Kevin."

"It didn't help that I was up until five o'clock this morning. I'm referring to my behavior, not my game, nothing could have helped that."

"Stop it, you weren't that bad. And why were you up until five o'clock? Did you go out last night?"

"No, unbelievably boring as it might sound, I was reading in my apartment, sad, but true."

"Five in the morning?"

"It's your mother's fault," I said, jokingly. "She recommended this book to me, *A Confederacy of Dunces.*"

Jolie began to laugh. It was a booming high-pitched laugh, resistant of censorship, despite our crowded surroundings. "Say no more," she said, struggling to regain her composure. "Ignatius J. Reilly, right? You didn't get any sleep because of Ignatius J. Reilly."

It turned out the book was one of Jolie's favorites. We both agreed reading about the chaos involved in Ignatius's life was akin to watching an accident develop; you were defenseless against your desire to find out what was going to happen next.

"So, now at least you know I'm not weird or anything, I just don't function well with no sleep," I said.

"But that doesn't have anything to do with the way you acted this morning."

"What do you mean?"

"Well, I don't know, there was just something strange about the way you looked at me. And I've caught you looking at me that way since then also." Jolie smiled, wagging her finger at me.

"If I told you the truth, you wouldn't believe me."

"Why don't you try me?" she said coolly, picking up her glass of juice and playfully twirling the straw with her tongue.

I thought for a moment. "Okay, but remember, you asked," I said slowly, shaking my head at the ridiculousness of the story I was about to tell. "A few weeks before Christmas I took a trip to Paris, and while visiting the Louvre, I came across a painting titled *Portrait of Negress*. It was of one of the most beautiful women I've ever seen. I ended up spending hours staring at it. It wasn't just her beauty that intrigued me though; there was something in her eyes, it was like a combination of strength, pain, honesty, I don't know, but whatever it was, it caused her image to, how can I put this, attach itself to my consciousness. Since then I've been having these dreams where I'm chasing the woman all over the city, but I can never catch up to her. I eventually lose her in Times Square, and go home, convinced my life will be empty until I find her."

"And I remind you of this woman?" Jolie asked, leaning in over the table.

"Physically, the similarities are staggering," I said, laughing. "Look, Jolie, I know we just met, and the last thing I want to do is freak you out or anything. It's just that, well, the reason there's something strange about the way I look at you, I think that's how you put it, right?" Jolie smiled, shrugging her shoulders. "The reason, as silly as it sounds, is that on some level I believe the dream to be true, and when I look at you, I can't stop considering the possibility that you are that woman."

Jolie, unintentionally mimicking my behavior from earlier, was speechless. She took a deep breath, placed her glass on the table, having to remove the straw from her mouth after it stuck to her bottom lip, sat back, and flashed a smile that caused me to melt into my chair. Mr. Frank told me when I met the right woman, I would know, and there would be no doubt in my mind. I did, and there wasn't.

Jolie and I spent the rest of the day together, most of it stretched out on a blanket in Central Park, talking. It was an unusually warm day for April, and with both of us suffering from cabin fever, the result of a harsh winter, we wanted to take advantage of the weather. We talked about our families, friends, past relationships, education, plans for the future, and everything else we could think of. The day flew by, and I dreaded having to say goodbye.

"So, you want to maybe grab some dinner?" I asked.

"Oh, I completely forgot, Maman wanted me to invite you back to the house for dinner."

"Okay, yeah, that sounds good."

"Maybe; depends on how well you hold up under interrogation."

"What does that mean?"

"Well, she kept me up for hours last night talking about you. I imagine she'll have lots of questions tonight. She is all over this."

As we left the park, Jolie reached out and grabbed my hand, swinging it back and forth like a child as we walked. It was such a simple gesture, but it made me giddy with excitement.

After dinner that evening, I talked with Jolie, Nicholle, and Ronald until after midnight. It was two a.m. by the time I walked out of the subway at my stop.

"Kevin, hey, Kevin, wait up," I heard a voice yell. I turned to find Beth running down the street towards me. Although we spoke on the phone a few times after our break-up, incredible as it sounds, considering we went to the same school, and lived on the same block, this was the first time we had seen each other.

"Beth, hey," I said, hugging her.

"Where are you coming from?"

"Me, oh, I was just out with some friends. How about you?"

"Same. I was going to stop by the diner and pick up something to eat, you want to come?"

"Well, yeah, why not, sure."

We walked a few blocks down to a twenty-four hour diner, one that we had frequented on many nights. After entering, we both instinctively went straight for a corner booth against the window, our customary spot.

"Hey, I haven't seen you two in here together in quite some time. Where have you been?" a waiter asked, approaching the table and instantly recognizing us.

"Yeah, it's been a while," Beth said, smiling.

"You guys need menus?"

"I don't, how about you, Kevin?"

"No, I know what I want."

"Me too."

"Let me see, two cheeseburgers, one well, one medium, two orders of fries, and two large chocolate shakes, right?" the waiter asked, remembering the only meal we ever ordered.

"Sounds good," Beth said. The waiter laughed and left to place our orders. "Guess some things don't change, do they?" Beth joked.

"Yeah."

"So, how have you been?"

"Good. You?"

"Crazy. I'm taking five classes, I took a research position with Pfizer, which is requiring longer hours than I ever expected, and I'm in the middle of moving."

"Moving?"

"My place is going co-op, it's a long story. How are your classes going this semester?"

"Good."

"And work?"

"Good."

"Kevin, are you going to give me anything more than one word answers?" Beth asked, smiling to put me at ease.

"I'm sorry, I'm just a little nervous."

"Why would you be nervous?"

"I don't know; guess I've got a somewhat guilty conscious when it comes to you."

"Hey, you weren't ready for a relationship. There was a lot going on in your life, I mean, you had just lost your mother."

"I was actually thinking about the other thing."

"I'm okay, really, I am."

"Do you regret it?"

"Honestly, yeah, I do."

"I'm really sorry."

"There's no need."

"No, you don't understand. I have to explain something to you."

"Kevin, there's nothing for you to explain," Beth said, placing a finger to my lips. "Whatever it is, I forgive you. It didn't work out between us, but you were very special to me, and I know I was special to you."

"You were."

We sat in silence, until the waiter returned with our milk shakes. "So have you met anyone?" Beth asked.

"No no, too busy."

"It's okay you know, you can tell me. After all, I did."

"Really? Who is he?"

"He's a researcher I met at Pfizer."

"A researcher you met at Pfizer, huh? No wonder you've been working long hours."

"He really is a great guy. We've been seeing each other since January. He actually knew who I was before we were formally introduced. You see, he graduated from Columbia, and apparently we took some classes together, although I didn't remember him. He said he recognized me right away after seeing me in the office."

"Well, Beth, you are hard to forget."

Beth and I finished eating, and then walked back to her apartment, sitting on the stoop talking until the sun rose. When I finally made it back to my apartment, I walked in with mixed emotions. I had enjoyed talking with Beth, but seeing her unsettled me. It reminded me of what a selfish person I could be. Having just met a woman who seemingly stepped out of my dreams, I questioned whether I had it within me to love, whether or not I was deserving of love. I had asked forgiveness of God, knowing his unconditional love guaranteed it would be granted. I had asked forgiveness of Beth, receiving it without her requiring the full knowledge of my offenses. I was all too aware that self-forgiveness would not come so easily.

PART III

FAMILY

"We Are Who We Believe Ourselves To Be"

"It feels a little weird being here," Jolie said.

"How long has it been?" I asked.

"It has to be over a year."

"Nothing's changed, I can tell you that. To be honest, not much has changed in this apartment for the past seventeen years. Well, I guess I did replace the milk crates."

"Actually, I replaced the milk crates." I thought for a moment, pretending to doubt her claim. "Kevin, don't even try it, if it was up to you those milk crates would probably still be in here," Jolie said, laughing and wagging her finger in my direction.

"I guess your moving in did help spruce the place up a bit. You want anything to drink?"

"No thanks. So, what did you want to show me?"

"Oh yeah, have a seat," I said, grabbing a gift from the kitchen table. "You didn't think dinner was your only present, did you?" It was November 15, 1996, Jolie's thirtieth birthday.

"Thank you, but you didn't have to get me anything."

"Why do people always say that? You know you want it."

Jolie smiled, slowly ripping open the wrapping paper. "Ignatius, you got me Ignatius," she said, giggling. I had given Jolie a first edition copy of *Confederacy of Dunces*.

"Hang on a second, open the front cover," I said, taking a seat next to her.

"Oh my God, where did you find this?" The book had been signed by Walker Percy, a noted novelist instrumental in getting the book published in 1980, eleven years after its author, John Kennedy O'Toole, committed suicide. Percy also wrote the book's foreword. "Thank you so much," she said, hugging and kissing me.

"The book almost doomed our first meeting, I was hoping it could maybe do the opposite tonight." Jolie leafed through the book as I began a battle with my nerves.

"Stop it," she said, placing her hand on my knee to stop it from shaking. "You're making me nervous."

"This is crazy."

"What?"

"Two people who have shared so much being this uncomfortable with each other."

"Yeah, I guess it is."

"What are you thinking?"

"Kevin, please don't analyze me."

"No, I'm serious. What are you thinking?"

"I don't know; nothing."

"Come on, Jolie, you have to be thinking something. I mean, did you have a good time tonight? Are you glad you came? How do you feel about seeing me?"

Jolie thought for a moment. "I had a nice time tonight, so yeah, I'm glad I decided to come."

"That's it? Wow."

"What?"

"I don't know; that just wasn't the answer I was looking for I guess."

"What do you mean?"

"Well, I haven't seen you in three months, I was hoping for a little more. It doesn't matter."

"Huh, interesting."

"What?"

"Nothing."

"Come on, what?"

"It's just, you didn't really care what I was thinking, did you? What I mean is, it really wasn't about me, was it?"

"What are you talking about?"

"You wanted to know if I missed you, right? You wanted me to say something to make you feel better. Of course you couldn't just come out and ask me that, you had to mask it with a question pretending to care how I felt."

"Jolie, that's not it, I wasn't doing that. I was just trying to figure out, you know, I mean, you know like, get an idea of, you know…,"

"I know what, Kevin?" Jolie slammed the book shut, her expression demanding a response.

"Okay yeah, you're right, I've missed you, and I wanted to know if you missed me too."

"Of course I did," Jolie said, suddenly calm. I stared at her, totally confused. "Somebody had to break the tension," she said, her attention returning to the book.

"And that's what you came up with?"

"We both acknowledged the fact that we miss each other, didn't we?"

"Well, yeah."

"That's as good a start as any. I'll have that drink now."

I wanted to be angry, but I wasn't. Truth is, at that moment I missed her more than ever.

❋   ❋   ❋

Jolie and I continued dating after meeting in the spring of 1984. Since Bennington was in Vermont, we didn't spend a lot of time together during the fall and spring semesters, but over holidays and in the summer we were inseparable. Jolie practically lived at my place, and even when apart, if the situation allowed, we were talking to each other on the phone. The amazing thing was that it was all so effortless. I always thought of relationships as hard work, but being with Jolie came so easily. I never felt the need to enter-tain or impress her, and she could make me laugh like no one else. It was a strange feeling, wanting, even needing to be with the same person every minute of the day, but I was in love.

Then in August 1986, two weeks before the fall semester started, Jolie told me she thought it would be a good idea for us to take a break and see other people. She said that she loved me, but didn't want to be tied down her senior year. "We can still see each other when I'm at home, but seeing other people will really put our relationship to the test. I think we owe that to ourselves, and to each other," she explained.

My initial reaction was shock, but it quickly turned to anger. I agreed to her proposal, not wanting to lose her altogether, but I soon found myself becoming obsessive and controlling.

"Jolie, all I'm asking is why you didn't call me back last night," I yelled into the phone, while pacing the room like a caged animal. It was a Saturday morning, and after being unable to reach Jolie the night before I was fuming. "You didn't call me back because you didn't come home last night, did you?"

"I am so tired of this," Jolie sighed.

"Just admit it; you didn't call me back because you didn't come home last night, right?"

"No, Kevin. I didn't come home last night. Is that what you want to hear? Well there, I admit it. Are you happy now?" I dropped down on the sofa, unable to muster a response. "Look, I have to go. I'm not going to be around tonight, so I'll call you tomorrow," she said.

As I hung up the phone, my mind was flooded with a blur of images picturing Jolie in bed with other men. Having visited Bennington's campus several times, I knew there was an unending supply of rich and privileged frat boys trying to get a piece of her. I had watched the way they greeted her when not in my presence, hugging and whispering in her ear. The image of her body intertwined with one of them sickened me. I've got to do something, I thought. I picked up the phone, and called Megan at Yale. "I have to use your car," I demanded.

I arrived at Bennington late Saturday afternoon. I had calmed down from earlier that morning, and now only had intentions of telling Jolie that our dating arrangement was not working for me. After phoning her room and getting no answer, I was seated in the lobby when Jen Wasserman, a friend of Jolie's who I'd met on previous visits, spotted me.

"Kevin, hey," Jen said, rushing over and hugging me. "You're up for the weekend?"

"Just came up for the day."

"Where's Jolie?"

"I was about to ask you the same thing. She's not in her room."

"Was she expecting you?"

"No, I thought I'd surprise her. Do you know where she is?"

"I do now, she's right there," Jen laughed, pointing out a window behind me. I turned and saw Jolie seated on the hood of a parked car laughing and talking with two guys. "You'll be around tonight?" Jen asked.

"Probably."

"Tell Jolie to give me a call. Maybe we can hang out."

"Okay, yeah."

"See you, Kevin." Jen hugged me goodbye, and headed upstairs. I continued staring out at Jolie. You only want to talk to her, I reminded myself.

"Kevin, what are you doing here?" Jolie asked, nervously jumping from the hood of the car.

"I thought we needed to talk," I said, purposely ignoring the guys she was talking to.

"Who's this, Jolie?" one asked, eyeing me from head to toe after sensing my unspoken hostility. I returned his stare. He was a good-looking guy; over six feet tall and well built. The other guy, who was around the same size, seemed indifferent, or maybe just unaware of the situation.

"This is Kevin, a friend from New York," Jolie said, positioning herself between us.

"What's up, man, I'm Brian," the second guy said, shaking my hand.

"What's up?" I said.

"And this is Evan," Jolie said. We reluctantly acknowledged each other with a nod of the head.

"Like I said, Jolie, we need to talk," I said, grabbing her hand and walking away.

"Guys, I'll catch up to you later, okay?" Jolie said.

"What about tonight?" Evan asked, leaning back against the car. "We're still on for tonight, right?"

"No, she's not going to make it tonight," I answered, turning to face him. Evan stood from the car, and Brian, who was now up to speed with what was going on, took a position next to him. This wasn't James and Josh I was about to take on. Although I was a few inches taller, these guys were roughly the same size as me, and more importantly, neither seemed intimidated.

"Kevin, let's go," Jolie said, attempting to pull me away. "Evan, I'll call you later."

"Just stop by, you know where I live," Evan laughed.

"You need to watch your mouth, man," I said, pointing my finger in his face.

"Get out of my face," Evan yelled, pushing me away.

I responded by throwing a right hook to Evan's temple. He countered with a blow to my stomach. Seconds later we were on the ground wrestling, both of us throwing wild punches at every given opportunity. Luckily for me, Brian decided to play peacemaker, grabbing Evan to pull us apart. Jolie threw her arms around me attempting to separate us. By this time a small crowd had gathered, seemingly coming from nowhere. Campus security arrived minutes later. When it was determined that I was not a student, the town police were called, and I ended up spending the night in jail.

The next morning I was released with nothing more than a warning. I had thrown the first punch, but Evan wasn't pressing charges. When I made it to the lobby of the police station, Ronald was there waiting.

"Are you okay?" he asked.

"Yeah, I'm fine. What are you doing here?"

"Jolie phoned yesterday to tell us what happened. Nicholle thought it wise that we drive up. I stopped by this morning to see how you were doing, and they told me you were being released. I knew you would need a ride back to your car, so I waited. Come on, let's go."

We left the police station, and rode back in silence, Ronald not asking for an explanation. When we made it back to Megan's car, which was parked in front of Jolie's dorm, Nicholle was waiting outside.

"Are you okay?" she asked, approaching the car as I got out.

"I'm fine."

"They told Ronald no charges were being filed, is that true?"

"Yeah, I'm free to go."

"Good, good."

"Look, I'm really sorry I caused you guys any problems." I was so ashamed that I avoided eye contact. "Ronald, thanks for coming to pick me up."

"You're welcome, Kevin." Ronald reached out, firmly shaking my hand. "You get home safe."

"Tell Jolie I'm sorry," I said to Nicholle. "I would go up and do it myself, but I really don't think she wants to see me right now."

"She knows, Kevin."

Nicholle hugged me goodbye, caressing the bruises on my cheek. When I finally found the strength to look her in the eyes, I was crushed by what I saw. I once asked Nicholle why Mama stayed with my father. She told me it was hard for her to answer, since the man Mama described seemed to be two different men; one selfish, controlling, and volatile, the other thoughtful, kind, and loving. I could see Nicholle analyzing that same dichotomy in me. No one had been more excited about Jolie and me dating, but I knew she was now left to search for answers as to why her daughter would stay with me.

Jolie and I saw each other a few times after that day, but I could tell she didn't have any interest in continuing our relationship. Nicholle and I spoke every couple of months, and I continued to regularly play squash with Ronald, but Jolie's name rarely came up. That was fine with me, since I was miserable without her. What made matters worse was the fact that I knew I had no one to blame but myself for losing her. When things didn't go my way in our relationship, I lashed out in anger, and even resorted to violence. It was a hauntingly familiar reaction.

I focused on school and work over the next few years, avoiding any serious relationships. Megan was busy as a first year associate at a Wall Street law firm, so we didn't see much of each other, and for the first time since eighth grade I was lonely. To fill this void I fell back into my old pattern of having numerous casual sex partners. For me, there was now an undeniable emptiness to these encounters, but I had allowed love to play a role in two relationships in my life; one resulted in nothing but heartache for Beth, and in the second I was introduced to that same hurt. Who needs that, I thought.

In the spring of 1989, I completed work on my PhD, and considered moving back to Louisiana. The research project I was working on with Dr. Reyas was scheduled for completion the following year, and after that, I reasoned there was nothing left for me in New York. Megan warned I would never forgive myself if I didn't at least talk to Jolie before leaving, but even though I never stopped loving her, I couldn't find the courage to do so, my fear of rejection outweighing all other considerations. I resigned myself to the idea that she was out of my life forever. As fate would have it, Jolie would not be so weak.

"Hi, Kevin, how are you?" Jolie asked, opening the door before I rang the bell. It was August 1989.

"Jolie, a…, a…, hi" I stuttered. It was raining, and as I attempted to close my umbrella I slipped on the stairs leading up to the front door.

"Careful, these stairs are slippery when it's raining," she warned, grabbing my arm to steady me. I knew the rain had nothing to do with me slipping. She did also.

"I just stopped by to pick up my squash racket. Ronald restrung it for me. I mean, well, he didn't restring it, but he took it to someone who did. I think it was a friend of his, you know, the guy who restrung it. Anyway, I called and asked Nicholle when was the best time to stop by and pick it up, and she said today. She didn't mention you would be home, so I didn't know you would be here when I stopped by, you know, to pick up the racket." Please shut up, Kevin, I thought.

"Kevin, come inside. You're getting soaked," Jolie said, pulling me into the house. "Wait here, I'll get you a towel." I waited at the door, struggling to get a grip on my nerves. Jolie returned with a towel, watching as I dried off, and unsuccessfully attempting to suppress her laughter.

"It's okay, you can laugh. Pretty pathetic, right?"

"It's not that."

"Then what?"

"Let's just say, your explanation sounded somewhat familiar." Jolie smiled, and as if nothing had changed, I melted on the inside.

Jolie asked if I wanted to stay and talk, and despite my rambling even more than in my explanation about picking up the racket, she understood I wanted nothing more. We spent the next few hours catching up on each other's lives. Jolie told me that after graduating from Bennington, she went on to Princeton and earned a Master's degree in Creative Writing. She had spent the past summer in France with her grandparents, and was now working part-time at Ronald's publishing firm until she could find something permanent. I told her that I'd finally earned my PhD, Jolie jokingly asking if she was now required to address me as "Dr." I also told her about my research project nearing completion, although I didn't mention my plans to move back to Louisiana. We ordered in a pizza for lunch, and to go along with it, tried out a bottle of wine Jolie brought back from some famous vineyard in France. Before we knew it, day turned into night.

"Well, tell Nicholle I'm glad she 'forgot' she wouldn't be around today, and that she 'forgot' to tell me you would be here to give me the racket," I joked before leaving.

"It wasn't Maman's idea this time," Jolie confessed.

"What do you mean?"

"I asked her to tell you to pick up the racket today, and I also asked her not to tell you I would be here."

"Why?"

"I don't know. I'm sorry, I know that wasn't fair."

"Oh, it's okay, I'm glad you did. I mean I'm really happy I got to see you."

"I've missed you, Kevin."

"You have?"

"Yeah, I have. Why would that surprise you?"

"Well, I haven't seen you since, you know, well, let's just say it's been a long time."

"I wanted to make sure I was ready before seeing you again."

"Look, Jolie, I know I've told you this before, but I really am sorry about what happened."

"You weren't the only one at fault."

"So, what do we do now?"

"Like you said, it's been a long time. Why don't we just try and get to know each other again."

Jolie and I stepped back into our relationship without missing a beat. We were engaged that Christmas, and she moved into my apartment. The place was small for two people, but neither of us was making much money at the time, and my rent over the years had only gone up to four hundred fifty dollars. After we were married in the fall of 1992, Megan lured us to the suburbs of Stamford, Connecticut, where she and her husband Morris had moved two years earlier. Financially, things had picked up quickly for us. Jolie was teaching at The Gallatin School, a small college within New York University, and had achieved success and a modest level of celebrity as a writer when her first, of what became a line of children's books, hit the New York Times Best-seller's List. The books in the series were titled: *The Adventures of Earl, The Friendly Rooster.* I was working two days a week as a counselor at Beth Israel Hospital, and had also started a private practice that was thriving. We bought a four-bedroom colonial white house with green trim. The house had big rooms with high ceilings, and a glass-enclosed patio that looked out onto a huge backyard. "House, Boy, you done bought a mansion," Mr. Frank joked after seeing pictures.

Jolie loved suburbia, and soon left Gallatin, taking a position at Fairfield University, which was only a fifteen-minute drive from our house. "I don't ever want to ride the subway again," she said. Since my practice was already established, I decided to commute to Manhattan. Jolie thought enduring the headaches of an hour-plus commute was crazy, but I enjoyed maintaining a connection to the city. To make things easier, we bought my old apartment when my building went co-op so I would have a place to stay if needed.

After being married a few years, with a home in the country, and both of us settled into our careers, we began hearing the inevitable whispers from family and friends that it was time to start a family. Logically, it was the next step.

"He is so precious," Jolie gushed, snuggling next to me in bed. She was referring to Tyler, Megan and Morris' son. It was July 11, 1996, and earlier that day we had gone to Tyler's fourth birthday party.

"Precious? Yeah right, you weren't the one trying to teach him how to play baseball," I said. "How many times do you have to explain that hitting someone with a bat is not funny. Kid's got homicidal tendencies if you ask me."

"Kevin, he's four, don't say that," Jolie laughed, playfully punching me in the side.

"Yeah, well, I don't know. He sure got a kick out of bonking me in the head with that bat."

"Don't be ridiculous, he loves his Uncle Kevin. He was following in your footsteps all day."

"And none of you were trying very hard to get his attention."

"Oh you love it. You're going to make a great dad." Jolie kissed me, sliding her hand under the covers. "You know, we could start tonight."

"I'm too tired to start anything tonight."

"How about I start? You just promise to finish," Jolie laughed, moving to crawl on top of me.

"Nah, not tonight," I said, stopping her. Jolie sighed in annoyance, and turned her back to me. "What? I'm just tired."

"Whatever, Kevin."

"Because I'm too tired to have sex tonight, you're pissed."

"This has nothing to do with having sex tonight, and you know it."

"Then what's the problem?"

"Don't play dumb with me," Jolie said, sitting up in bed. "I went off the pill almost three months ago, and since that time you've mysteriously been tired each week that I'm ovulating. And don't lie and tell me you don't know when that is, because I do everything except put up signs around the house."

"I don't know what you're talking about."

"Kevin, if you don't want to have kids, why don't you just say so?"

"I'm not against having kids."

"You're not against having kids? Hey everybody, my husband isn't against having kids," Jolie shouted to an imaginary audience. "I'm the luckiest woman on the planet."

"You're twisting my words. I didn't mean it like that and you know it."

"Then how exactly did you mean it?"

"Forget it, I can't talk to you when you're like this." I got out of bed to leave the room.

"Don't you dare walk out on this conversation," Jolie demanded, standing from the bed. "We both agreed, in this very room, that we wanted a family. I'd like to point out to you that wanting something, and not being against it, are two very different things."

"Look, I said I wanted a family, I didn't say I wanted one now."

"And you didn't feel the need to share that little tidbit of information? Not even when we discussed my going off the pill so I could get pregnant. Instead, you decide to just secretly orchestrate the timing of our lives without including me."

"First of all, we never discussed your going off the pill, you announced it. And second of all, we've only been married four years. That's not very long, I don't know what the big rush is."

"Only been married four years?" Jolie thought for a moment, placing both hands on her hips. "Well, exactly how much time do I have to put in before you decide I'm worthy of starting a family with?"

"All I'm saying is, we don't want to have kids until we're certain."

"Certain of what?"

"Certain of us." Without warning Jolie slapped me across the face, and then, wearing a confused and hurt expression, stood silently staring at me, tears welling in her eyes. "Look, Jolie, I didn't mean that the way it sounded," I explained. "I mean I love you."

"Don't say that to me," Jolie said, placing a finger to my lips. "Don't ever say that to me again, not until you're man enough to back it up."

The next day, Jolie asked me to move out.

*   *   *

"Okay, we miss each other, so what do we do about it?" I asked, handing Jolie a glass of wine.

"We try to fix it."

"It being us?" I joked, sitting next to her.

Jolie smiled. "Yes, it being us."

"And now for the tough part, how do we fix it?"

"Well, I'd say that's pretty simple. We find out if we want the same things." I could tell from the trembling in Jolie's voice, that she too was now nervous. She took a sip of wine, put her glass on the coffee table, and reached over taking my hand. "You know how I feel, Kevin. I want to have children. I love you, but that's not something I'm willing to give up."

"I love you too. But, I don't know, what happens if one of us decides some day that they're no longer in love?"

"What?"

"Well, it could happen. I mean look what happened your senior year. I thought we were in love then. I'm not blaming it all on you. I mean I know I acted like a jerk."

"Kevin, that was over ten years ago. We were kids. How can you compare that to what we have now?"

"I'm not doing that. It's just that my childhood was a lot different than yours. I know firsthand that love isn't always enough. And if things don't work out, it's going to be the child that suffers."

Jolie looked at me stunned. "There it is. That's what this is all about, isn't it?" she asked, her hands clasping her face, as she shook her head in disbelief. She then stood, and walked over to the window looking out. "Well, I can't do this. I won't."

"You won't do what?" I asked, following her to the window.

Jolie turned to face me. "I won't sacrifice having a family because of how your father treated you." I was speechless, the effect more due to my own guilt than Jolie's words. "Kevin, I love you, and despite what you might think, I always will. But you will never be able to love me the way I need, the way I deserve, until you come to terms with the fact that we are not your parents, and you are not your father."

"What are you saying?"

"I'm saying that we are who we believe ourselves to be, and sometimes nothing can change that." My mind searched frantically for the right words to say, but the weight of her statement muddled my thoughts. "Look, it's getting late, I better be going. Thanks for dinner, and thank you for the book, it was very sweet," Jolie said, squeezing my hand, and kissing me before turning to leave. I stood motionless, my body crippled by the moment, and watched as she gathered her things, and walked out the door.

The apartment never felt so small. It was as if the building was being loaded into a gigantic trash compactor collapsing the wall onto me from all angles. If I don't get out of here I'm going to be crushed, I thought. I waited a few minutes to give Jolie some time to get out of the building, then left my apartment, and headed for *Smoke*, a neighborhood bar that featured nightly jazz. I hoped the music, in combination with some vodka, might somehow save me from a nervous breakdown.

"Dr. K, how you doing, brother?" Carl asked, shaking my hand as I took a seat at the bar.

"I'm okay. What's up with the music?" I asked, seeing the bandstand was empty.

"Set just ended, next one starts in about twenty minutes." Carl placed a napkin on the bar in front of me. "Usual?"

"Yeah, thanks."

It was a Friday night, and the place was packed. Clouds of cigarette smoke wafted through the air masking the faces seated at the bar, and a din of conversation echoed around the room, as I sat struggling to maintain my emotions.

"Stoli Gimlet on the rocks," Carl said, returning with my drink. "You want to start a tab?"

"Yeah, I'm probably going to hang around for the next set."

"Cool. Oh, a fine young sister at the end of the bar asked about you."

"Asked what?"

"Asked if you were Kevin Matthews."

"She knew my name? Who?"

"Me," a voice said, tapping my shoulder. I turned to find a familiar, yet unrecognizable face. "Kevin, you don't know who I am, do you?" the woman asked.

"No, I'm sorry, I mean, you look familiar, but I'm drawing a blank on the name."

"And to think I wanted you to be my daddy," the woman said, laughing.

"Excuse me."

"It's me, silly, Amber." It was Amber Martinez, the little girl I met working with Dr. Reyas.

"Amber?"

"It's me, I'm just all growed up," Amber said, hugging and kissing me.

"I can't believe this," I said, standing to get a better look at Amber, who modeled for me, twirling with both arms stretched above her head.

Amber was definitely all "growed" up. She was much taller than I would have guessed, close to six feet in heels, with a lean shapely figure. She was wearing a short black halter dress, and her hair was pulled back in a ponytail, revealing diamond earrings, and a matching diamond choker.

"How have you been, Kevin?"

"Okay."

"You still live around here?"

"Same apartment. How about you?"

"No, I live in Tribeca."

"How's your aunt?"

"She's good."

"How old are you now?"

"Twenty-two."

"Twenty-two?"

"Yeah, it's been a long time. You look good, Dr. Matthews. It is Dr. Matthews, right?"

"Yeah, yeah, it is. My office is actually right around the corner."

"Are you ready?" a man asked Amber, placing a coat around her shoulders. The man was white, appearing to be in his fifties, with a horseshoe pattern of short gray hair surrounding his shiny bald crown. He was well dressed, and handsome, but the two made an unlikely couple.

"Baby, come and meet a friend of mine," Amber said. "This is Dr. Kevin Matthews. Kevin, this is William, ah, William, okay, this is embarrassing."

"William Sisler, nice to meet you, Kevin," the man said, shaking my hand.

"William Sisler," Amber repeated. "In my defense, Sisler is an unusual name."

"Nice to meet you also, William," I said.

"Kevin was the first of my many shrinks," Amber said. "He's known me since I was nine."

"Really," William said.

"I don't know if I qualify as her first therapist, I was a student at the time," I said.

"Well, student or not, you're definitely the only one I ever liked," Amber said, poking me in the chest, and losing her balance. Amber was tipsy.

"How long have you guys known each other?" I asked.

"Tonight's our first time meeting," Amber said.

"Oh, first date?" I asked.

"I guess you could call it that," Amber said, giggling.

"Trinity, I think we better get going," the man said to Amber, checking his watch.

"Okay, Sweetie, give me one second," Amber said.

"Nice to meet you, Kevin," the man said, shaking my hand, before making his way to the door.

"Kevin, I've got to run, but it was really good seeing you. Let me give you my number, maybe we can get together for a drink sometime." Amber went into her purse and handed me a business card, which read *Madison Modeling Agency* in the top left corner, and the name *Trinity* centered with a phone number below.

"Who's Trinity?"

"It's just like a stage name, you know."

"So, you're modeling now?"

"You could call it that," she said, with a wink. "What can you do, it pays the bills, you know."

"Oh, yeah."

"Kevin, it was really good seeing you."

"Yeah, it was good seeing you too." Amber kissed me goodbye, hugging me tightly, before turning to leave.

As I watched her walk toward the door, Jolie's words rang in my head, "We are who we believe ourselves to be, and sometimes nothing can change that." Amber had not escaped her mother's shadow, just as my father's lingered over me. I gulped down my drink, and signaled Carl for another.

Long Ball

"Kevin, you can't chase after him around the entire backyard," Megan said. "Tyler, Baby, go and get the ball, then choose one spot to play in."

"Hey, maybe we should take a break. Maybe go in and watch some television, or something. I mean, doesn't this kid ever get tired?" I asked, out of breath, collapsing in a lawn chair next to Megan.

"No, he doesn't. A day like this, you'll have to drag him inside." It was Saturday, April 26, 1997. The temperature was in the mid seventies, and after being cooped up for the winter, Tyler was making the most of the warm weather.

"What time are you guys getting back tonight?" I asked. Megan and Morris were going to a wedding, and I was babysitting.

"Why, nervous?"

"I'm just asking a question. It might not look like it but I've got this situation under control."

"Mommy, Mrs. Burns has cookies and she needs me to go and get some," Tyler yelled from across the yard, pointing to the neighbor's back door.

"She needs you to go and get some, does she?" Megan yelled back, standing and looking toward the house. "Hi, Mrs. Burns, how you doing? Okay, Tyler, since Mrs. Burns needs you, go and get some cookies, but then come back outside, okay?" Tyler disappeared into the house.

"Kid's got a way with words," I said.

"You have no idea," Megan said, laughing and sitting back down. "So, are you coming to the party next week?"

"Nah, I don't want to have to drive that far home at the end of the night."

"Stamford is a forty-five minute ride from the city, thirty from the upper West Side. And it's not like you can't sleep here if you don't feel like driving home."

"I still think I'll pass."

"You know, it's been almost a year since you and Jolie split up, and all you do is stay cramped up in that shoebox of an apartment. It's not healthy."

"It is what it is."

"Oh, please."

"What?"

"That is so pathetic, 'it is what it is,' will you stop being a baby?"

"Excuse me?"

"Kevin, it is what you make it. And you're making it into your own little pity party."

"Thanks, Megan."

"All I'm saying is, if you and Jolie don't want the same things, if you can't make each other happy, then move on."

"I can't believe you're telling me this."

"I told Jolie the same thing."

"You what?"

"Kevin, you know what Jolie wants, what she needs, but you're either unwilling or unable to give her that. So what, you want her to sacrifice her happiness for you?"

"That's ridiculous. I want her to be happy, I mean, I want to be happy too."

"No, you don't."

"What?"

"You remember back in school, that Christmas we spent together when I told you what I was going through, about how I felt all alone, and you were feeling the same way, and you said we were basically the same person."

"Not really, but what's your point."

"I think the reason we connected so much as friends, you know, why we became so close, is because in a lot of ways we really were the same person. We were both allowing ourselves to be trapped by the past."

"So you're saying my past won't allow me to be happy."

"No, I'm saying you choose not to be happy, and your past is an excuse to justify that choice."

"Well, that's all very profound, Megan, but life is not that simple. Being happy, or unhappy for that matter, is not a choice."

"True, but wanting to be happy is a choice."

"You have no idea what you're talking about. I mean why on earth would I not want to be happy."

"Because you don't trust happiness. You're convinced it's something that for you will never last. I'm not even certain it's something you think you deserve."

"That's nonsense."

"It wasn't for me. For years I felt that way, and just like you it had a lot to do with my father. But the difference is although I didn't trust happiness, I never stopped wanting it; and when I saw the opportunity to have it, I grabbed hold and didn't let anything or anybody get in my way."

"And what was your opportunity?"

"Morris."

❋   ❋   ❋

Morris Goodman was average height, about five feet ten inches, bean-pole skinny, with thick jet-black wavy hair, and dark brown eyes. After meeting at Yale, he and Megan had been dating for close to a year before she introduced us.

"Now he talks a lot. And sometimes he makes really inappropriate comments, but he doesn't mean anything by them, okay?" Megan nervously explained to Jolie and me in her backyard, after inviting us over for a cookout to meet Morris. "Oh yeah, and he eats a lot also."

"So does Kevin," Jolie said.

"No, you don't understand. Morris eats a lot, like an embarrassing amount. I have no idea why I'm introducing you guys at a cookout."

"Megan will you calm down?" I said. "I mean, I don't know about Jolie, but you've got meat on the grill, beer in an ice chest, and the Yankees on television; Morris and I will get along just fine."

"Hey, everybody," Morris said, walking from the back door to join us.

"Baby, you're here," Megan said, greeting Morris with a kiss. "Ah, this is Kevin and Jolie."

"Kevin, nice to finally meet you," Morris said, shaking my hand.

"Same here. I was beginning to think Megan was embarrassed of me."

"More likely it was me, but I know what you mean."

"Hi, Morris. It's really nice to meet you," Jolie said, shaking Morris' hand.

Morris paused for a moment, staring at Jolie. "Holy crap, you really do look like that damn painting," he blurted out.

"Morris!" Megan yelled, slapping him on the back.

"I'm sorry, Megan. I mean she's beautiful, but it's a little freaky," Morris said, ducking.

"Don't worry, man, I know the feeling," I said, laughing and pulling Morris to safety.

Morris and I hit it off immediately. He was the first and only guy Megan ever introduced me to, and I was thrilled that he seemed willing to accept our friendship, considering our past. Jolie never had a problem with it, but we knew men were a lot less understanding when it came to such things. The two of us meeting also gave Megan a trusted and honest observer to discuss their relationship with, something she was starved for.

"So he seems like he likes me, but we've been dating for almost a year, and he hasn't said anything about where he sees this relationship going. What does that mean?" she asked over the phone, the day after introducing us.

"It doesn't mean anything."

"But he just graduated. He's going to be moving into the city, I've got another year of school, don't you think he'll want to stop seeing each other, you know, exclusively?"

"Did he say he wanted to stop seeing you?"

"No."

"Then why would you think that?"

"Well, I don't want to pressure him. I mean if he wants his freedom for a while, I'm fine with that."

"What the hell are you talking about?"

"I just don't want to be one of those women who hangs on when they know it's over."

"Megan, the guy seems like he's crazy about you."

"Really? You think?"

It was apparent to me from day one that Megan and Morris were made for each other, but many took on another view. After dating several years, the two were married on September 24, 1990, amidst a storm of controversy after both of their families opposed the wedding. "He's Jewish, you two have nothing in common. I know his family won't accept you, and I will never accept him," Megan's father told her. "You will always be our son, but we will never accept your choice for a wife," Morris's parents responded to news of the wedding. It wasn't the south, and it was over thirty years later, but in many ways, things were much the same.

"I'm really sorry your parents didn't come," I said to Megan and Morris at their reception, seemingly more upset by their family's abandonment than either of them.

"Hey, if they can't accept the woman I love, then they don't really love me," Morris said, smiling, and kissing Megan.

"But this is one of the most important days of you guys' life; I mean, to not have family share it with you, that's just not right," I said.

"Kevin, never forget, family is not determined by blood," Megan said.

The two never looked back, and set out creating their own family with Megan giving birth to Morris Tyler Goodman, Jr. on July 11, 1992. He was named after his father, but was the spitting image of his mother. Tyler had the same cocoa brown skin, high cheekbones, and almond shaped green eyes. "Kevin, unlike you and me, Tyler has been blessed with some color," Morris joked. The only traits Tyler appeared to have inherited from Morris were his thick wavy black hair and slight frame. Megan had to punch extra holes in Tyler's belt to keep his pants from drooping down around his waiflike waist.

After Tyler's birth, Megan's mother attempted to repair their relationship, apologizing to Morris, and even making trips to visit her grandson. But even with Morris urging her to patch things up, Megan was never able to fully forgive her mother.

"Maybe you should go to the funeral. Your mother's all alone; at her age, that's a scary feeling," I said to Megan, after her father died of cancer in March 1996. "I don't know, maybe you should try and be there for her."

"Like she was there for me?"

"Well, your father had a lot to do with that. It's not like she had a choice."

"I'm her only child. She had a choice."

"She's your mother, Megan. She loves you."

"No, Kevin, she needs me, she doesn't love me. It took me a long time to accept that; it was always easier blaming my father for everything."

"Come on, Megan."

"You know, at eighteen years old I remember my mother standing by silently while my father told me I was responsible for being raped. She never once told me otherwise, not even in private. For a long time after that, I didn't feel I was deserving of love. I certainly never thought anyone would love me the way Tyler and Morris do, and to be honest, I never thought I would love anyone the way I love them. Our life is here. And you, Jolie, and our other friends are the only family we need."

✳   ✳   ✳

"No no no, that's not how you do it," Tyler cried later that evening, after striking out.

"Really, then how am I supposed to do it?" I asked.

"You throw the ball, and then I hit it."

"But I just threw the ball, only you didn't hit it."

"But you threw it the wrong way."

Tyler and I were in the last inning of a heated baseball game. It was a game with very unique rules: Tyler, who'd given himself the nickname

Long Ball, was the only player who batted, tagging him out before he reached first base constituted cheating, and his strikeouts were nullified due to my ineptitude as a pitcher. Long Ball had hit countless homers during the game, scoring a total of fifty runs, a number that he alone calculated. The game had lasted over three hours, and endured delays such as multiple water breaks using the garden hose as a fountain, an ice-cream break, a bike-riding break, a tree climbing break, and a looking for bugs break. Nonetheless, we always returned to the game, and were determined to finish it.

"Okay, Tyler—,"

"No," Tyler said, stopping me.

"Sorry. Long Ball, this is the last pitch. It's getting dark."

Tyler looked out steely eyed from under his cap, his bat waving above his head. I let the pitch fly, and Tyler connected with a towering fly ball.

"Homerun! Homerun! I win, sixty-five to nothing," Tyler yelled, rounding the bases.

It was a humiliating loss for me, but considering the last homerun counted as fifteen runs, and my not being allowed to bat the entire game, the score wasn't that bad.

Once we were back in the house, Tyler tried to convince me that his mother didn't make him take baths on Saturday because he never went anywhere or did anything. We eventually compromised when I suggested that he take a shower. He really went for the idea, and remained in the shower for fifteen minutes, until I finally coaxed him from the bathroom with the promise of hot dogs and French fries.

"What do we do now?" Tyler asked, stuffing his mouth with the last fry.

"I don't know? What do you want to do?"

"Let's play guys."

"Guys" was Tyler's name for his collection of action figures, which he stored in an old mop bucket. The game began with Tyler dumping his "guys" into the middle of the living room floor. He then picked out Wolverine and Buzz Lightyear, and I chose two action figures to do battle with them. After several skirmishes requiring repeated chases from one end of the house to the other, my combatants suffered defeat.

"But this is Batman and Superman, two of the most powerful superheroes ever, how can Wolverine and Buzz Lightyear beat them?" I asked.

"Because Wolverine has claws that are sharp, and when Superman tries to fly, he cuts his cape, and then Superman falls. And Buzz Lightyear has laser rays, and they can burn Batman," Tyler explained. It was an argument that was difficult to refute.

Tyler and I played "guys" for a couple of hours, after which I was exhausted. Luckily, I possessed an ace in the hole; a videocassette of *Toy Story*. The tape had not been rewound from a previous viewing that was never completed, so the movie started somewhere in the middle when I pressed the play button. Tyler could have cared less. We both grabbed a pillow from the sofa, and settled in front of the television with a bowl of popcorn. I knew I was home free.

The doorbell woke me sometime after three that morning. Did they lose their keys, I thought. I stumbled to the door, opening it to find Jolie, who was trembling and crying.

"Jolie, what's wrong, what happened?" I asked.

"It's Megan and Morris," she cried.

"What? What happened?"

"There was an accident."

OUR DAILY BREAD

"So, how's Tyler?" Dan asked, greeting me in the lobby of the mortuary on the morning of Megan and Morris' funeral. Dan was Morris' best friend.

"He's okay, but more and more he's starting to question where his mom and dad are, why they haven't come home yet."

Megan and Morris were less than a mile from home when the accident happened. They were driving along a two-lane highway, when the hitch on the back of a truck in oncoming traffic broke loose. The truck was towing a boat, which swerved into their lane, crashing head-on into their car, and killing them both instantly. The police had contacted Jolie after finding her name listed as an emergency contact on papers in the glove compartment.

Tyler went to stay with Jolie after the accident. I decided to stay at the house for a few days to make things seem as normal as possible. All we told Tyler was that he would be spending some time at our house. He was excited about the idea for the first couple of days, but on Tuesday morning, he awoke wanting to see his parents.

"Are Mommy and Daddy coming to get me today?" Tyler asked Jolie.

"Not today, Baby. Don't you want to spend another night with Uncle Kevin and Aunt Jolie? That would really make us happy."

"Okay, but I have to go home soon."

There were few decisions to be made when it came to the funeral arrangements. Megan and Morris listed explicit instructions in their wills regarding how the services should be handled, even accounting for such an unexpected tragedy. Jeanie Marks, Morris' close friend and law partner, was the will's executor. The wills stipulated in the event that both Megan and Morris died at the same time, their wake and funeral should be held jointly. I smiled when Jeanie told me of this instruction, knowing that this was Megan's and Morris' way of saying to the world that in death, just as in life, you would accept them together, or you would not accept them at all. Sadly, Mrs. Waters, Megan's mother, was the only blood relative at the funeral. Da-dee and Ms. Bertha came to pay their respects, and Jeremy, who had moved back to New Orleans, also flew in, although Monica couldn't make the trip since she was eight months pregnant with their fifth child. Dan's wife, Nina, babysat Tyler the night before during the wake, but today Jolie decided to stay home with him instead of going to the funeral.

The funeral was scheduled for ten a.m. Megan was Catholic, and Morris was Jewish, but neither practiced their respective religions. "We believe in a God that is accepting, forgiving, and loving of all his children, no exceptions. When we find a religion that agrees with us, we'll join it," Megan once said to me. We respected their beliefs by conducting the services with no religious rituals. Dan and I arrived an hour early to make sure everything was in order.

"Okay, we'll both say a few words, and then we'll head over to the cemetery," I said to Dan.

"Yeah, yeah, and I think they have enough chairs set out, don't you?" Dan asked, rubbing his hands together as if he were trying to wipe them clean.

"I think so."

"You know what though, I'm just going to have them set out all the chairs, I mean just in case."

I knew Dan was in as much pain as I was. He and Morris were roommates at Rutgers University, and then both went on to Law School at Yale. Dan was a big guy, about six feet tall, with a wide barrel chest, and thick arms and legs that were the result of years spent in weight rooms. With sandy blonde hair and light blue eyes, he and Morris couldn't have been physically more at odds, although you would have been hard pressed to find two people who were more alike, or two who shared a deeper friendship.

People began to arrive at nine-thirty, with the services starting promptly at ten.

"I was friends with Morris for close to twenty years," Dan said, addressing the room, his left hand tapping the top of Morris' coffin, while his voice choked with emotion. "I'll never forget the day we met; I was having lunch, and Morris walks into our dorm room at Rutgers, we had been assigned as roommates, and the first thing he says to me is, 'Are you going to eat that whole sandwich?'" The room filled with laughter. "For those of you who knew Morris, that's probably not a big surprise. Despite how skinny he was, to this day he's the only man I've ever known that could out-eat me," Dan joked. "But I guess I shouldn't say 'for those of you who knew Morris,' because if you knew Megan, you knew Morris. They were inseparable. I'm sure we all remember him introducing Megan as 'the beautiful Egyptian Queen——,'"

"'Who has taken pity on a homely Jew,'" everyone chimed in, finishing Dan's last line, laughter again filling the room.

"Megan and Morris loved each other, and I loved them. We will all miss their physical presence, but I know spiritually, neither will ever be absent in our hearts and lives," Dan said, kissing the tops of both coffins, before taking a seat.

It was my turn to speak, but I sat motionless, unable to move from my chair, my body trembling, as tears raced down my cheek. I was furious, my insides feeling like they were on fire. Da-dee was seated next to me, and I could feel his stare, as he attempted to gauge my thoughts.

"This is not about you, Kevin," he whispered, firmly gripping my forearm.

I looked him in the eyes, nodded, and then stood, walking to the front of the room. "Megan and Morris were two of my dearest friends, and I'd like to share some of my memories of them with you today."

After the funeral, Jolie and I held a small gathering at our house. Mrs. Waters, Ms. Bertha, and Da-dee spent time with Tyler, while Jeremy and I took some time to catch up.

"So, how's Monica doing?" I asked.

"Three weeks, man, three weeks," Jeremy said.

"Is this it?"

"Yeah, Monica will have her little girl. This is it," he said, laughing. I tried to laugh along with him, but the most I could manage was a smile. "So, Mrs. Waters, she's okay with you guys adopting Tyler?"

"I don't know. I haven't talked to her about it."

Megan and Morris' will provided that Jolie and I become Tyler's legal guardians should anything happen to them. We were prepared to seek custody, but knew that a blood relative could challenge the will. Jeanie took on the task of telling Morris' parents about his death. In doing so, she pointed out to them that Morris had a son, and asked if they would be interested in seeking custody. Jolie and I knew the answer before she asked, but Jeanie felt it would be prudent to do so anyway. We weren't so sure about Mrs. Waters. She knew her grandson, and had made an effort to be a part of his life.

"It's what Megan and Morris wanted. I'm sure she'll be okay with it," Jeremy said. "Have you and Jolie considered getting back together?"

"Right now it would be for all the wrong reasons."

"So what are you going to do?"

"For now Tyler is going to live with Jolie. I'll spend as much time as I can with him on weekends. Ironic, isn't it?"

"What?"

"My wife and I separate because we can't agree if we should have children, and then our two best friends get killed and we adopt their son."

"Who knows, maybe this will bring you and Jolie back together."

"Like I said, us getting back together right now would be for all the wrong reasons. It may never happen. What can you do, some people just weren't meant to have families."

Jeremy had a flight out that night, so he left around three, but most people didn't leave until that evening. Dan and Nina stayed to help Jolie clean up, while I drove Mrs. Waters back to her hotel.

"It was really a beautiful ceremony," Mrs. Waters said to me, riding back in the car.

"It was," I said. "Mrs. Waters, I've been meaning to talk to you about something."

"Tyler. You want to talk about Tyler."

"Well, you see, Megan and Morris asked that Jolie and I take care of him should anything happen to them."

"I won't fight you for custody, Kevin."

"You won't? I mean, thank you," I said, relieved. "Now, I should tell you that Jolie and I are currently separated, and to be truthful, I don't know if we'll be getting back together. But we love Tyler, and I promise we'll take good care of him."

"I know you will. Besides, if Megan and Morris wanted it any other way, I'm sure they would have changed their instructions." Mrs. Waters nodded her head, confirming in her mind that she was doing the right thing. She then became lost in thought, staring blankly out the window. "He meant well, you know."

"Excuse me?"

"Her father, he thought he was doing what was best for her."

"I'm not sure he wasn't, but I don't think that's what the problem was."

"I know. He shouldn't have said the things he said; I shouldn't have let him. But it wasn't her he was angry with. He just couldn't look at her without seeing those boys on top of her. He couldn't look past what they did to his little girl."

"That wasn't Megan's fault."

"No, it wasn't."

"You know, the thing that hurt her the most was his rejection of Morris, and in essence Tyler."

"He never rejected Tyler."

"He never met Tyler."

"You're right. I don't know, Kevin. Prejudice, maybe arrogance, sometimes we judge what's best for our kids by what was best for us. I mean, why did I agree with him, losing my daughter for all those years in the process? And now she's gone." Mrs. Waters reached into her purse for a handkerchief after giving in to her tears.

"Well, I'd like to thank you again," I said, parking in front of the hotel lobby.

"No, Kevin. Thank you. Megan and Morris had good friends in you and Jolie. I know my grandson will have a good home."

When I made it back to the house, Da-dee was alone in the living room watching television.

"Where's everybody at?" I asked.

"Bertha in there packing, and Tyler and Jolie are upstairs in the bedroom watching movies."

"I better go on up, we're going to try and explain to him what happened."

"You know, Tyler's go'n be looking to you to let him know that everything will be alright. Even at four years old, you can't convince him of that if you don't believe it yourself."

"Things will be fine. It's going to take some time, but everything will be okay."

"When a man gives up, things will never be okay."

"When a man gives up? What are you talking about?"

"Son, I've been ministering to folks for close to fifty years, I know when a man has given up."

"I'm just upset, okay?"

"No, you're angry, and there's a big difference. Anger is a selfish emotion."

"Da-dee, I lost two of my best friends."

"And there's a little boy upstairs who lost his parents. A little boy who's depending on you to help fill that void. You don't have time to feel sorry for yourself."

"Have I ever felt sorry for myself? When I had a father who didn't love me, did I feel sorry for myself? When he took my mother away, did I feel sorry for myself? So now I've lost my best friend, why should anything be different?"

"The Lord never gives us more than we can handle."

"And he also doesn't give some people what they need." Da-dee sat silently shaking his head in dismay. "What?"

"Son, that's a very dangerous path you heading down. God responds to faith, not to need."

"What are you talking about now?"

"I'm talking about faith being the tool by which we find the strength to face life's storms, and once you lose it, you're defenseless."

"Faith?"

"Kevin, this world promises us nothing, not even our daily bread. But Jesus said to us, 'what things soever ye desire, when ye pray, believe that ye receive them and ye shall have them.'"

"And what is that supposed to mean?"

"It means to get the things we want in this life, the things we need, we must never doubt in our heart that we deserve them, or lose faith that we will receive them." I knew Da-dee was trying to help, but his words meant nothing to me, and I didn't have the energy to pretend otherwise. I left the room, saying nothing.

When I walked into the bedroom, Tyler and Jolie were lying on the bed watching *Toy Story*. Over the past few days, Tyler was in the habit of excitedly jumping up whenever a door opened. When I walked in this time, he didn't move.

"Hey, guys," I said.

"Hey," Jolie said, standing from the bed. "Say hello to Uncle Kevin, Tyler."

"Hey, Uncle Kevin, we're watching *Toy Story*."

"It's getting late, you think we should maybe wait until tomorrow to do this?" I asked Jolie.

"No, we should do it tonight."

"Okay."

"Tyler, Baby, Uncle Kevin and Aunt Jolie need to talk to you, okay?" Jolie said, sitting back on the bed and pulling Tyler onto her lap.

"Okay."

"Let's turn off the movie," Jolie said, clicking off the television with the remote. "We'll finish watching it tomorrow." Jolie motioned for me to join them on the bed, but I didn't move. "Tyler, we need to talk to you about your mommy and daddy," she said.

"They're coming to get me?"

"Well, Baby, actually, you're going to be staying with us from now on," Jolie said.

"Mommy and Daddy aren't coming home today?"

"No, Baby, they're not," Jolie said.

FIFTEEN HUNDRED MILES AWAY

"Okay, Mister, time for bed," Jolie said, walking into Tyler's bedroom. It was July 11, Tyler's fifth birthday. I walked over to the door, listening and peeking in. "Did you have a good time at your party?" Jolie asked, tucking Tyler in.

"Yeah, did you see the guys that Uncle Dan brought me? Let me show you," Tyler said, climbing from under the covers.

"Hold on, hold on. You can show me tomorrow. It's time to go to sleep."

"How about a story first?" This I'd learned was one of Tyler's nightly tactics at extending his bedtime.

"What kind of story?"

"How about an Earl story?"

"One story, and then lights out. Deal?" Jolie stuck out her hand to shake.

"Deal," Tyler said, slapping her hand.

I slipped away from the door, and went downstairs to clean up. There had only been eight kids at the party, but the mess they left suggested ten times that amount. After rounding up all the toys from the backyard and putting them away, I started taking down the decorations. Tyler was an active participant in planning the party, which resulted in not only the backyard being decorated, but also every room downstairs. There were even balloons and streamers in the bathroom. After taking down the decorations, and sweeping up the living room and kitchen, I went to get some garbage bags. I looked in the pantry, their normal location, but couldn't find any. There were none in the cabinets under the sink, either. I started rifling through all the drawers and cabinets in the kitchen, becoming angrier each time I came up empty.

"That kid has to be Earl's biggest fan," Jolie said, coming down the stairs.

"Jolie, where the hell did you put the garbage bags?" I shouted. Jolie stopped at the bottom of the stairs, shocked by my outburst. "I mean, we used to keep them in the pantry. Why did you move them?"

"I moved all the cleaning supplies to the cabinet above the refrigerator so Tyler couldn't reach them," she answered.

"That doesn't make any damn sense, they're garbage bags, not poison," I mumbled under my breath, while getting the bags.

"What did you say?"

"I said it doesn't make any damn sense, at least not to me."

"Well, since you don't live here, I really didn't give that any consideration. And if you're going to spend time here, please don't use that language."

"What do you mean if I'm going to spend time here? This is my house."

"No, Kevin, this used to be your house."

"Who the hell do you think you're talking to?" I asked, moving face to face with Jolie, who didn't flinch. "My name is still on the mortgage, and until a court says otherwise this is still my house."

"Continue acting like this, and that day isn't far away," Jolie said, brushing past me.

"What, is that a threat?" I asked, grabbing her arm.

"Take your hands off of me," she yelled, pulling away, and slipping down in the process.

"Aunt Jolie, are you okay?" Tyler asked, standing at the bottom of the stairs. The sight of him froze me.

"I'm fine, Baby, go back to bed," Jolie said, standing.

"But you're bleeding," Tyler said, pointing to her lip.

"It's okay, Aunt Jolie's fine," she said, wiping the blood away. "You go back to bed. I'll come up and say goodnight again in a little while." Tyler looked at Jolie, and then stared at me for a few seconds, before running back up the stairs. Jolie went into the kitchen, and got some ice for her lip. I didn't move. "Don't worry, I'll finish cleaning up," she said, walking past me and heading back upstairs.

"Jolie, look, it was an accident. It wasn't my fault."

Jolie stopped, and turned to face me. "Well your father's locked in a cell fifteen hundred miles away, so we certainly can't blame him."

My Father

"Forgiveness by God of man's sin is the atoning death of Christ Jesus," Da-dee said, sternly peering down from the DoRight Baptist Church pulpit. He was ninety-six years old, but he still delivered a sermon every Sunday morning. His delivery was subtler these days, but his messages possessed more power than ever. "Throughout the Bible we are commanded to forgive. Let's all turn to Matthew, chapter six, verse fourteen," Da-dee said, flipping through his bible. "'For if ye forgive men their trespasses, your heavenly father will also forgive you;' verse fifteen goes on to say 'But if ye forgive not men their trespasses, neither will your father forgive your trespasses.' Amen?"

"Amen," the congregation responded.

"And I'll tell you something else, church, forgiveness is not a one or two times thing. We must always be in the attitude of forgiveness. In Matthew eighteen, twenty-one and twenty-two, Peter asked Jesus 'how often shall my brother sin against me and I forgive him? Should it be seven times?' You know what Jesus told him? Jesus said 'I say not unto thee, until seven times: but, until seventy times seven.' Therefore, church, I say to you as often as there is a need for forgiveness, we must be willing to forgive."

I was so shaken by my actions the night of Tyler's birthday that the next day I flew to Louisiana. I recognized the path I was headed down, and felt there was only one way to avoid it, confronting my father. I was going to at least attempt to understand how he became the man he was.

"Nice sermon," I said, after we returned home from church.

"I thought it appropriate considering your visit. You got the directions out to the prison?"

"Yeah, shouldn't be a problem."

"And you sure you don't want me to come with you?"

"No, I need to do this alone."

"Well, you better get going. It's already after eleven, and you got a long ride ahead of you. Here you go." Da-dee handed me a brown paper bag. "Bertha done made you some lunch for the trip. She said she'll send some supper over here for when you get back this evening."

"Tell her I said thanks." I took the bag, and headed for the car. Da-dee stood at the door and watched as I pulled out of the driveway. I knew he was as nervous as I was.

"I put your name on the visitors' list close to thirty years ago, but like they say, better late than never," my father said, smiling and shaking my hand in the visitors' room at Angola State Penitentiary. Aside from the streaks of gray in his hair, he looked just as I remembered. "It's good to see you," he said.

"Good to see you too," I said, cringing upon hearing the words escape my lips.

"Damn, boy, you really grew into your own, didn't you?" he said, patting me on the shoulders.

"Yeah, I guess so."

"Guess, hell you bigger than me now," he said, laughing. My father led me to the other end of the room, and motioned for me to sit at the end of a cafeteria-style table, which was positioned next to a gated window. He took a seat directly across from me. "Preacher say you a doctor, psychiatrist, right?"

"Actually, I'm a psychologist."

"Well, sounds like you done good for yourself. Hear you married too."

"Yeah, her name is Jolie."

"I know. Preacher done showed me pictures, beautiful girl. She a writer, huh?"

"Yeah."

"What she write?"

"She writes children's books."

"Ya'll just adopted a little boy too, right?"

"Tyler, he's five. His parents were killed in a car accident. They were close friends of ours."

"That's good of ya'll, give that boy parents. Every child deserves a family." I tried not to react, despite the irony of his statement. "I was surprised last night when Preacher told me you was coming today."

"He didn't even know until I showed up unannounced at the house yesterday."

"Well, I guess there's a reason for your visit," he said, leaning in over the table. "No sense beating around the bush."

"I want to know why you treated Mama the way you did." The bluntness of my statement surprised my father. The smile he was wearing disappeared, and his eyes narrowed, as he shot a familiar icy stare in my direction. Only this time, I didn't blink.

"Now, what the hell is that supposed to mean?" he asked, leaning back in his chair. "I treated your Mama fine, just wasn't nothing, or nobody for that matter, ever good enough for her. You know how white folks is."

"She didn't think you were good enough for her, yet she gave up her entire life to be with you? Is that what you're telling me? Because that doesn't make much sense."

"She married me 'cause she ain't had no choice."

"That's not what I was told."

"Not what you was told?"

"She was going to leave you, wasn't she? That's why you hurt her."

"Boy, what the hell you talking about? And what makes you think you know what was going on between me and your Mama? You wasn't nothing but a kid."

"'You ever try to leave me woman, and I'll kill you.' I heard you say that to Mama the week before she was attacked."

"We was arguing. I had too much of that alcohol in me." My father chuckled to himself.

"Is there something that you find amusing about this conversation?" The intensity of my tone silenced him. "Look, all I want to know is why you hurt Mama, you owe me at least that much."

My father took a deep breath, and thought for a moment. "Boy, I don't know who you think you are walking in here after all these years and talking to me like this, but I don't owe you shit."

"I'm your son," I shot back. "You treated me with nothing but contempt when I was a child, and before this day, I've never asked you for one damn thing. All I'm asking is why did you take my mother from me?"

My father sat silently, shifting nervously in his chair as we became locked in a staring contest. After a few seconds, he broke his gaze, turning his head away, and looking out the window. "Kevin, I loved your mama."

"Tell me what happened that night," I demanded.

My father squinted from the streaks of sunlight that filtered through the gate, while a single tear crept down his cheek. "I snapped."

"What?"

"I had been out drinking, and when I got home, Sarah had a suitcase out."

"So she was leaving you."

"She was still upset about the fight we had the week before. Said she couldn't live that way any longer, and that she wanted a man who loved her. A man who loved her," my father repeated, shaking his head. "Ain't a man on this earth could have love that woman more than I did."

"What happened next?"

"I saw her lip was all swollen, so I asked her what happened. She said Boutte had been to the house, and she had asked him to loan her some money to get a place for you and her. Said they got in an argument when he told her he'd give her the money if she left you with me. Told her she'd never be able to live a respectable life with a half-breed for a child. You know your mama; she ain't allow a soul in this world to say a bad word about you, so she went after him. Said he pushed her away and she fell and hit her lip." Johnny saw exactly what he claimed, I thought. "For some reason, probably 'cause I was drunk, I started laughing when she told me what happened. I knew she didn't have nobody else to turn to, and I told her so. That made her mad, and she told me Boutte and me weren't the only two men in her life."

"What did you do?"

"Sarah knew saying something like that was go'n piss me off. Before I knew it, I had her by the throat. I was yelling and screaming, asking her what she was talking about. She ain't even fight back. She just looked at me and said it meant there was somebody else out there who loved her, and she was go'n let him." My father turned and looked me square in the eyes. "I told her, 'ain't no other man go'n love you, not as long as I'm breathing.'" We sat in silence after that, me digesting what I'd heard, my father spent after reliving it.

"That's when it happened, isn't it?" I finally asked. "That's when you hurt her?"

"Yeah, I guess. I don't remember much after that. I must have left the room and passed out, cause the next morning I woke up in the living room on the sofa. When I went back in the bedroom, I found her lying there in bed, all bloody. She was barely breathing," my father said, completing his confession, and staring off into space. "Why did she have to tell me she was leaving me for another man? She knew I had that alcohol in me. That was Sarah's problem, she just never knew when to let a man be."

I was dumbfounded. After all these years, my father somehow blamed Mama. He married a woman he didn't think he deserved, and faulted her for making him feel that way. He pledged to love her, but through his own insecurities became her abuser. And when she decided to no longer suffer him, he all but ended her life. My father did all these things of his own free will, and yet, he was too much of a coward to accept responsibility for his actions. I looked across the table at him, and for the first time in my life there wasn't the slightest doubt in my mind that, genetics aside, I would never be anything like this man.

"Six-thirty, you back earlier than I thought," Da-dee said, checking his watch and looking up from his recliner when I walked into the house.

"It was a pretty quick ride home. The highways were empty," I said, taking a seat on the sofa.

"So, how did things go? I mean, probably was a little strange, being the first visit and all."

"A little."

"It's good the two of you are talking. He'll be coming up on parole next year. "

"He confessed."

"What?"

"I confronted him about what happened to Mama, and he confessed." Da-dee was silent. He stood from his recliner, and walked to the living room window, looking out into the backyard. "I get no pleasure in telling you this, but I can't lie to you about what happened."

Da-dee thought for a moment, and then turned to face me. "And you shouldn't have to," he said, walking back over to the sofa, and taking a seat next to me. "Kevin, I'm sorry."

"Da-dee, there's nothing for you to be sorry about, there's no way anyone could have known for sure what happened that night."

"That ain't what I'm talking about. It's a horrible thing for a son to live with knowing that his father committed such a monstrous act, and you done had to live with it since you was ten years old. It got to be a burden, living with that legacy." Da-dee reached over, patting me on the knee.

Da-dee never stopped believing in his son's innocence. The news I delivered must have been devastating. But true to form, his concern was first and foremost for me, and not himself.

"No, Da-dee, I'm proud of my legacy," I said, taking his hand. "You see, I'm sitting next to my father."

PART IV

HOME

BLESSED

"Happy birthday to you, happy birthday to you, happy birthday dear Da-dee, happy birthday to you," I sang, along with over two hundred people gathered around a picnic table in Ms. Bertha's back yard. Da-dee blew out the candles on his cake, with Tyler assisting him in what was no small task.

It was Sunday, August 27, 2000, Da-dee's one-hundredth birthday. Ms. Bertha invited the entire church congregation to her house to celebrate the occasion. Nicholle and Ronald flew in for the event, and Jeremy and his family drove out from New Orleans. Jolie suggested that we have the party catered, but Ms. Bertha wouldn't hear of it.

"I been cooking meals for Preacher for the past thirty years, ain't no stranger making this one," she said.

Ms. Bertha set out a buffet table that included: Red Beans and Rice, Crawfish Etouffee, Fried Chicken, Barbecue Ribs, Candied Yams, Macaroni and Cheese, Potato Salad, Gumbo, and Cornbread. Mr. Frank provided beverages for the party.

It was a great day, sunny, and with the temperature in the low seventies; cool for that time of year in Louisiana. People set up lawn chairs and laid out blankets across the back yard. As a birthday present, the church members, under Melvin's direction, hired a local artist to do a portrait of Da-dee standing in the pulpit, bible in hand, and dressed in his traditional black robe with a red sash around his neck. The picture was to be hung in the lobby of the new DoRight Baptist Church, which was currently being built, and would be twice the size of the old church.

"I'll tell you the truth, I never thought I was this handsome, but I ain't go'n argue with the artist," Da-dee joked, after seeing the picture. "You know, I was go'n wait until we moved into the new church, but since I have you all here, I'd like to make an announcement."

"Make it quick, preacher, you already done gave one sermon today," Ms. Bertha said, everyone laughing.

"Amen," Da-dee said. "First, let me just say thanks to all of you. This really means a lot to me, everybody coming out like this, to share in this day. I been Pastor at DoRight for the past fifty years, and I want all of you to know that every single day I served in that position has been a blessing. But the time comes when a man recognizes that it's time to step down, he only hopes there is someone to take his place. Well, almost twenty years ago, God sent me a soldier in Minister Melvin Lawes."

"Amen," several people shouted.

"Melvin, come over here." Melvin walked over and stood next to Da-dee. "When the doors to the new DoRight Baptist Church open, I'll be putting you in the hands of that very soldier."

"Amen," people once again shouted, as everyone gave Melvin a round of applause.

Melvin shook Da-dee's hand, and embraced him. "Pastor, I don't know if I'm worthy to replace you in the pulpit."

"The man standing in the pulpit is of little importance, it's the message that comes from it that matters. Now, they tell you never argue with the cook, so, Bertha, I'm go'n shut up," Da-dee said, laughing, and taking a seat at the table.

"Wait a minute, Preacher, you got to cut the cake," Ms. Bertha said, handing Da-dee a knife. Ms. Bertha baked a chocolate pudding-filled vanilla cake, with chocolate icing, Da-dee's favorite. Da-dee sliced down the middle of the cake, as everyone applauded.

"Alright, now, Preacher you just sit down. I'm go'n fix you a piece," Ms. Bertha said, pushing Da-dee aside, and taking the knife. "What you want, vanilla or chocolate ice cream with it?"

"I'll take vanilla, but Bertha, don't give me too much ice cream. You a little heavy handed when it come to serving."

"Now ain't that ungrateful. I offer to serve him dessert, and he go'n insult me," Ms. Bertha laughed, addressing everyone within earshot.

In addition to Da-dee's cake, Ms. Bertha also baked an assortment of other cakes, pies, cobblers, and bread puddings.

"You know her kitchen isn't that big, how long do you think it took her to make all this stuff?" Jolie asked.

"I have no idea."

"I don't know, Kevin, it seems like too much work. The woman is almost ninety, you should have insisted that we hire a caterer."

"Are you kidding me, feeding people is Ms. Bertha's specialty," I said, biting into a huge piece of Devils' food chocolate cake. Ms. Bertha had not forgotten my favorite dessert, either.

The party started before noon, but was still in full swing three hours later, with a softball game taking place in the field behind Ms. Bertha's house.

"Strike three!" Mr. Frank yelled, calling Melvin out on strikes.

"Now, come on, Mr. Frank, that ball almost hit me," Melvin pleaded.

"Melvin, it ain't the pitcher's fault that your midsection is sticking out over the plate," Mr. Frank laughed.

"Now, Pastor, you go'n allow him to talk to your successor that way?" Melvin yelled to Da-dee, who was watching the game from the sidelines.

"No no, Melvin, don't get me involved in this mess, I'm just a spectator. Besides, Bertha done warned you about that UC diet you on," Da-dee yelled back.

"UC diet? What you talking about, Pastor?"

"Everything UC, you eat." Both teams burst into laughter.

"That's three away, next team is up to bat," Mr. Frank yelled.

"Uncle Kevin," Tyler yelled.

"What is it?"

"There's a man here to see you. He's waiting in the driveway at Da-dee's house."

"Mr. Frank, somebody's over at the house to see me. I'm up sixth this inning, but Tyler can bat in my place if I'm not back."

"Okay," Mr. Frank said.

"Me?" Tyler asked. "But there's nothing but big people playing in this game."

"Oh, come on, Long Ball, you can handle it." Tyler smiled, and grabbed a bat to warm up.

"Kevin, how are you?" Mr. Boutte asked, meeting me under Da-dee's garage, and shaking my hand.

"I'm good, Mr. Boutte, I'm good."

"I heard you was in town, when did you get in?"

"Got in Friday night. You stop by for the party? Why don't you come on out back to the field? Da-dee's back there, we're playing softball."

"Thanks, but that's okay, I don't wanna disturb anybody. You tell him I said Happy Birthday though, you hear?"

"Sure, sure. What can I do for you?"

"Well, I stop by to——,"

"Papa, Papa," a voice called out from behind the garage.

"Out here, Baby," I said.

"Is that her?" Mr. Boutte asked, nervously looking around the garage wall to see where the voice was coming from.

"Yeah, it is. Mr. Boutte, I'd like to introduce you to Sarah Ann Matthews," I said, picking Sarah up in my arms after she made her way under the garage. Jolie and I had reconciled in the fall of 1997, and one year later, we celebrated the birth of a daughter. "Sarah, this is your great grandfather. Say hello."

"Hi," Sarah said bashfully.

Mr. Boutte's eyes lit up. "Hi, Sarah. My, what a pretty girl you are."

"Say thank you, Sarah," I told her.

"Thank you," Sarah said, hiding her face by burying it in my shoulder.

"How old are you?" Mr. Boutee asked.

"Two," Sarah said, holding up two fingers to make clear her answer.

"Two, huh? My, you are a big girl," Mr. Boutte said, laughing.

"Okay, Baby, why don't you go out back with Tyler, Papa will be there in a little while." I kissed Sarah, and put her down. She looked at Mr. Boutte for a moment, and then ran off behind the garage toward the softball game.

"She's beautiful, Kevin."

"Thank you."

"Preacher told me about her when she was born. Tyler, that the little boy you adopted, right? I think I met him earlier."

"That was him, he's filling in for me in the game, you sure you don't want to come and watch?"

"No no, I just heard you was in town, and I wanted to drop something off to you." Mr. Boutte went into his pocket and pulled out a small jewelry box. "This was originally my mother's," he said, opening the box to reveal a beautiful cameo pendant. "It was a gift from my daddy on their twenty-fifth anniversary. I was the oldest, and since I didn't have any sisters, my wife inherited it when Mama died. Sarah, that is my Sarah, well, it would have rightfully gone to her next after my wife passed." Mrs. Boutte had died one year earlier after suffering a stroke. "So anyway, when I heard about little Sarah being born, well, I figured it was only right that it should go to her, and I was hoping you would accept it, you know for when she grows up." Mr. Boutte handed me the box. "I guess it's kind of like a family heirloom."

"Thank you, Mr. Boutte," I said, looking at the cameo.

"Kevin, I want you to know that I loved your mama, and I'm sorry about the way I treated her," Mr. Boutte said, exhaling as if unloading a heavy burden.

"I appreciate you saying that."

"I won't try to make excuses for the things I did, we both know they was wrong, and I know I'll have to answer for them one day soon. I'm sorry for the way I treated you too. You turned yourself into quite a man, your mama would have been proud."

"Thank you. And thanks again for the cameo, I'm sure Sarah will love it when she gets older."

"Well, like I said, I figured it was only right. Okay, I better get going. You tell Preacher I said Happy Birthday." Mr. Boutte shook my hand. "It was good seeing you, Kevin."

"Good seeing you too, Mr. Boutte."

Mr. Boutte patted me on the shoulder, and headed for his truck. "Little Sarah, she got that silky curly hair just like your mama," he said, stopping and turning back to face me.

"What can I tell you, genetics, they're something else."

"Yeah, yeah, I guess so."

"You know if you like, I can get your address from Da-dee, and maybe send you some pictures of Sarah."

"That would be nice, Kevin, and while you at it, why don't you send me a picture of the entire family, that is, if you don't mind."

"Be happy to."

"Thanks, I sure would appreciate that. Well, ya'll enjoy the rest of your visit. How long you staying?"

"We leave tomorrow morning."

"Tomorrow, quick trip, huh?"

"Yeah, Tyler has school this week, so we have to get back."

"I guess it's still good to spend time with family, even if it's only for a couple of days."

"It is, Mr. Boutte, it really is."

The party wrapped up around six that evening, with Ms. Bertha recruiting Melvin, Mr. Frank, Jolie, and me for the clean-up detail.

"Should I load these into the dishwasher?" Jolie asked, picking up the empty dessert trays from the picnic table.

"Dishwasher? Baby, you looking at the dishwasher," Ms. Bertha laughed. "You just bring them in the house and set them on the counter."

"Ah, no, no, I can get started on them," Jolie said, embarrassed.

"I'll be right in there to help, Baby," Ms. Bertha said, smiling. "Melvin, you pull Preacher truck around back. We need to load up these picnic tables to bring back to the rec center tomorrow."

"What about supper?" Melvin asked.

"Lord, Melvin, I ain't never seen a man eat much as you," Ms. Bertha said.

"When you asking a man to do strenuous labor, you got to feed him first."

"Come on in the house, boy, let me fix you a plate," Ms. Bertha said, laughing. "Frank, Preacher, Kevin, ya'll want anything else to eat?"

"No indeed, Bertha," Mr. Frank said, rubbing his stomach. "I can't eat no more today."

"No thank you, Bertha," Da-dee said.

"I'm okay, Ms. Bertha," I said.

"Alright then, let me go help this child with these dishes. Come on, Melvin."

"I'm go'n take all those leftover sodas back to the store," Mr. Frank said, standing from the table. "Tyler, you wanna help your Uncle Frank? I got a new flavor ICEE I want you to try out, blueberry crush."

"Okay. Is it better than the strawberry?" Tyler asked, following in Mr. Frank's footsteps.

"I doubt it," Mr. Frank said.

Da-dee and I were left seated at the picnic table alone, with Sarah asleep in my arms.

"Who was that come by here for you earlier?" Da-dee asked.

"Mr. Boutte. He stopped by to tell you happy birthday, and to drop this off for Sarah." I pulled the cameo from my pocket, and showed it to Da-dee. "He said it was his mother's, and with Mrs. Boutte and Mama gone, he thought Sarah should have it."

"That was nice of him."

"He apologized to me too. Told me he was sorry for the way he treated Mama and me."

"What did you say?"

"I thanked him, and told him that I appreciated his words."

"Did you?"

"I did. 'For if ye forgive men their trespasses, your heavenly father will also forgive you.'"

"Looks like you learned something hanging around me all these years after all," Da-dee said, with a smile.

"I learned a lot."

"Preacher, I done saved this last piece of cake for you, so you might as well come on in here and get it," Ms. Bertha yelled from the house.

"Alright, Bertha," Da-dee yelled back, standing from the table. "That woman ain't happy unless you eating."

"So, one hundred years old, how do you feel?"

"Blessed," Da-dee said, thoughtfully. "Kevin, I spent my life preaching the gospel, loved and married a good woman, had friends who cared about me, and raised a son that any man would be proud of," he said, patting me on the back. "Yeah, as far as this life goes, the Lord done give me more than any man can ask for, and I'm grateful, I truly am."

"This life? That sounds like you're ready for the next one."

"Now, I didn't say that," Da-dee laughed, turning and walking toward the house. "No, I ain't planning on going nowhere any time soon."

As I sat at the table holding Sarah, the wind began to pick up, and I noticed clouds inching toward the sun. I didn't move though; just like Da-dee, I wasn't going anywhere, it felt too good finally being home.

CPSIA information can be obtained at www.ICGtesting.com
Printed in the USA
BVOW081442300912

301758BV00003B/4/P